VV *ŋɑt* ıs

Forever?

Joel McIver

Tonyah,
Thank you for
your support.
God bless !!
Joel McIver

4 Unity Publishing

What is Forever?

By: Joel McIver

Published by:

4 Unity Publishing
PO Box 548
Pfafftown, NC 27040
336-923-2849
www.4unitypublishing.com

Cover Design: William Bryant McIver II

Editing: Motivated Proformance Inc.,

Printed in the United States

Library of Congress Number: 2003111958

ISBN: 0-9753708-0-4

Dedication

In Loving memory of my first inspiration

Ellia G. McIver

for

My wonderful supportive wife Ann. I love you and look forward to spending my forever with you.

What is Forever?

About the Author...

Joel Eli McIver is a graduate of Winston-Salem State University where he earned a Bachelor of Arts in Mass Communications. He has worked in television production, in an art gallery, education and in the legal field.

His life long dream has been to write a great novel that moves people. His debut novel: What Is Forever?, has been regarded by readers and critics alike as that and much more.

Joel Eli McIver is currently working on his second book Dancing With My Shadow. It is expected to be released in early 2004. He lives in Winston-Salem, North Carolina, with his wife and three children.

ACKNOWLEGEMENTS

I Give honor to God without whom no good thing can be. It is with great respect, honor and love that I thank my father, William Bryant McIver Sr. for all of his love and support. He is the man who taught me through his example the true meaning of manhood. I pray that one day I will be the kind of man you are.

To my wife Ann; I love you, I love you, I love you. I can not believe the way you put up with me through out all of this. I know I had to have gotten on your last nerve but you never let on. You are absolutely my better half. Keep loving me because I'll never stop loving you.

To my beautiful children: Christian, Krista and Ellia you are blessings from God and I thank him for you every day. My family is my inspiration to wake up each morning and strive to be a better person than I was the day before. I love you all more than words could ever say. Remember, never give up on a dream and never settle for good enough. Because it never is.

To my big brothers Bryant and Todd, thank you for all of your help on this project, it couldn't have been done without you. Bryant the cover is beautiful and Todd the check is in the mail. I have spent my entire life looking up to both of you and you both have always had and deserved my respect. To my stepmother Gloria, God bless and keep you.

I want to thank my "other" brothers: Bill, Andre, Big John, Eric, Derrick, Carl. We have traveled the long road from boyhood to manhood together and man what a trip.

What is Forever?

Y'all hold it down.

To Bryan Fiese of Motivated Proformance and my editor Tracy; thank you so very much for guiding me through this long and arduous process you made the insurmountable almost easy. You have found a friend for life.

Chasity Conrad, thank you so much for all of your help and support with this book. Thank you for your insightful critiques and endless encouragement.

Special word of thanks to Robert and all of the guys and the girl at Reprotech graphics, we finally got it right.

Special Shout Outs to: the Brothers of Omega Psi Phi Fraternity Inc. be out dogs!
Literary Voices: Terry, Tracy, Tish, Rob, Sean, Tracy, Kim...,

To my sisters Jennie, Trixie, Cherise, Robin, Patrice, Carroll, Cathy, Mshai and all the reds of Gamma Phi I'm sending all of y'all much love,

Just so no one else asks, this book is 100% fiction. That's right the people and events are just figments of my imagination.

I especially thank you the reader for taking the time out of your busy schedule to read my first novel. I pray that you enjoyed it and that you will equally enjoy the books I write in the future. With God's help they will only get better. I must not forget to thank every person who came into my life that contributed to the person I am today I pray for your happiness and success. Finally, to every one who has found or is still looking for that special someone, I wish you a Love

What is Forever?

that lasts forever.

CHAPTER 1

The music played softly as Alexis entered the church. She could feel her heart beating strongly in her chest. The ankle length dress she wore hugged her womanly hips. They swayed in a manner that would make even the most pious man stand in need of redemption. Her body moved with a natural rhythm, as if she were walking to the beat of a smooth Caribbean melody. She wore a big brimmed hat with a 1930's style veil that came down past her eyes and ended at the bridge of her nose. Her countenance revealed the African nobility that ran through her veins. In a word, Alexis was class.

She had put drops in her eyes just before the limousine picked her up. She wanted her big brown almond shaped eyes to remain round and bright. As Alexis proceeded down the aisle toward the alter she felt the stares of the people who crowded the large sanctuary of the New Zion Memorial A.M.E. church to the point of standing room only. The new sanctuary had been opened less than a year ago and today it was beautiful. There were purple, gold, red and white flowers hanging everywhere. Golden sunlight poured in through the large stained glass windows. A huge mural of a black Christ looked down upon the congregation like a loving father over his baby's crib.

Alexis looked into the faces of the people who had come to show their support. She was happy to see her family, James Damon's policeman friend and everyone else who had been there for her and Damon. She could feel their love and support.

She had planned and paid for everything. She wanted to make sure that everything went perfectly. Alexis gave Keisha a slight smile and nod of her head. The supportive smile that was returned made her heart lift a little. Although Keisha was the mother of Damon's daughter she was still a friend, and her presence was comforting.

****

It was a warm April afternoon when she and Damon pulled up in front of Keisha's house to pick up his daughter Ebony. Alexis was about to meet Keisha for the first time and she was nervous. She had already spent a couple of weekends with Ebony when Damon had her, but she had never met the child's mother. She tried to convince herself that there was nothing to worry about. She needed to believe that even if the woman didn't like her, it wouldn't have any affect on her relationship with Damon. In her heart she didn't feel confident about that. Although Keisha and Damon's relationship had been over a long time, in a way she would always be the "woman" in Damon's life. There was a strong possibility that Keisha would resent another woman barging in on her territory. She felt wings of uneasiness flutter in her belly.

"Damon, how do you think Keisha will react to me?"

Damon chuckled. "Come on Baby, we've already been through this. I've told Keisha all about you. She's looking forward to meeting you."

Alexis felt doubt gnaw at her. She had many friends who had endured "Baby's Momma drama." She had heard more than her fair share of war stories: mothers calling fathers in the middle of the night, frantic that the baby was terribly ill when the baby hadn't even sneezed. For some reason it seemed the babies' mommas always decided they wanted the man back when a new love interest entered the scene. Alexis wondered what kind of "drama" she was in for. Whatever it was going to be, she had prepared herself for war if necessary.

"Look baby, don't even worry about it. Keisha is nothing like that. I'm telling you she is cool."

She was hoping that Keisha was as cool as Damon said but she wasn't about to take any shorts from the woman. If need be she would just let her know that she was the new woman in his life and there would be no "mess."

And then there was Ebony. Although she knew how to deal with a jealous woman, dealing with a child and the problems that might come with one would be delving into unknown territory. Alexis was not sure how to deal with any difficulties on that level. Still, Keisha was the real trial right now.

"Maybe you should have left me at your house." Alexis placed her hand on Damon's leg as she looked at the front door of the small house. "I mean, it's probably not a good idea for you to spring me on her right at her doorstep. Maybe she needs more time before we meet."

Damon placed his hand over Alexis's. "Come on, Baby. We've already been through this. I just know in my heart that she will like you. Just like Ebony did."

He looked into her eyes and gave her an easy smile. The sound of his voice eased her tension a little. Alexis looked down at Damon's dark brown hand covering her lighter one. Seeing the contrast of their skin sent tingles through her body. There was something about the contrast of their skin that always made her feel comfort and warmth. It was almost as if his darkness was an outward sign of his strength. With muscular arms to protect her and a broad chest to comfort her, he was a dark, beautiful, powerful man with the soul of a poet. Alexis loved to listen to him speak. His deep, rich voice had a way with her. Yes, this man was her dark prince, and she loved him.

She waited while Damon got out of the black BMW and walked around to her side and opened her door. "Don't you think I should at least wait in the car?" She was hoping she sounded enough like a baby to keep him from insisting she go with him. It didn't work.

"Alexis, come on. I can't believe such a strong, independent woman could be so afraid. Xena would be ashamed of you right now. Where's the warrior princess I fell in love with?"

Alexis knew he was just trying to goad her, but there was just something in her that couldn't turn down a dare. She took his hand as he helped her out of the car, took a deep breath and walked with him toward the house. Before they could reach the door it sprung open. A very attractive woman stuck her head through the opening.

"Boy, you always late. Shoot, you gonna end up being late to your own funeral."

"That's my plan." Damon smiled.

Keisha laughed and playfully slapped him upside the head. Alexis felt a twinge of jealousy at the playful way she touched Damon, but brushed it off. He had told her that they had a good relationship.

"Keisha, I want you to meet Alexis. Alexis, this is Keisha."

Keisha gave Alexis a warm smile and stuck out her hand. "Well it's nice to finally meet you. Damon's told me a lot about you. It's about time he found somebody decent to spend his time with. At least since me." She laughed at her joke.

Alexis tried desperately to manage a smile back. "It's nice to meet you."

"Come on in the house. Ebony's just finishing her dinner. Y'all have some? I've got plenty. Fried Pork chops, string beans, sweet potatoes and home made biscuits."

Alexis found herself smiling a bit more easily at the southern hospitality. She found it hard to picture Damon and this woman as a couple.

"No thanks. We've already eaten and we're stuffed."

"You look stuffed." Keisha patted him playfully on the belly.

Alexis was not completely comfortable with the familiarity between them, but again she brushed it aside. She trusted Damon. He had never given her reason not to.

"You look like you've gained a few pounds around the middle." Keisha laughed again.

They walked through an immaculate living room. The furniture was simple, but elegant. They walked into the kitchen and Alexis immediately saw the small female version of the man she loved. It had been over a month since she had seen the child, but from their first meeting Alexis had fallen in love with her. When Ebony saw her daddy her face lit up like a Christmas tree. She sprang from the table into his arms.

"Daaaaaddy!" She was tall for four years. Ebony had a golden brown complexion perfectly in the middle of her mother and father. The child had her mother's full lips, but other than that it was as if her father had made her without any help. "What'cha bring me?"

"Girl, if you don't carry your tail back to that table and finish your dinner you're not going anywhere," Keisha admonished her.

Damon put her down and she hurried back to the table to finish her vegetables, but she kept expectant eyes on her father.

Damon reached into his pocket. "What makes you think I brought you something?"

"Cause you always bring that spoiled tail something," Keisha huffed. "That's why I can't do nothing with her now." Keisha patted the little girl on the head.

"Well I didn't bring anything today, but I was going to ask you if you wanted to go to the movies."

Ebony's face lit up with the same beautiful smile that her daddy possessed. "Yes, please Daddy. I wanna go to the movies."

The three adults smiled at her good manners.

"Hey, Lexxus." Ebony bashfully smiled up at her as if she just noticed she had been standing there next to her father.

"Hello there, Miss Ebony." She walked over to where the child was seated and squatted down to her level. "It's so nice to see you again."

"Do you want to see Patches?" Ebony asked with her mouth full of the last of her vegetables.

"Not until you stop talking with your mouth full." Damon responded before Alexis could answer. "I swear girl, you have the worst table manners. I know you didn't get that from me." He glanced at Keisha.

"Don't look at me."

"Who's Patches?" Alexis asked.

Ebony allowed another sunshiny bright smile to spread over her soiled face and grabbed Alexis's hand. "Come on! I'll show you!"

Ebony nearly pulled Alexis's arm out of its socket as she exploded from the chair and down the back hall with Alexis in tow. It was all she could do to keep up with the little spitfire without falling over in her heels.

Ebony led her to a laundry room that was just big enough to hold a washer, dryer and a couple of plastic shelves over each. Instead of a door there was a small baby fence across the doorway. There, standing on his hind legs with his front paws draped over the little gate, stood Patches. A pink tongue hung out one side of a tiny mouth. The little dog's eyes focused on Ebony like she was all that was good in the world.

The Shitz-su was the most adorable thing Alexis had ever seen. Fur swirled in beautiful patches of black and white.

What is Forever?

When Ebony approached he let out a pitiful whimper and two small yaps.

"Oh Ebony, what a beautiful puppy! Where did you get him?" Alexis sat down on the floor in front of the gate. She loved dogs, especially little fru-fru ones. Patches gave another pitiful whine. He was really playing up to his new and sympathetic audience. "Awww, I think he wants to get out. Can we take him out?" Now she felt like the child, asking Ebony for the puppy's pardon.

"Sure, we can. He only hasta stay in there while we eat dinner. Momma don't want 'em in the kitchen while we eat, she says it's nasty. But he takes a bath every week. He's almost clean as me."

Alexis looked into the child's eyes and smiled. Just then Damon and Keisha came down the hall. "You can pick him up if you want. He doesn't bite." Keisha's invitation was all Alexis needed to hear before she swooped the lump of fur up into her arms and cuddled him like a baby.

"Oh whatacuetlilpupikinsyouare...yes you are! Oh Keisha, he's lovely."

"He's not my dog! Damon brought that mutt over here for Ebony. I'm just the maid that takes care of him."

"Now you know you're lying." Damon laughed. "You love that dog as much as Ebony does, probably more."

"No, I'm just responsible, unlike some people I know. I won't name any names, though."

"What are you trying to say, Keisha? I'm irresponsible?"

"You said it, not me."

"Well, I'm not. I am a free spirit."

Alexis saw the smile she liked so much spread over his face. She didn't like it going toward someone else. "Baby, don't you think it's time we go? The movie starts at six."

"See, that's exactly what I'm talking about Y'all supposed to be going to a six o'clock movie all the way

13

across town and you sitting here running your mouth. Mmmm hmmmm irresponsible."

"Well that's why I have Alexis. She keeps me on point." He leaned over and planted a kiss on her lips. "That's just one of the reason's I love her."

"Eeeewww, that's yucky." Ebony hid her eyes and crinkled up her nose.

"Good, that's exactly the attitude I want you to have toward kissing boys....yucky!" Damon imitated the look on his daughters face. "All right Keisha, I guess we'll get out of your hair. By the way where's Junior?"

"He's out with Skee and them. They supposed to be playing basketball down the street at the school, but ain't no telling where they really are. He should be back in a little while. At least he better come on back, or he ain't eating here tonight. Shoot, he know once I clean this kitchen up nobody's gonna be in here messin' up no more tonight."

"I know that's right," Alexis agreed.

"Come on, baby girl." Damon picked his daughter up in his arms. "The air is getting cold in here. Keisha where's her bag?"

"Oh, don't try to run out now, just cause the sista's in here about to testify."

Alexis laughed at him. "I think we can go to a later movie."

"No, no that's all right. Ebony doesn't need to be out that late. She needs her rest. Ya'll know that. Come on so we can go." Damon grabbed Ebony's small pink power puff girls overnight bag and slung it over his shoulder. "Don't you want to see that new Disney movie?"

"Yeeeeeahh! Alexis do you want to come with me and Daddy to the movies?"

She couldn't help but smile one more time. "Yes, Sweetheart. I'd love to go with you and your father to the movies."

What is Forever?

***

After they had arrived and the tickets were purchased, as they were walking through the lobby Ebony pulled on her daddy's jacket. "Daddy can I have some sour skittles?"

"What are you supposed to say anytime you say, 'Can I have,' young lady?"

"Pleeeeeease," she said showing off her two missing front teeth.

"I'll get you some baby, but after we go in and get our seats. You don't want to have terrible seats do you pumpkin?"

"No daddy, I wanna have good seats."

"So let's go on in there and find us some good seats."

By the time they reached theater five it was already getting crowded.

"It's a good thing we did come early huh?"

"You're right." Alexis agreed.

"I appreciate your coming to see this with us, Alexis. I'm sure there's something a little more grown up you would have preferred to have seen."

"Are you kidding? I love Disney movies. And at least now I don't have to be the only adult in the theater without a child."

They both laughed then gave each other a little kiss. Immediately Ebony made the yucky face.

"Daddy can I have my sour skittles now?" Before he could respond she added, "Pleeeease."

"All right, Baby, I'll be right back. Now y'all don't pick up any sailors while I'm gone."

With a wink he was gone, leaving Alexis and Ebony alone together. Alexis felt the awkward nervousness creeping back into her gut.

"So, Sweetheart, how old are you?"

15

"I'm four years old. How old are you?"

The child's quick comeback caught her off guard. "Oh let's just say I'm a little older than you."

"How old?"

"So did you see part one of this movie last summer?" Alexis tried to change the subject.

"Yes I did. Daddy even bought it for me on video. But you still didn't tell me how old you are."

At that moment the movie screen lit up with bright colors as the previews for upcoming children's movies started. Ebony's attention was immediately fixed on the screen. Alexis was grateful for the timely deferment.

By the fifth trailer Alexis was wondering why they had to show all of the best parts of the upcoming movies. Why did they have so many previews anyway? Damon returned with his arms full of popcorn and soda's. "Let's see here, large soda for my baby, medium cherry for my other baby and a diet for me. And one large popcorn with extra, extra butter."

"Daddy you forgot my sour skittles!"

"Sour Skittles? Hmmm. Did you say Sour Skittles?"

Alexis noticed Damon pull a small pink jewelry box out his right pocket and a pack of sour skittles out of the other.

"Here, Baby. Pick one. I'll let Alexis have the other."

Immediately Ebony went for the sour skittles.

"Thank you, daddy. I knew you wouldn't forget them." The little girl gave him a big hug and a kiss on the cheek.

"I guess that means this must be for you." Damon handed Alexis the box.

Her heart pounded in her chest like a drum. Her hands trembled as she touched the box and began to open it. She could not control the loud scream that forced it's way from her mouth when she saw the sparkling princess cut diamond set in a beautiful white gold setting. Every head in the theater turned toward the commotion, but Alexis was too excited to care.

"Oh, Baby! Oh I just can't believe it! Yes, yes of course I'll marry you!"

"Well, then would you at least give me a chance to ask you?" Damon slid off his chair and put one knee on the sticky floor. "Alexis, I love you with everything within me. I wouldn't have anything worth waking up for if it weren't for you and Ebony. You complete me and my life. Alexis will you be my wife?"

"Will you shut up back there? The movie's starting." Some man sitting in front yelled.

A woman sitting closer yelled back, "Shut up! He's back here proposing to her! You're ruining the moment!" She turned to Alexis. "Go on, Honey, now you can answer him."

Alexis blushed, suddenly becoming aware of her surroundings and much quieter said: "Yes, baby, of course I'll marry you. You complete me too."

The two rows of moviegoers on either side of them began cheering and clapping. The woman who had spoken before said, "That was the most beautiful thing I've ever seen in my life. I wish my Harry was that romantic. He won't even come with me to take the kids to the movies."

They kissed again, deeply, lovingly. Then Damon sat back in his seat, said pass the popcorn and fell into the movie just as Ebony had. Alexis may as well have been staring at a blank wall. All she could think about was that after all this time everything was coming together perfectly. And it was coming together with the man she loved.

By the time they reached Damon's house after the movie Ebony was in the back seat sounding like a miniature chain saw. Damon carried her toward the front door.

"Now that's what you call bustin' a slob." Damon said.

"No, this is what you call bustin' a slob." Alexis pulled him in close and pressed her lips to his. She felt his mouth open as she pressed her tongue against his lips. The heat of the kiss almost made him drop the little girl so she allowed him to pull away, then she led the way inside.

"Why don't you put our little girl to bed so that we can spend some quality time together." She hoped he got her meaning and wouldn't take too much time putting Ebony down for the night.

"I'll be right back." He carried Ebony up the stairs two at a time.

"Hurry up. I'd hate to fall asleep on you," she called up the stairs behind him.

After he disappeared onto the second floor of his condo Alexis walked into the bedroom to find something special to put on. She looked in the weekend bag that lay at the foot of the bed. As she reached for the lavender camisole and panty set she had packed, the diamond on her left hand caught her eye. A smile equally as bright spread across her lips. She stared at the ring and began to giggle.

"I can't take it. I've got to tell someone." She reached across the bed and picked up the phone. She barely noticed that the dial tone indicated that Damon had messages. Alexis dialed her best friend's number in Charlotte. It seemed like the phone rang a hundred times before Sonya's familiar voice came over on her answering machine. "We can't take your call right now, but leave us a message. Ciao." Beeeep.

"Girl, where in the world are you when I need to talk to you! Oh my God, I..." Alexis realized she didn't want to leave this kind of news on the machine. "...I'm at Damon's. You have the number. Call me. Love ya." Alexis hung up the phone, frustrated that she couldn't share her news with her girl.

She thought about calling her parents, but decided against it. They had only met Damon once, and would have too many questions. Alexis could hear her father now.

18

What is Forever?

"Do you know him well enough?" and "What kind of lifestyle can he provide you with?"

She'd call and tell them in the morning.

"Oh well." She sighed as she picked up her lingerie. She held it up, admiring. It was a near replica of one they had seen in a movie. She had noticed how much Damon seemed to appreciate it on the actress. When she found it in her favorite lingerie store, she bought it. Looking at the small amount of material, she knew it would be just the thing to cap off this perfect night. Alexis went into the bathroom of the master bedroom and turned the shower on. She took off her clothes and stepped under the powerful spout. The sensation of the hot water coursing across her body released the tension that had built up in her muscles. She felt like her whole body had just exhaled, allowing her to relax. When the potent stream from the shower nozzle hit her breast, it set a smoldering fire inside of her. She felt her nipples stiffen. She let her mind wander to intimate times she and Damon had shared. She imagined his hands, those dark hands running across her body, his perfect lips kissing her from head to toe and all points in between.

She generously lathered up her body and washed herself slowly and thoroughly, allowing her hands to linger in sensitive places. When Alexis closed her eyes and thought of Damon she knew that tonight their loving would be special. When she finished showering, she stepped out of the tub and dried herself with a plush purple and green towel.

She stepped in front of the large vanity mirror and used a hand towel to wipe the steam from it. She looked at her reflection as it became clear. She examined her ample breasts, placing a hand under each and lifting slightly.

"You guys are still standing firm after all this time. I just want you to know I appreciate that."

She knew that for her age and the size of her breasts they should have retreated south a long time ago. She was proud of her body and worked hard at the gym four times a week to keep it in good shape. Still, she was very self-conscious of her little "pooch." She was in constant battle with the tummy she had unknowingly picked up somewhere along her travels. Damon had told her again and again that it just gave her a womanly look and that it was one the things he found sexiest about her. Alexis refused to believe it. Why would any man find any amount of fat on a woman sexy? He had to just be saying it for her sake, but then again there was something about the look in his eyes when he said it that made her want to believe him. Anyway, it didn't matter. The war would continue until all signs of the enemy pooch were destroyed.

Alexis finished drying and proceeded through her nightly woman's regimen of cleansing her face, brushing, flossing, gargling and applying moisturizer. Once she completed that, she slipped into the little teddy. In a flash she was in the bed on her side facing the wall with the covers pulled up around her ears. Three minutes later Damon entered the room looking exhausted. He flopped onto the bed with his hand over his eyes.

"Baby? You're not asleep are you?" he asked, lifting his head and looking at the lump Alexis's body made out of the covers.

"No," she said softly, "but I'm on my way in a minute. Why?"

"Oh, no reason. I just thought maybe we would talk or something. Um, anyway, I need to take a quick shower. I'll be back in a minute."

"Okay, Baby." She answered him while yawning.

Alexis hunkered down in the covers a little more, trying to make him think she was really about to pass out from exhaustion. She laughed on the inside. Why couldn't he just come out and say it? She found it amusing and somewhat frustrating that Damon had trouble discussing sex with her. It had something to do with his attitude toward her. He felt she was too good to use certain language with. She had told him countless times that they could discuss anything together, but he still seemed too uncomfortable verbalizing his sexual desires and needs.

She didn't mind too much. What he didn't say with his mouth, he screamed with his actions. He had a way with making love that was beyond description. He was an artist, her body his canvas and his hands and tongue his brushes and paint. Damon would lovingly swirl and slap the paint of his love over her until together they created a masterpiece every time.

After he closed the bathroom door she sprang from the bed and lit the scented candles she had placed in his room a month ago. She turned on a Sade CD, keeping the volume down so that he wouldn't hear the music until he left the bathroom. Once she felt the mood was right she slid back under the comforter and waited for him to reappear. She couldn't decide if she would be sexier on top of the comforter or underneath it or with it only covering her legs. She was just climbing out from under the covers, trying to get on top without making the bed look messy when Damon opened the bathroom door and a cloud of steam was released. Alexis was caught in an awkward position with her bottom up in the air, while her arms and hands were twisted under her pulling the blanket in place.

"Now that's a view I could get used to."

She spun around, desperately trying to strike a sexy pose. The result was something that resembled a break-dancer. She felt her cheeks flush with embarrassment. Damon walked over to the bed and took her face in his hands.

"I love you, Alexis. I love you more every time I look at you." He moved in close and kissed her gently on her lips.

Alexis felt the warmth of love sweep over her body as she pulled him closer still. She could feel waves of pleasure and happiness fill her as they made love. She could feel them unite in a way that only soulmates could. Afterward, they lay tangled in each other's arms and legs. Perspiration glistened on their bodies. Alexis would normally run to the bathroom after making love to freshen up, but tonight was different. Tonight she wanted to just lay there with him, feel him in, on and around her.

The phone startled them. Damon started to reach for it when she stopped him.

"Baby, just let it ring. I don't want any thing to stop this moment. Right now everything is as perfect as it can be."

"Whatever you want, Baby." He kissed her gently on her forehead.

A moment passed after the phone stopped ringing. Damon sat up. " I hate to ruin the moment, but I really have to pee."

"Can't you just tie it in a knot?"

"I like to think well of myself in that area, but I'm afraid I don't have enough rope right now." He looked down at his sleeping manhood and shrugged his shoulders.

Alexis looked down. "Okay, you can go, but only if you promise to let me wake him up when you get back."

I'll see what I can do." Damon smiled as he rushed into the bathroom. He didn't bother to close the door.

Alexis thought about the phone ringing and remembered that it might be Sonya calling her back.

"Baby," she called, "what's the code for your answering machine?"

She heard the strong stream of urine hitting the water in the commode. There was a pause before he responded so she added, "I think it might have been Sonya that called. I left her a message while you were putting Ebony down."

"Well, I guess since you will soon be the new Mrs. Black it's okay for you to be able to check the messages." He rattled off the numbers.

What is Forever?

"Oh yeah, that's original."

"With only you in mind baby." He laughed. "Damn this is like a 40 0unce of Malt Liquor piss."

Alexis picked up the phone and dialed the code. As she listened her eyes widened then cut to slits.

"So, you ready for round two, Baby? 'Cause the pharaoh is ready to rule." He stopped in his tracks when he saw the look on her face and the phone pressed to her ear.

CHAPTER 2

Keisha watched Alexis walk past. Their eyes met. She smiled and gave a look of what she hoped was support. They had been through a lot in the last few days. There were times when she wanted to rip the woman's head off and times when she felt like Alexis was the only person who understood her. She really wished that she could talk to her now. Keisha pushed the thought out of her head. She knew that it would be totally inappropriate to speak to Alexis about the way she felt.

She looked down at Ebony sitting next to her, reminded of how much she looked like her father. Keisha thought of how this beautiful blessing came to be born and of the life the three of them could have lived if it were not for her own foolishness. She closed her eyes and remembered the day she'd met him. She thought of the young arrogant college Junior with so much charm as he strode into State's student union grill.

****

She instantly hated him. One thing she could never abide was an arrogant man, and Damon Black was the epitome of arrogance. She watched him as he walked with an easy confidence, flashing that cinematic smile of his at people. His outgoing personality had made him one of the most popular "frat" boys on campus. He spoke to almost everyone he passed as he walked to the counter to order his chili-

24

What is Forever?

cheese fries and grape Ocean Spray. Everyone, that is, except Keisha. He walked past her without so much as a glance. He made her feel invisible, and she hated him even more for having the power to do that. Damon went and sat at a booth with three Deltas. Keisha despised those stuck up bitches, too.

"What's up Keisha?" Cecil was standing over her with a stack of books in his arms. She hadn't even noticed him walk up. It was almost like he was invisible.

"Nothin' much, Cecil. How you been?"

"Everything's everything." His typical response. "Do you mind if I sit down? I just came in here to get a bite to eat before I head over to the library."

"Sure, have a seat. Did you finish that lab for Dr. Sing yet?"

"Yeah, I stayed after class and got it done. Did you?"

"Naw, that dern Indian is speaking Greek to me. Do you mind if I get your results from you later?" She knew he would say yes. He'd liked her all semester but never had the nerve to speak up. So she'd decided to continue to let Cecil do things for her, like her homework or cleaning her car, until he grew some balls and spoke his mind. Then she might consider letting him take her out.

"Yeah, sure that's no problem. I'll just have to get them to you tomorrow. I have something I have to do tonight."

"What in the world do you have to do? You never do anything other than go to library." Keisha knew from all of their conversations that Cecil had no social life. She figured he must be dating his right hand, from what she could see that was the only action he might be getting.

25

What is Forever?

"Well, I'm really not supposed to talk about this..." He paused and looked around, lowering his voice to a whisper. "I'm going to the Que's interest meeting."

Keisha couldn't believe her ears. Not Cecil. He was just not cut out for frat life, especially the life of a "nasty Que dog." They were the big men on campus. The college ruff necks. She just couldn't see it. "Get the hell out of here! You wanna be a Que?" She spoke louder than she'd intended, but she was totally blown away by his revelation.

"Please Keisha, don't talk so loud." Cecil ducked his head down as if trying to hide. "Don't you see Damon Black over there? He's supposed to be my sponsor. If he finds out I've been talking to anyone, especially a female about my plans I can forget about it."

They looked over to the booth were Damon had been sitting just in time to see him get up and head their way. Cecil's fidgeting increased with each of the other man's steps towards them. What a turn-off. How could he let another man turn him into such a punk? Damon Black wasn't no damn body. She did have to admit that he was nice looking and had a certain presence about him, but there was no need for him to have this effect on another man. Shit, didn't they both piss standing up?

"What's up Cec?" Damon nodded at Cecil while turning a chair around, straddled it and leaned his elbows across the back.

"Nothing much. Just talking about a science lab we're working on for Dr. Sing."

"Dr. Sing, huh? He can be tough. I had him last year. I barely came out of there with a B. He almost messed up my

26

What is Forever?

GPA. That's one person in my life I'm glad to leave in my past. You better really stay on your game in his class. So when's the lab due?"

"Tomorrow. We were just talking about getting together to work on it." He motioned towards Keisha. It was the first time Damon seemed to acknowledge she was sitting at the same table.

"Well damn, Cec. Don't act like she isn't even sitting here with us. You could have introduced me." He turned to her with that notorious smile of his. "Hi. I'm Damon."

Yeah right, like I don't already know who you are, she thought. Everybody on campus knows who his stuck up ass is. Mr. class president, most likely to succeed, frat boy. Puhleeese!

"Oh... oh yeah, my fault." Cecil looked like he had just failed some secret test. " Keisha, this is my boy Damon. Damon, this is Keisha."

Keisha saw Damon quickly survey her body. His eyes lingered on her sweater. A breast man. She was certain not to meet his standards in that department, not that she cared.

Damon reached for her hand. His shake was firm, almost businesslike, not the soft prissy grip of a junior player trying to impress a woman. He also failed to use one of the tired lines that seemed to be floating around campus like discarded newspapers.

"It's nice to meet you." There was a genuine tone to his voice when he said that. It made Keisha let her defenses down a little. Maybe he wasn't the dog everyone said he was. Maybe he was just a regular guy that had a lot of friends. After all, he had just greeted her the way any person

who was just meeting a new person for the first time would.
Other than checking her out a little, he had not come across
too bad.

"It's nice to meet you too." She tried to appear unfazed.

"So, do you stay on campus? I don't remember seeing
you around."

"No, I'm from the city so I commute. I stay with my
Momma."

"Oh yeah, that's cool." He nodded his head. "I bet that
sure cuts down on expenses. I wish my parents lived here."

"Were do your parents live?"

"They're both dead actually. So I guess first of all I wish
they lived anywhere. Then I'd wish they lived in town. It
must be nice to have home cooked meals and your mom to
look after you, huh?"

"I'm sorry to hear that." She found that she genuinely
was. She had never really taken the time to think about how
close she and her mother were, and how nice it was to have
those things she so often took for granted. Her mom had
been there for her since her daddy left, which had been a
long time ago. In fact, she hadn't seen him in years and
barely knew him. Most of her memories of him were of him
stopping by from time to time. He'd pat her on her head, tell
her how much she had grown and drop some cheap gift on
her. Then he'd tell her he needed to "talk" to her momma
alone for a minute. It was funny that their talks always lasted
until the next morning. Before he left he'd pat her on the
head again, then disappear out the door until the next time he
needed to "talk."

What is Forever?

When she got older and realized what their conversations were really about, Keisha lost some respect for her mother. She could never understand why her mother let her father use her like that. Still, in spite of everything, her mother had always been there for her, no matter what.

"I hadn't thought much about it, but now that you mention it I guess it is nice to be with my mom, when she's not getting on my nerves."

"Maybe you could invite me to your mom's sometime. I'd love to have something other than food from the pit." He paused, then looked at Cecil "Unless you and Cec here are kicking it or something."

Ah, here came the pickup line after all. He had just been taking the round-about route.

"Nah... Nah, me and Keisha, we're just friends." Cecil volunteered.

Keisha shot a quick look at Cecil. It was true that they were only friends, but they both knew that he had been working hard all semester to get next to her. Now he was all but inviting this guy to make a play for her. She made a mental note right then to scratch Cecil off her list of potentials. Any man that would kiss another man's ass thoroughly enough to give the woman he wanted away so he could get into a club was no man for her. Truth be told, Cecil's chances of getting with Keisha had been slim to none anyway, but for the cowardly way he was behaving she decided to teach him a lesson.

"Yeah, sure. I could talk to her about that. Do you want my number?"

What is Forever?

"I think it would be best if I gave you mine. I'd hate to keep calling begging for food. This way you can get in touch with me when it's cool with your mom."

Keisha didn't know how to take his turning down her number. Part of her felt insulted. Did he think he was too good to pursue her? If that was what he had in mind. She still couldn't tell. With most men she could tell in five seconds not only what their intentions were, but also how successful they'd be. With this guy she just couldn't tell. He may actually just want a home-cooked meal. She looked him in the eyes and then, bam! There was that smile again. It weakened her defenses another notch and she took the number and put it in her purse. She shot a glance at Cecil. "See, idiot? It's not that hard," she tried to tell him through telepathy.

"It was very nice to meet you, Keisha. I hope to hear from you soon. Cecil can I holla at you for a second." He motioned with his head and started toward the front door, never once looking back. Cecil was up and following behind him before Keisha could have said goodbye, which she did not plan on doing anyway. She was definitely through with Cecil. This Damon on the other hand, he was a mystery she would have to figure out.

***

Keisha had gone back and forth in her mind as to whether or not she really wanted to invite Damon to dinner. She wanted to convince herself that she would only invite him to prove a point to Cecil's stupid ass, but there was something about him that had her too curious not to follow up. Two weeks passed before she called to invite him to dinner. She dialed the number, assailed with a sudden urge to hang up before he could answer.

"There is no way he is interested in me. Not with those hoochies that are sniffing behind him."

"Hello?"

"Hey, can I speak to Damon?"

"Keisha? Yeah, this is Damon."

She was impressed that he remembered her. She also noticed that he broke one of the cardinal player rules. A real player would never call a woman's name over the phone if he wasn't certain who she was. He either was not a player or he had taken the game to another level.

He continued. "I'm glad you called. I thought maybe you had forgotten about me."

"Nah, I didn't forget. I been a little busy with class and work that's all."

"I can relate to that." She could almost see that smile of his through the phone. "So how have you been?"

"I'm fine. Like I said, swamped with my books, but everything's starting to slow down a little now. Anyway, I called you because I promised you dinner."

"That's right, you did. What time should I be there?"

Keisha laughed. "I wasn't talking about tonight." She thought about the prospect of seeing him and decided that she didn't have anything else to do. Besides, her mom wouldn't be home until late anyway. "But if you wanna come on by tonight I guess that will be all right. Just don't expect anything fancy." She could feel butterflies beginning to flutter around in her stomach.

"That's cool. I'm not looking for anything fancy. I'm looking for some good down home cooking. What's your mother making?"

"Who said my mom was cooking anything?"

"So what are you telling me? You're gonna cook?"

"You have a problem with that?"

"Not really, it just depends."

"Depends on what?!"

"It depends on if you know how to cook." He was teasing her.

Keisha smiled. "Well you know, they are still serving food in the cafeteria."

"Nah, that's all right. I've eaten there for three years. I'd rather take my chances with you."

"Good choice."

They shared a laugh. Keisha gave him directions to her house and told him to be there around six-thirty. He impressed her again when he asked if she needed him to bring anything. She had never had a guy do that before. She liked it. She told him not worry about it though, everything was covered.

Damon showed up at six-thirty on the dot. When Keisha opened the door, she definitely liked what she saw. Damon was not what she would refer to as fine, but she didn't like pretty boys anyway. He was handsome but thankfully had just a little edge to him. She noted the thin scar under his left eye and thought that it was sexy. She wondered how his face had been cut, but was scared to draw attention to it by asking. He was dressed in a white T-Shirt that had the college's crest embroidered on the chest, jeans and boots. He looked like an educated rough neck. She really liked the way he filled out that shirt.

"Hey Keisha, it's good to see you again." He gave her a quick hug that took her off guard. "Sorry about my appearance I was running late and didn't have time to change.

"Don't worry about it. You look fine." She wanted to tell him just how fine he looked, but didn't want it to go to his head. "Trust me, this ain't no fancy restaurant. Come on in and have a seat. Dinner's just finishing." She caught herself checking out his ass when he walked over to the couch and plopped on it.

"Well it smells like one up in here. What did you cook?"

"Let me see. I cooked some southern fried steak with gravy, rice and collard greens."

"Oh, you know how to hook a brother up."

"Don't get too excited. The collards are out of a can." "I don't know you well enough to be cutting up, washing and cooking fresh collards."

"Not yet, but give it time." He flashed his winning smile.

"Hmmph, we'll see."

She walked toward the kitchen to finish cooking. She let her hips sway a little more than normal, just to make sure she had his attention as she walked away from him. She had on her catch-a-man tight jeans, so she knew that he was checking out her plump ass.

What is Forever?

Less than fifteen minutes later they were seated at the small kitchen table. She was taken off guard when Damon took the liberty of saying the blessing. That was something done only on holidays in her Momma's house.

She was also impressed with his table manners. She struggled to keep a chuckle from escaping when he laid his napkin neatly in his lap. She wasn't used to a man who knew how to use a knife and fork better than she. Much better, in fact. But what she enjoyed most was the way that he dug into the food she had prepared with such abandon.

"Mmmmm! Keisha, this is good. You better believe they don't serve food like this on campus."

"Don't try to butter me up to just impress me," she laughed.

She could tell by the way he ate that his compliment was sincere.

"I don't have to fake liking this. It has to be the best meal I've had all year, if not longer."

Keisha had to admit that she'd really outdone herself, but it was a bit more difficult than usual for her to enjoy the dinner. She was overcome with the need to use her knife and fork properly. She didn't want him to think she lacked class.

She was delighted when he asked for seconds.

After dinner Damon helped her wash the dishes, then they went back to the living room and sat on the floor. They talked about school, watched television, listened to a few of her CD's and debated over who was the greatest rap artist in history. It was ten o'clock before she knew it. Her mother would be home by eleven and Keisha really didn't want her mother to be asking her a bunch of questions or

34

embarrassing her. As she tried to think of an excuse to ask him to leave without making him think she didn't like him, he spoke up.

"Well Keisha, it's getting kinda late. I have an eight o'clock test tomorrow and I need to get some studying in."

She wasn't sure if he had picked up on her thoughts or if he was being honest but she was glad he was leaving. Well, not glad exactly, more like relieved. As she walked him to the door she wondered if he would try to kiss her. She also wondered if she would let him. As he walked out the door he turned to her and gave her a warm hug. This time she hugged him back.

"Thanks again for the dinner." He paused a moment, then added, "by the way, you can burn."

She laughed "Well you're gonna have to come back sometime and get some fresh collards."

"I'd like that a lot." He turned and walked to one of the ugliest cars she had ever seen. When he turned the motor over she found that it was the ugliest sounding one she had ever heard too.

"So he drives a hoopty. Nobody's perfect," She told herself. She also knew that she definitely would have let him have a kiss if he had tried.

***

After that, Keisha found herself spending a lot of time with Damon. They made an odd couple. She was a southern girl, born and bred. She spoke with a southern twang and had never been outside of North Carolina. In fact, she had

What is Forever?

rarely left her hometown. Damon was the paragon of what a Yankee should be, with his proper northern talk. Keisha loved to hear him enunciate every syllable of every word. Over time she had learned that Damon had been raised by his aunt. Apparently the old girl was far from broke. He grew up going to Broadway plays and cultural events. She found out that he had traveled to three different countries and thirty of the fifty United States.

Growing up, the biggest cultural event Keisha ever experienced was the annual county fair that came to her town. And she had never been any further away from her front door than Charlotte. They were very different people from very different backgrounds, but for some reason they complimented each other. Over the course of less than a month she regarded Damon as her best friend and confidant other than her girl Rolanda. In a lot of ways he was better than Rolanda. Damon helped Keisha with her schoolwork. He exposed her to things that she had never taken the time for: reading, plays, being socially and politically conscious, he even had a way of making the simplest, everyday things seem important.

She took him around the city, introduced him to her family and friends. She provided him with a surrogate family and many home cooked meals. It didn't take long before she knew that she was falling for him.

But even after all of the time they spent together, the personal thoughts and feelings they shared, Keisha was no closer to understanding what he wanted from her. It had been three weeks and he had not made the first romantic move on her. This was a very different experience for her. The guys

What is Forever?

she was used to dating made their move early, often on the first night.

Damon was a different story. Always an enigma. He liked to spend time with her. As a matter of fact, most of his free time was spent with her. He confided in her. He told her his plans for the future, how he wanted to be a movie producer and director. He wanted to make movies that would make a difference in the black community. He wanted to tell stories about people who had made a difference. People that the average American had never heard of, such as Lewis Latimer and Benjamin Mays.

Keisha would have thought that he just wanted to be her friend if it were not for the little special things he did for her. He always opened doors for her. On occasion he would use pet names like baby or sweetheart. When he said goodnight he even kissed her on the lips. But that was as hot as it had been.

The fact that he had not attempted anything with her made Keisha feel unattractive. It made her feel like she didn't measure up to the other women he had been with. She had spoken to some of her friends and had them check the grapevine about Damon. From the reports she received there were two things she knew. One, he was not gay. Two, he was not the type of guy to go this slowly. For the life of her she couldn't figure out what was going on with him. If he wasn't trying to get some from her it must be because he wasn't attracted to her. She could see no other reason.

Things came to a head one night when they went to the Flamingo Drive In to see a double feature. The flamingo always played old movies. That night Boomerang and The

What is Forever?

Nutty Professor were playing as tribute to Eddie Murphy. Keisha was restless all through Boomerang, which was one of her favorite movies. She could not contain herself after Eddie Murphy showed up in his fat make up. She decided to put her cards on the table.

"Why haven't you tried to have sex with me?"

Damon almost choked on the grape ocean spray he was sipping. "What? What kind of question is that?" he sputtered as he wiped the sticky juice from his thick lips.

Keisha imagined herself licking the juice from his lips. She had become so hot while waiting for him to make his move that she found herself fantasizing about him constantly. She was shaking off the feeling when she realized it had been over six months since she last had sex. She had received numerous phone calls from past partners attempting to reignite flames long dead, but she just couldn't see herself getting with any of those guys. This was really out of character for her. She had never been the type to turn down good sex when she was single, and since she and Damon didn't officially have a relationship she knew she was free to do her thing. She was all but sure he was doing his. Still, for some reason she just didn't think anyone else would do.

"I mean it. I thought you liked me. I thought maybe you were just building up your nerve. Maybe deep down you were really shy or something. But I asked around and one thing I found out is you're not is shy. From what I hear there are plenty of girls on campus that you've been with. I just want to know what it is about me that turns you off so much. Why don't you want to get with me like that?"

What is Forever?

Damon looked her in the eyes and that smile of his spread across his lips until he suddenly burst out in laughter. He had himself a good hard belly laugh while she sat there almost in tears.

"Stop laughing at me! I can't believe you are such a damn asshole." Keisha pulled the door handle, prepared to walk home. He grabbed her by the arm and pulled her gently back toward him.

"Wait a minute, Keisha."

"Get the fuck offa me, nigga. I don't care if you don't want me no way. Trust me, there are plenty of guys trying to get with me."

"Keisha, will you chill? I'm sorry. I'm not laughing at you, Baby. I was laughing at what you said. Now please sit here so we can talk about this."

She pulled her arm out of his hand and slid as far away from him as possible, leaning on the passenger door, but she did not attempt to open the door again.

"Look, Keisha. I didn't mean to laugh. It's just I've never had a girl come at me so bluntly. It kind of took me off guard, that's all. I know you're not crazy so I'm not even gonna front like I haven't been with my share of women." That comment did not ease her already fragile ego. She turned her head and gazed out the window.

Damon continued. "It's just that you're different from any girl I've ever known. I know it sounds corny, but it's true. There's just something about you that makes me think differently, act differently. It's the way we vibe with one another. It's the way I can talk to you about anything. I like the way you're always yourself. You never put on airs or act phony. I'm tired of people who sweat me because I'm a Que or because I'm class president. I'm tired of people who want to be my friend because it seems like the thing to do. You never treat me like I'm special because of those superficial things. You treat me like I'm special because I'm me. I like that, Keisha." He paused and took a deep breath before continuing. "I've never said this before... at least I've never meant it... I love you Keisha. I guess I have since that first dinner."

She turned her head and looked at him. She was confused. If he loved her, why didn't he want to have sex with her? How could he love her without that?

Damon seemed able to read her thoughts. "I know I haven't really shown my feelings for you, but I wanted to show you that I respect you. I didn't want you to think I was just trying to get in your pants."

"Well maybe I wanted you in my pants!" she yelled.

He just smiled at her, then looked down at his hands. "Keisha, I just spilled my heart out to you. You haven't really responded to what I said. At least not in the way I hoped you would. I told you that I love you. Do you love me?"

She wanted to say "hell yeah," but instead she said "I don't know, Damon. I mean, we are still getting to know one another. There are a lot of things about you that I don't know, and things about me that you don't know. Can you truly say that you love me?"

She was still protecting herself. She knew it, but she just could not make herself tear down her walls and leave herself defenseless. She looked into his eyes and for a brief moment thought she saw a tear well up. He looked away before she could be sure.

"Damon ... I'm just scared. I'm scared you're not sincere. I'm scared if I give you all of me, you'll leave me. I don't think I could stand it if you left me." She heard the words coming out but didn't know where they came from. She heard herself opening her soul and it scared her to death, but it was too late to turn back.

"But you just got mad because we haven't done it yet. You're confusing me. I thought you knew how you felt."

"I was talking about sex. I never said anything about love. I wanted to know why you didn't want me."

"So all you want me to do is fuck you?" His eyes turned dark with anger. "Is that what all of that yelling was about? Hell, I can fuck you. Take your pants off. Come on! I'll fuck the shit out of you." He began to unbuckle his belt. She could see disappointment in his eyes. "I thought you were special, someone I could respect, but hell, sex is fine too. Well what are waiting for? Come on."

"No, that's not what I meant, that's not what I want." She was flustered and confused. The tears began to stream from her eyes. I just meant I wanted you to want me, to care about me. When you never tried, I couldn't tell how you felt about me, about us. Damon I wanted you to want me. I wanted you to love me because... because I love you." Her eyes focused on her lap. "I do love you. I've known it for a while. It's just like I said, I'm afraid. I'm afraid of what you think of me. I'm afraid of how you feel about me. I've never had a guy who treats me the way that you do. Sometimes it's overwhelming. It takes me off guard. I feel like I don't deserve all of this. I mean..." she paused, "you are such a special person. You are going to be someone great someday. I know that. Me, I'm just a regular person. Average. But that's cool with me. I like things simple. I don't want to be rich and famous. I just want to live an average life. I want a couple of kids, a small house and a decent job. You've already told me about what you want. You want to change the world and I believe that you can. I just don't think that I could fit into your future world and I know that you wouldn't want to fit into mine. If we got together, years from now you would regret it. You'd realize that I'm not good enough for you. That's when you'll leave and I don't think that I could stand that. So I'm afraid to put myself into that position in the first place."

"Keisha, this is crazy. You love me, but you don't want me because you love me and I *might* leave. I can't believe this." He took a deep breath. "Look Keisha, no one knows the future. You don't know what I'm destined for. I could die tomorrow. You say you want an average life now, but by the time you graduate that may change. Your future may be brighter than mine will ever be. We just don't know. What we do know right now is that we love each other, and right now that's all that matters." He lifted her head in his hands. "We should be kissing now, not arguing. Lets live in this moment, right now and let tomorrow take care of itself." He leaned in and kissed her. Not a friendly goodnight kiss, but a warm deeply passionate kiss that made Keisha's heart race.

She had waited months for this moment and she knew that it was worth every second. She still felt apprehensive about their future together but she decided to take his advice

What is Forever?

and to live in the moment. They left the movie and drove to his dormitory. That night she let herself go and totally gave herself to him. Keisha had been with several men, but making love to Damon could only be described with one word: perfection.

***

After the night at the drive-in, Keisha and Damon became inseparable. They grew closer; they shared their dreams. Keisha had confided in him that she only went to college after high school because that's what her mother wanted her to do. She had hoped that after she began taking courses she'd be able to figure out what she wanted to do with the rest of her life. She'd been there almost two years and had no more of a clue as to what she wanted to be than she had the day she'd stepped on campus. She thought Damon would think less of her for not having a life plan, but he didn't. He told her that most of the people at State were in the same boat. He told her that the secret was to find what she liked and figure out how she could make a career of it.

"But I don't need a degree to make money having sex," she joked.

"Unfortunately you can't have a career having sex if you want to be my wife."

That was the first time he had actually mentioned her becoming his wife. She liked the sound of it. "Well, if I am going to be the future Mrs. Big Shot, why do I even need a career? You are going to make plenty enough money for the both of us."

43

"I hope you're right, but you still need to have your own career. Hopefully not for the money but for your own self worth. How could you be content just keeping house and watching the twelve children?"

"I don't know what you're talking about. I ain't shooting no twelve kids outta my kitty kat. Two. That's it. A boy and a girl. Then I'm done. Shoot, after twelve kids you'd be useless to me. I'd have to get a baseball bat to scratch my special itch." She laughed out loud.

"Well since you put it like that, maybe two will be enough."

"That's what I thought. But anyway what's wrong with tending house and taking care of the kids? Lots of women love being housewives."

"You're not lots of women. I know right now you think you're just an average person, but you don't have to be just average. Your only limits are the ones you set for yourself. You can be and do anything you want. I want you to stop selling yourself short. You are a beautiful, intelligent young lady. You have so much inside of you to offer to this world. You just need to start believing that and then start shooting for the stars."

His words soothed and inspired her. It was not long after that conversation that Keisha noticed a change in her attitude. Her grades gradually began to improve and she began to understand and learn the information she was given in her classes. Along with the change in attitude she noticed a change in the way people treated her. It wasn't that they had not been friendly before she started dating Damon. In fact most people were almost too friendly. People had a way of approaching her in a too personal way. Guys approached her with "Hey, Shorty," or "Pssst Psst." Although she always hated that, she had never given any thought to it being disrespectful. After she and Damon got together she noticed everyone seemed to treat her with more respect. She never realized that this would be a perk of being the BMOC's girl. She had to admit, she enjoyed it.

Their relationship went smoothly for the next three months, until Keisha missed her period. Her cycle was like clock work. In fact she often joked with her girls that you could set your watch by it. When it was overdue by more than two weeks, she knew that she was pregnant. She just couldn't figure out how. She'd been on the pill since she was fifteen and almost never missed it. In addition to that, they almost always used condoms.

Keisha called her best friend Rolanda and told her what was going on.

"I bought the test already. I've been staring at it for an hour. Please Rolanda, will you come over? I can't do this alone."

"Girl, why don't you call that Q-Dog that did this to you?" She emphasized the word dog.

"He's already got a lot on his plate, Rolanda. I don't want to worry him with this if it turns out to be a false alarm, which it has to be. I just need someone here with me while I take the test. Please, Rolanda. Don't let me down."

"Come on, Keisha. You know I'm here for you. I'll be there in ten minutes."

As always, Rolanda was true to her word. She and Keisha had been best friends since the third grade and had

What is Forever?

always shared their secrets. Keisha was there when Rolanda
got pregnant at fifteen. She went to the abortion clinic with
her when she terminated the pregnancy. She was also there
when her friend got pregnant again at seventeen, and was
there when her godson Jaquan was born. They had double
dated on many occasions and in everything except blood
they were sisters. Keisha had not spent as much time with
her friend since she and Damon had gotten together, but she
knew when it came down to the wire her girl would have her
back.

When Rolanda walked into the house, Keisha's mother
was laying on the purple couch in the living room. She was
wearing her pink flowery housecoat and had her hair tied up
in a green silk scarf. She was watching her soap opera. She
taped it every day while she was at work.

"Hey, Ms. Jones. How are you today?"

"Child, I'm fine. I just wish this crazy story didn't take
so damn long to get to the point of its story lines. That boy's
been looking for that girl for two years. I wished he'd go on
and find her already."

"I know that's right, Ms. Jones. I think he's 'bout to get
with that new girl they got on there now, what's her name,
Charlie? Yeah, I think them two is gonna hook up."

"You know, I bet you're right. She looks just like his
wife, with them big lips. It cracks me up how these white
folks spend all that money injectin' shit in they lips so they
can have black folk's lips. Then they want to make us feel
like our big lips are ugly. They need to be ashamed."

"Don't forget how they lay out in the sun cooking they
skin so they can get dark. It don't make no sense."

46

What is Forever?

"I know that's right, Child. They want to look like us, and if they has to, they give themselves skin cancer to do it. They don' even care."

Both the women laughed.

"If you looking for Keisha, she back in her room. She been back there all evening. She been round here acting all strange since she got with that boy over there at that school. Shoot, you ask me she shoulda stayed with Willie. He got that good job with the city. He got benefits and all. That's the kind of man I would pick for her, someone stable."

"You right, Ms. Johnson. I told her she was crazy when she put him down. Have you seen that new car he got? It got rims and every thing."

"I saw him driving it the other day. Now that's a good boy. I don't know what she see in that ole sedity boy she bringing round here. He sittin' up in my house more than I do. I figure if he got that much time on his hands, he need to get a job somewhere."

Just then Keisha entered the room. "Momma, you don't even know what you talkin' about. He ain't even here that often, and for your information he does have a job. It's just part time 'cause he's in school full time. In a few years Damon will be able to buy and sell ten Willies. Willie ain't about nothing. The only reason he could afford that car is cause of the drugs he's selling. He'll be in jail before long, paying someone like Damon to get him out."

"Willie sellin drugs?" Rolanda feigned shock.

"Girl, don't even go there trying to act like you didn't know just cause my momma sitting there. You know good and well that's how he keep all that money in his pocket. The

What is Forever?

city ain't paying that much money. That's why I quit that sorry man. Walking round here thinking he Scarface or something."

Ms. Jones spoke with her eyes glued to her video. "Well Keisha, I ain't saying he should be selling no drugs, but men gonna do what they feel they hafta do. He'll get hisself together, you watch and see. At least he don't think he better than everybody else. He down to earth, and that's what counts."

"Momma, I ain't even gonna argue wit you about all this. Ro, come back to my room."

"You gonna listen to me one day, Girl. That boy don't care nothin bout you. He just getting what he can get then he'll be gone. You just watch what your momma say. Then you'll be in here crying on my shoulder," she called after them.

"Whatever you say, Momma." The girls walked down the hall to Keisha's room. Keisha closed the door and locked it.

"Damn girl, your momma don't like Damon. What's up wit that?"

"I don't know. It's like she can't stand for me to be happy. When I was with Willie she couldn't stand him. Now she's all sweatin him like he Jesus or somethin."

"Well he is fine, Girl. You gotta admit that." Rolanda reminded her as she flopped on the full sized bed. It sported the same pink comforter set that had been on it since Keisha was a little girl.

"If he's so fine, why don't you take him?"

What is Forever?

"You know I don't want none o yo' sloppy seconds. I don't even roll like that."

"If you decide to, it ain't no skin off my apple is what I'm saying. Anyway I don't have no time to be worried 'bout that trifflin nigga anyway. Here let me have the test." She snatched the bag out of her friends hand and ripped it from the plastic wrapper. She tore the package open and began reading the instructions.

"I don't know why you reading them instructions. Everybody know all you gotta do is piss on the thing and wait for it to change colors."

"Thank you Dr. Ruth, but if you don't mind I'd rather read the instructions to make sure I do this right."

She read the entire instruction sheet which basically told her to urinate in the cup, dip the stick in, and wait for 10 minutes while the color changed from white to pink or blue. If it turned pink, her period was just late. If it turned blue she was indeed pregnant.

"See, I told you. You think because you in college you smarter than me, but now I guess you know that don't make you no smarter."

"Any smarter," Keisha corrected her.

"Now I know you trippin. That's exactly what I'm talking about. Like you always speak perfect English. Sometimes folks just want to chill and not worry about conjugating they verbs right."

"I know, Girl. I was just playing with you. Why you all sensitive? Shoot, if I didn't know better I'd think you was the one taking the pregnancy test. What's up with you?"

What is Forever?

"Nuthin, Girl. It's just that every since you started college and dating Damon," she squished up her nose when she said his name as if it had a bad smell to it, "you just don't seem to be the same Keisha. I mean, I know you got a white girl's name, but now you starting to act like it."

They both laughed. Keisha hit Rolanda in the head with her pillow.

"Come on now, Girl. I haven't gotten that bad. Look Ro, I really care about this man. He's a special guy and he makes me feel special. You know what I mean?"

"I can't say that I do. What's so special about him? Ain't he just a man like any other? They all just like buses..."

"You miss one another will be along in ten minutes." They finished in unison and laughed.

"Ro, I know we always say that, but Damon ain't no bus. If anything, he's a Benz. They don't come by every ten minutes. As a matter of fact, most people never get to ride in one. I have the chance to have one of my own and I just don't want to blow it. Now I might be pregnant. I just don't know what to do. I don't want Damon to think I'm trying to trap him. If he thinks I got pregnant on purpose there's no telling what he'll do."

"Hell, he better take care of his responsibility. I don't care if you did it on purpose or not. You didn't get pregnant by yourself. He's just as responsible for this as you are. I can't believe he has you so whipped that you're afraid of what he might think. What in the world has he been doing to you? You're not even the same person anymore."

"Well, for one thing he knows how to put it down in the bedroom. He's so sensitive and tender. But he still knows

50

exactly when to put it on me Mandingo style. Giiirrrl, mmmmh! I'm telling you, that brother is holding. But really that's not all of it. It's like I said, he treats me like I'm special. He makes me feel like I'm important, what I think is important. I love him and that's the bottom line."

"If it's like that then I'm happy for you, but if he really loves you he'll be happy about this and he'll love you and the baby."

"Well let's hope we don't have to put him to the test."

The girls waited in silence for the next three minutes. Keisha walked over to the desk where she had set the pregnancy test. She could not make herself look at it. She closed her eyes and turned her back to it.

"You look at it for me. I can't do it."

Rolanda picked up the stick and looked at it for a moment. "Well Girl, I guess congratulations are in order. You gonna be a mommy."

CHAPTER 3

While the family was entering the church, Tara leaned her head back and wiped the tears that streamed from her eyes.

"How did everything come down to this? We were supposed to end up together," she thought to herself. "Oh God, I'd rather be dead than to have to sit and watch this. How am I supposed to live without him?" She was perfectly aware of how inappropriate her thoughts were, but she couldn't stop them.

Tara watched Alexis walk toward the alter. She tried to figure out how she felt about the woman. She didn't hate Alexis, but she definitely couldn't say that she liked her. The only emotion she could pinpoint was jealousy. She hated to admit it, but she was jealous of her. Of course, she had reason to be. After all she and Damon had been through together, after all the promises that had been made, he still chose Alexis. Tara didn't know if she could ever forgive him for that.

***

Tara had met Damon two years earlier while he was still in film school. It had been a cold blustery day in October. She had been sitting in The Corner Coffee House crying. It seemed before she met Damon she spent most of her time crying. On this particular day, she had just been cursed out by her fiancé – no new thing.

What is Forever?

She had met Gabe there for lunch. They had only been seated fifteen minutes before he lashed out at her. Gabe was a very smart man. He was a lawyer and he knew how to argue. Whenever they got into it he always knew just what to say to make her feel stupid. She couldn't even remember now why they had been arguing that day. Probably the way she looked at the guy behind the counter, or maybe it was the amount of sugar in his coffee. There was no telling what it had been about. All she could remember was that he had left her feeling alone and worthless, which was the way he seemed to prefer her.

After reducing her to a crying mess he had walked out and left her sitting there with her eyes and nose running. She wanted to get up and leave, but Gabe's verbal assault had left her too weak to move. All she could do was sit there and cry.

She saw a shadow over her, but couldn't even look up to see who was standing there until she heard the deep, clear voice.

"Excuse me, Miss. Are you all right?"

What a stupid question. Did she look all right? "Yes, yes I'm fine."

She moved to pick up her cappuccino and knocked her purse off of the round table onto the floor. The contents of the bag spilled out onto the black and white tile floor. Before she could bend to gather her things he was on one knee picking up her belongings and placing them back into the bag.

"It's okay I'll get it." She put her hand on the purse.

It was then that she truly noticed him for the first time. He was a very attractive dark-skinned man about three years younger than she. The loose fitting purple T-shirt did not hide the fact that he was well built with broad shoulders. She looked at his face and was instantly mesmerized by the most beautiful brown eyes she had ever seen. The handsome stranger picked up the pack of birth control pills that had fallen out of her bag. When he realized what he had in his hand, he blushed and lowered his eyes as he placed them in with the other items.

She managed to smile. She liked his modesty. It was refreshing.

"I'm Damon."

"Hello, Damon. My name is Tara." She reached to shake his hand. "Thank you for helping me with my things. I'm such a klutz."

"Don't mention it. You seem upset so it's understandable. Are you sure you're all right? Can I get you anything?"

"A new life maybe. Other than that I have every thing I need."

"A new life, huh? What's wrong with the one you have now?"

"I think the question should be what's not wrong with it."

"Would you like to talk about it?" He sat down across from her, folded his hands and looked at her as though he really expected her to spill her life story.

"No, thank you. That won't be necessary. I was actually getting ready to leave."

"Oh, okay. I just think sometimes it helps to get out what's bothering us."

What is Forever?

"Do you really think a person would share personal problems with a stranger?"

"Well technically I'm not a stranger anymore. You know my name's Damon and I've had your birth control pills in my hand. How can I be considered a stranger after that?" He smiled a smile that made Tara want to smile too. "Not to mention, sometimes it's better to talk to someone totally removed from the situation. They tend to have fewer biases."

"I really appreciate the offer, but I think I must pass." She placed her purse over her shoulder and stood to leave. "It was nice meeting you Damon, take care of yourself."

"I think I should be saying that to you. So you take care of yourself, Tara. Remember, we have the power to create new lives for ourselves every day."

She smiled a little, then turned and walked toward the door. As she reached it she caught her reflection in the mirrored glass. Her eyes were swollen and her nose was red. Yuck! He must have really thought she looked a mess. Inside her gold convertible Saab, Tara turned up the radio and sang along with Whitney Houston's *The Only Man I Need*. She decided she wouldn't go back to work. She used her cell phone to call the office and tell her boss she wouldn't be back in. She didn't feel like going straight home, either. She ended up just riding around the city attempting to get her thoughts together.

As Tara drove, she thought about the stranger from the coffee shop. How gentle his mannerisms were, and of the way he blushed when he saw her pill pack! And those eyes. They seemed to pierce her. She'd been impressed by his kindness. Gabe would never take the time to be so kind to a stranger. He felt that people who were weak deserved to be sad. She began to think about Gabe again and how cruelly he had treated her. She was fed up with it. She was not going to allow him to treat her like shit anymore. She didn't need him. She had a good job as a real estate agent. She didn't need his money and she damn sure didn't need his shit. It was definitely time for her to make a change.

By the time she reached the townhouse she shared with Gabe, she was resolved to tell him she was leaving him. She pushed the button to the remote garage door opener and pulled her car in next to his black Lexus LS 400. As she walked up the stairs to the main floor she prepared herself for battle. Tara was determined not to allow him to twist her words and make her feel like she was not smart enough to argue her point. Gabe was one of the best domestic attorneys in the city. One thing that he was very talented at was twisting any argument his way, but not this time. She knew she was right and he was not going to get her to back down. When she opened the door and stepped into the living room she was overwhelmed by the scent of roses. She looked up to see the living room completely covered in roses of every variety and color. In the middle of all that color sat Gabe on the cream colored leather sofa. He was wearing the green Calvin Kline pullover she had bought him for his birthday with the black slacks that fit him oh so well. He was holding a single red rose in his hand.

The roses instantly weakened her resolve. Before she could speak he had gotten up and handed the rose to her. He put his finger over her lips.

What is Forever?

"Before you say anything baby, please let me say that I'm sorry. I was thinking about our fight and I know that I was wrong. I haven't treated you like the queen you are, and I'm sorry for that. I know that this is no excuse, but work has me so stressed out lately I just can't think straight. Everything has me on edge. I know I've been taking it out on you. Tara you are the only thing in this world that keeps me sane. I don't know what I'd do if I lost you, but I also know that all I've done lately is push you away. I'm sorry, Baby. I promise it will never happen again."

Tara listened to his words and the sincerity in them. Maybe she had overreacted. Gabe could be verbally abusive at times, but he did have a very stressful job and sometimes he probably needed to vent. She told herself that he had never actually hit her. That was something she'd never stand for. Maybe if she was more understanding and was there for him more he wouldn't speak to her so harshly. Maybe she was partially to blame for their problems.

Gabe had been on her about the long hours she put in at the office. She had explained to him that she was still considered the new kid on the block and she had to put in extended hours in order to prove herself and to get the quality properties. He always felt that he made enough money so that she shouldn't have to work. The whole situation was the root of half of their blowouts. Tara was starting to think that he was right. Maybe she should stay home and take care of the house.

Gabe put his arms around her waist and kissed her on the forehead. She looked into his eyes and saw the stress in them. He leaned down and kissed her lips. She allowed his

What is Forever?

tongue to wash over hers. Gabe unbuttoned her blouse and let it fall on the plush carpet. She pulled his shirt over his head. It took only moments for her to find herself on the floor with Gabe. Tara closed her eyes as he entered her. For just a moment she imagined she was looking into the eyes of a stranger. Big beautiful brown eyes that captivated her spirit.

Things went well between Tara and Gabe over the next few weeks. She reduced her hours at work and spent more time at home. Gabe seemed to be happier and yelled less. Tara decided to have lunch at the Corner Coffee shop while she reviewed some new listings that had been given to her that morning. She was eating a tuna fish croissant when someone walked up behind her.

"Well hello again. Tara, isn't it?"

She was totally caught off guard when she looked up and into Damon's beautiful eyes. She had a mouth full of Tuna, and mayonnaise on her fingers. She quickly wiped her hands on her napkin and attempted to swallow the big wad of food she had been chewing. She almost choked as she forced the food down. When she'd composed herself she looked up and smiled at him.

"How are you?" She gave him her most businesslike voice. "Yes, it's Tara. I'm surprised that you remember."

"I never forget a face or a name. So how have you been? I must say you look much happier than the last time I saw you. I guess you created a new life for yourself after all."

"No, I can't say that, but I have made some improvements to the old one." She didn't know why she felt so happy to see him, but she did know that she was happy that she didn't look like an escaped lunatic this time. "Would you like to sit and have a cup of coffee with me? I'd like to say thank you for your thoughtfulness that day."

"I'd love to, except for two things: one I don't drink coffee and two, you don't have anything to thank me for. I'd love to have a hot chocolate though." He sat in the chair directly across from her. "So how are things going these days?"

"Oh, everything is fine."

They sat in the coffee shop and talked for over an hour. Tara found that they had a lot in common. They were both only children. While Damon's parents had both died and he was raised mostly by his aunt, Tara's mother had been a drug addict and gave her up for adoption when she was three. She'd never heard from her again. Tara never knew her biological father. She suspected that he was white due to her light complexion, green eyes and silky hair.

Eventually she'd been adopted by an upper middle class white couple, and raised in a predominately white area in Long Island, New York. Her parents had given her a lot of love, but for as long as she could remember Tara had suffered from feelings of not fitting in. She always felt like an outsider or a visitor with her black counterparts, and she could never really click with her white friends. From elementary school through high school she spent most of her time as a loner. Her adoptive father died her senior year of high school. Because of some bad business deals he left Tara and her mother in a tough financial situation.

She worked hard in high school, and after graduation she received a scholarship to the University of North Carolina at

What is Forever?

Charlotte. Like Damon she had been very involved in campus life. She pledged AKA and participated in student government. Although Tara never felt the need to run for any offices she had been appointed to several important supportive positions.

She and Damon discovered that both of them had pretty much worked their way through college. Damon turned out to be three years younger than she and currently in his first year of film school. She found his personality refreshing and unpretentious. When she found out that he was single she told him that she had several girlfriends that she would love to introduce him to. He politely turned down her offer, explaining that he'd had bad experiences with blind dates. She was having a great time when she happened to notice the time.

"Oh my, I'm late for an appointment. Damon it has been such a treat talking with you. You've been a joy."

"The pleasure has been mine." He smiled at her as he shook her hand.

When Tara looked in his eyes it made her feel warm and comfortable. "Well I hope we see one another again." She stood to leave.

"How about Wednesday night?"

"Excuse me?" She wasn't sure, but she thought he just asked her out on a date. "I'm sorry Damon, but I'm engaged." She held up the big diamond ring as proof.

"Bring him along."

What? "Uh, we're not really into that kind of thing." She hoped he was joking.

What is Forever?

Damon laughed a big laugh. "There's a poetry reading here this Wednesday. They have them every first Wednesday of the month." He pointed to the bulletin board by the restrooms. On it was a large poster advertising the event. "Do you really think I could have missed that rock on your finger? It's been blinding me the whole time we've been sitting here."

"Oh." Her cheeks burned. "Well, maybe. Gabe is very busy these days, but maybe we'll be able to make it. I really love poetry."

"That's great. I hope to see both of you there."

"I hope so too. Take care, Damon." She turned and walked out the shop.

She could feel his eyes on her back but did not allow herself to turn around. She walked out with a big smile on her face, but for the life of her couldn't figure out why.

That Wednesday morning as she and Gabe got ready for work she decided to ask if he would go to poetry reading.

"Honey, I met this guy at the Coffee shop on Fourth Street the other day, and he invited us to a poetry reading there tonight." She noticed him tense up when she said she met a man so she added, "I think he's gay, but he's a nice guy." For some reason she had always had many homosexual friends. She knew Gabe wouldn't feel threatened by a gay man. "So what do you think, Baby? It might be a nice change of pace, huh?"

"I don't know Tara, I've got a lot going on down at the office. I really don't have time to go listen to a bunch of your fag friends recite poetry."

What is Forever?

Tara knew he would react like this. She thought of the words "use what you got to get what you want." She walked up behind him and wrapped her arms around his waist. She placed her hand in the waistband of his briefs and began to fondle him. They had not made love since the day on the floor in the living room. She felt his body respond immediately.

"Don't worry. I won't let my homosexual friends get you. I'm gonna keep you all to myself." She purred into his ear. "Don't you think we need some special time together? We haven't been out to something like this in a long time. I don't complain when you drag me around with your boring business friends who pretend not to be gay. It would really make me happy. When we get home afterward I'll show you how much." She gave him a firm squeeze and kissed him on the back of the neck.

"I know you're not going to let me go to work like this." He gestured toward his erection.

"Don't worry I'll take care of it tonight after the reading."

"I'll tell you what, you take care of this now and I'll try to get enough done at the office today so that we can go tonight."

Knowing that was the best offer she was going to get she slid to her knees in front of him. "Okay, Baby. Just don't forget that there's a lot more where this comes from if you come through for me."

After she made sure he was happy, they finished getting ready for work. There was little more conversation as they headed downstairs to the kitchen. Tara worried that now that

What is Forever?

he had gotten what he wanted he would renege on their deal. Gabe fixed his usual cup of black coffee in his green travel mug. He gave her a quick kiss on the side of her mouth and walked out the door.

Tara fixed herself a cup of coffee and a wheat English muffin. She sat at the counter and tried to figure out why she was having such mixed emotions about her relationship. Gabe always made her jump through hoops when she wanted something from him. It wasn't that she didn't like to flirt with him or that she hadn't missed his touch, she just didn't like having to use sex as a tool to get what she wanted. She was starting to feel like the "sex tactic" wouldn't work much longer anyway. Earlier in their relationship she had a strong grip on the sexual strings. Lately he seemed to have lost his desire to make love. He was always too busy with something else. More often than not he was either dragging her here or there to socialize with his boring black republican crew, or he just wanted stay home in front of that damn computer working on a case. His attention had become focused on everything except her.

At the same time she had to give him credit. He was a good provider and he took care of any and all problems that had ever arisen. She liked knowing that she would be taken care of. Tara considered herself far from a gold digger. She didn't care what her man did for a living as long as he was a real man. He had to be able to take care of problems, make her feel safe and he had to be capable of leading the way. Those were traits she always wanted in a man and Gabe possessed them. The fact that he was financially successful

What is Forever?

was just icing on the cake. What she couldn't understand was why she felt so unfulfilled.

She decided to put her problems out of her mind and go to work. Once she got there she would put on her big "I'm so happy to be at work" smile and make it through another boring day. She told herself there was no need to worry about how mundane her life had become. She was just in a rut and everything would be better soon enough.

That afternoon Tara left work early. She wanted to go by the Fresh Market and get something special for dinner. If she put Gabe in a good mood maybe he'd keep his promise to go to the Corner Coffee Shop. Tara walked into the upscale grocery store and inhaled the aroma of fresh coffee beans. She slowly made her way around the store and to the meat counter. She had the attendant give her the thickest, reddest ribeyes in the case. She picked romaine lettuce for a salad, and a bottle of their best Merlot. She returned to their condo, unpacked the groceries and began preparing the meal. She made a marinade for the steak using Worcestershire sauce and honey butter, submerged the steaks in it and placed it in the refrigerator. She cut up tomatoes and cucumbers after shredding the lettuce. She mixed them and added croutons, bacon bits and covered it all with shredded cheese. She decided to prepare the pasta and put the steaks in the oven later.

She went upstairs to her bathroom and took a hot shower. While in the shower she finalized her plan. She would make everything so perfect that there would be no way Gabe could say no to the poetry reading. After her shower she wrapped herself in her fluffy red robe and slipped on matching slippers. She stepped into her walk-in closet. It took a long time for her to pick out the perfect outfit. She finally settled on her black halter top party dress. She took it out and laid it across the bed. She decided not to put it on yet so that it wouldn't capture the aroma of the meal she was cooking.

Tara put a John Coltrane jazz CD in the stereo. She loved his music. There was just something about his melancholy style that she related to. Tara opened the vertical blinds to the large porch. She toyed with the idea of serving the dinner alfresco but thought about how Gabe always complained about bugs when they ate outdoors. She didn't want to take the chance of putting him in a sour mood. She decided to set the dinning room table in front of the big glass window instead. She used his grandmother's china to really make it special.

After she put the steaks in the oven and finished preparing her pasta she went back upstairs to change. It had been some time since she had put this much effort into a dinner for just the two of them. It made her feel good to put something special like this together for her man. She was very proud of herself. She put the dress on, then carefully applied her make up. When she was finished she stood in front of the full length mirror. The dress showed the perfect amount of cleavage to make her look sexy without looking trashy. She admired her shapely legs as she twirled in front of the mirror in her black high heels.

She only had to wait another ten minutes after she placed the last dish on the table before he came in through the front door.

What is Forever?

"Hey baby!" She was genuinely happy to see him. She threw her arms around him and kissed him on the lips. "How was your day? Come on in the house let me take your briefcase." She was starting to get into the June Cleaver role. Tara took his satchel and set it by the counter.

"Mmm. What smells so good?" Gabe loosened his tie as he allowed his nose to lead him into the kitchen. He opened the oven door and took a big whiff of the steaks as they sizzled in the marinade. "You've outdone yourself this time. This is just what I needed after the day I've had. I want to eat a good hot meal then take a shower and chill." He turned to face his fiancé and noticed her outfit.

As soon as she heard him use the word "chill," tears welled up in her eyes. She felt her bottom lip tremble as she tried to force the tears not to fall. She turned her back on Gabe and busied her hands straitening the already straight ceramic dogs on the counter top. She tried to keep her voice steady.

"Did you forget about the poetry reading tonight?" She turned toward him again hoping that her plans had just slipped his mind.

"The poetry reading... yeah, I did forget. No wonder you're so spruced up. I'll tell you what, Baby. I'm really beat. Can't we just catch the next one?"

She wanted to cry, wanted to scream. She just couldn't understand why he always refused to do the things she wanted to do. She thought of the countless times she had allowed herself to be dragged off to functions by him when she was cramping or sick or just dog tired. She wanted to

66

yell at him "hell no, we can't go next time!" but instead she just went into the kitchen and took dinner to the table.

"I guess that's fine," she muttered as she sat down.

She felt like a beaten dog retreating with her tail between her legs.

"Don't worry, Baby. You know I'll make it up to you."

They ate in silence. The only sounds came from Gabe as he devoured the food in front of him. Tara hardly touched her plate other than to move pieces of tomato back and forth. Gabe didn't seem to notice or care that she was not eating. She consoled herself with the wine. In fact by the time Gabe finished his second helping, Tara was finishing her third glass. When he finished eating he gave her a greasy kiss on the cheek.

"The dinner was great, Baby. We should eat like this more often." He dropped his underused napkin in his plate and headed up the stairs. "I'm just gonna take a quick shower. Anything good on T.V. tonight?"

When he was out of sight she dropped her head. She sobbed heavily, uncontrollably until there were no more tears to cry. She rose from the table, cleared and washed the dishes. She was not sure what she was feeling. Basically she just felt numb. She moved like a zombie, washing, rinsing then drying. She was pulled from her stupor by the phone's third ring. She moved to answer it when it stopped as suddenly as it had started. She didn't know if the caller had hung up or if Gabe had answered the other line. Either way she really didn't care. She just felt stuck.

What is Forever?

Tara finished in the kitchen and began climbing the stairs so that she could take off her dress. As she walked through the bedroom door she heard Gabe talking.

"Yeah, I'll be over in a few minutes." She must have misunderstood what he said. There was no way he could have said that he was leaving. That could not have been it.

He hung up the phone. "That was Joseph. He and the fella's are getting together to play some cards. I'm gonna head over there for a couple of hours. I should be back around eleven."

Something inside of Tara snapped. She looked at the man sitting on the bed with a blue towel wrapped around his waist as if he were a complete stranger.

"Oh, hell no you didn't!" With the help of the wine she felt herself growing what she could only describe as a tremendous pair of balls. Tara put her hand on her hip, her finger waved back and forth just inches from his nose. "I asked you, no I begged you to go to the poetry reading with me. I made you that great dinner and put on my sexiest dress for your yellow ass. That's not to mention the way I took care of you this morning. And what did you say? You came in here talking about you were too tired. Too tired to do what your woman asked you to do, but you can run your ass out the door as soon as one of your tired ass friends calls. That's fucked up, Gabe!"

"Wait one fucking minute, Woman. Don't come at me like that. I pay the bills in this house and you're going to treat me with some fucking respect."

His forceful counterattack took the wind out of her sails for a moment, but only a moment. "Mother-fucker I'll speak

68

to you any damn way I want to speak to you! You know you're wrong. How can you treat me like this? Yeah, you pay the bills, but I take care of this house. I clean, wash your nasty drawers *and* I go to work every day. You don't own me. I contribute just as much to this relationship as you. And I don't ask for half as much." She was definitely pissed. "Just this once I asked you to go out with me and do what I want to do, but you couldn't even do that for me. Matter of fact, you know what? Go on. Go on out with your friends. I have a car, I can go by my damn self." She was breathing hard, but managed to calm her voice to almost her normal tone. "You go do what you want to do and I'll do what I want to."

Tara was serious and she could tell by the look in his eyes that Gabe knew it. She didn't know if it was male pride or if he was just stupid, but he called her bluff.

"That's fine with me." His voice was as cold as ice. He got off the bed and lightly bumped her as he walked past to his dresser. He pulled out a blue Calvin Kline T-shirt and a pair of blue jeans. As he was walking out the door he said, "I guess I'll see you when I see you." He didn't turn around or wait for a response.

Tara was dumbfounded. He had done it again, used her anger against her. She couldn't figure out how every time she was mad at him he could turn the situation around and make her feel like the bad guy. Tara sat on the bed like there was a truck load of bricks in her underwear. She had reached behind her to unzip her dress and get ready for a night of Kleenex and the tonight show when she thought about those eyes, those beautiful brown eyes. Hell, if Gabe was gonna

What is Forever?

play the game she was gonna play it better. She zipped the dress back up, walked to the vanity mirror, freshened her make up, grabbed her purse and headed for the door.

The coffee shop was packed. The smell of incense wafted through out the open room. The lights were dimmed and votive candles burned on each of the small tables that surrounded the small stage that had been erected along the back wall. The scene immediately put Tara in the mind of the beatniks from the sixties. There was a brother with long dreads seated on the stage with a bongo between his legs. Beating a smooth rhythm as a white poet who also had dreads went on about The Man, and black people rising up against him. The sight tickled Tara. The poet and drummer were both dressed in traditional African garb, as were about a third of the crowd that sat closely together around the small tables. Tara searched the crowd for Damon as she moved to an empty seat toward the back. She didn't see him and was afraid he may not have come. She ordered a White Zinfandel when the waitress came by and took her order.

The next poet called to the mic was a petite girl. If she was any older than eighteen, it wasn't by much. Tara scrutinized her frail form. She was just a little over five feet tall, and couldn't weigh more than a hundred pounds wearing a sponge in a monsoon. She looked terribly afraid standing in front of the microphone. She reminded Tara of a little bird. Tara couldn't imagine the young thing would have the nerve to speak in front of an audience. Then the young poet opened her mouth. She possessed the clearest, richest speaking voice Tara had ever heard. The girl spoke of the

70

What is Forever?

evil of wars and how governments were responsible for children dying. She asked what would become of the children if the world they were supposed to inherit was destroyed by greed and self service. By the time she had finished her poem Tara's eyes spilled rivers of tears. The poem was so fraught with honesty and passion that it truly touched Tara's heart.

The next poet was no comparison to the girl as far as Tara was concerned. She listened to four more poets and drank two more glasses of wine. There was still no sign of Damon. She was about to give up on seeing him. After all she hadn't come to see him, she was there to listen to poetry and prove a point to Gabe. She had done both. It would just have been nice to see him and thank him for inviting her.

She was about to leave when she heard them announce the name of the next poet.

"Damon Black."

She looked up to see Damon striding toward the mic. Instead of traditional African garb, he wore all black. His tight-fitting shirt showed off his chest and arms. Tara had always had a thing for men in black. It was such a masculine color. A good looking man looked even better in black.

Damon greeted the crowd with a loud "Harambee."

They replied in turn.

"I'd just like to say good evening to all of you, and thank you for coming out tonight. I'd like to do a new poem for you; in fact I think of it as a work in the making. It was inspired by someone that I met recently who touched me in a way that I can't quite explain. Anyway, here it goes.

What is Forever?

"Sadness, loneliness, hurt, despair. You long for a lover who will be there. No, a companion. Someone with whom your life you'll share. The trappings of wealth, Prada, Gucci and such, are empty promises because you long for the touch... of a man, a lover, a friend, a safe harbor until life's storm finally ends. But today Life is so unkind. So bitter, so unfair, so caustic no matter how you try. Too often alone in your sad life you cry.

"The devil's stranglehold pulls you down; you're tethered to despair as in the ocean of pain you drown. You smile, but it's transparent. Your laugh is empty of true bliss. Your beauty fails to hide the pain, your need for true love's kiss. Never look out, for what you need, look in. God lives inside you, yes He dwells deep within. His love will sustain you, comfort and hold. You must keep your head up, live life and be bold.

"Never give in to sadness. Each day you begin, remember love lives inside you. He will be your provider, your companion, your friend. When loneliness attacks find strength in your heart, for with each new day a new life you can start."

Damon's voice was strong and melodious. His words wrapped around Tara and picked her up and rocked her like a mother's child. The thought that this man had written a poem for her gave her a feeling she hadn't experienced in a long time. It made her feel important. No man had ever done anything so special for her before.

When Damon finished the crowd gave him a loud round of applause. Only the young girl had received more. He walked from the stage directly to Tara's table. She thought that he hadn't seen her. It made her feel warm that he came directly to her after leaving the mic. She greeted him with a friendly hug and a Kool Aide smile.

"Oh Damon, thank you so much! That was beautiful. I can't believe you wrote a poem for me. I'm so very touched." She placed a hand over his and touched her heart with the other. She savored the feel of his skin. It was soft.

"I'm glad you liked it. I've been working on it since the first day we met. Something about your spirit just stayed with me." He looked around. "So where is your fiancé? I thought you were going to bring him?"

"He couldn't make it. He had a prior engagement." The thought of Gabe sent a bevy of emotions whirling through her mind. She was mad at him for not coming. Part of her wanted him to hear the warm words another man had put together for her, but she was also glad that he was not present to hear. The poem may have just created additional problems in their already strained relationship.

"Well I'm glad that at least you could make it."

There was something mesmerizing about the way he looked into her eyes. She felt like a deer caught in a car's headlights every time he looked at her. They spent the next two hours talking and listening to poetry. They laughed and joked until the last poet left the stage. During their conversation Tara had two more white wines, while Damon drank just one Corona. When she stood to leave she felt her head spin and she stumbled a little.

"Are you okay to drive?"

"Sure, I'm fine."

"Let me at least walk you to your car."

What is Forever?

"Thank you, Damon. That would be nice."

As she was walking toward the door her mouth began to water uncontrollably. Her head throbbed. When the night air smacked her in the face she felt her stomach lurch.

Oh God, please don't let me throw up in front of him. Please, please not now.

Her prayers went unanswered. Before she could make it four more steps she was doubled over the curb spewing almost clear liquid from her empty stomach.

"Oh God, Oh God no. This can't be happening," she wheezed in between eruptions.

She felt Damon's hand on her back, rubbing gently. "It's okay, Tara. It's okay. Just let it out and you'll feel better. Don't fight it. Let it out." His voice consoled her.

By the time her stomach stopped revolting against the wine she had consumed, her makeup was running, her legs were weak and her whole body was feeling shaky. Damon put an arm around her waist to support her and gave her a handkerchief to wipe her mouth and face.

"Please, let me drive you home."

She knew she couldn't make it home alone. She nodded weakly and leaned on him as he walked her down the block to his car. Through the haze in her mind she realized that they had walked quite a ways. She started to get a little nervous. After all, she really didn't know this man very well. In her state there was no way she would be able to defend herself if he tried something. She started to feel anxiety swell in her chest. They began walking down an incline on a dark street. She was forming her get-away plan when he announced that they were at his vehicle. Tara looked at the

What is Forever?

old Toyota Corolla and wondered if referring to it as a vehicle was not false advertising. The car's body was a faded shade of silver and the doors were each a different shade of blue. The car looked like it was ten years late for an appointment with a junk yard. The passenger door gave a rebellious cry when he opened it. Obviously it didn't get used very often. Damon carefully deposited her in the passenger seat. It leaned awkwardly to one side. He placed the seatbelt around her and she heard it click.

After getting in the other side, he left a foot dangling out as he forced the stick into second gear and released the parking brake. With his left foot Damon pushed the car away from the curb. He held the clutch in with his right. When the car began to coast down the hill, Damon quickly let out the clutch. The car lurched forward then chugged to life.

"I've been having some problems with my battery so I have to kick start the engine. That's why I parked so far away on that hill. It's a lot easier to get it started on a hill." His grin was only the slightest bit embarrassed. "So where do you live?"

When she gave him the address, he told her he was familiar with the area and commented on the affluence of it. She tried to tell him how much she appreciated the ride. The next thing she knew he was shaking her and telling her that she was home. She woke up startled, not recognizing her surroundings. Finally, she figured out where she was and who she was with. She also realized there was a spot of drool on the side of her face. She was mortified. The slob on her face was even more embarrassing than throwing up in front of him had been. She quickly used the handkerchief that was still in her hand to wipe it away.

She looked out the window. "Damon I want to thank you again for all you've done for me tonight. I can't tell you how sweet you've been or how embarrassed I am at the way I've behaved in front of you. There's really an explanation for it but I just don't have the energy to go through the story right now."

"There's no need to explain. I really had a good time tonight. If you want to talk about what's going on though, here's my number. Give me a call sometime and we can talk over a cup of coffee for you and a soda for me."

"I'd like that." She opened the loud door. She winced, worried that Gabe might have heard the noise. The last thing she wanted to do tonight was to explain why a strange man was dropping her off.

"Can you get in alright?"

"Don't worry I'll be fine, thanks."

She stumbled up to her bedroom, relieved to see that Gabe had not come in yet. She looked at the clock. It read two thirty seven a.m.

"Wait a damn minute. Didn't he say he'd be in by eleven? Where the hell is that bastard?"

Tara was too tired and disoriented to spend many brain cells worried about Gabe. She made her way into the bathroom and took a shower. She brushed her teeth until her gums were sore. She didn't bother with nightclothes, she just slipped under the cover and immediately fell asleep.

An insistent buzz pulled her up from the depths of a dream. She felt for the clock's alarm but couldn't find the off switch with her eyes closed. She cracked one eye. It was seven-thirty in the morning. She pulled the clock off the nightstand and flung it under the bed. Her brain bounced around in her head. She rolled over to find Gabe snoring in her face. She struggled to roll back over. Damn clock. Seven-thirty—Oh, no! She was still alive and due at work in less than an hour.

Tara sat straight up in bed. She had to get ready for work! Unfortunately, her hangover was her only boss at that moment, and it ordered her back to bed. Her head fell back into the down pillow. It felt like cracking her head on a cement wall. Moaning, she closed her eyes, thinking she would never be able to get back to sleep in this condition.

When Tara awoke again it was noon. Gabe's side of the bed was empty. A note lay on his pillow.

Baby,

You seemed to have had a rough night last night. I've never heard you snore so hard. Anyway, I called your job and told them you had a virus. Coffee's downstairs along with some bagels. I'll call this afternoon to check on you.

Love,
Gabe

He was normally a big pain in the ass, but at that moment she appreciated the hell out of him. She gently laid her head back on the pillow and slept for another hour. When she finally pulled herself out of bed, she was just too worn out and sick to do much around the house. She restlessly wandered from couch to bed, bed to patio, always too tired to move very far, too restless to lie in any one place too long.

What is Forever?

She replayed the events of the previous evening over in her mind. She thought of Damon and how sweet and kind he had been. She was trying to keep her thoughts on a friendship level, but she knew her interest was deeper than that.

She had never been the kind of woman to be unfaithful or even flirty. She had always looked down on women who got involved with more than one man. She did not consider herself a snob, but she did hold fast to some old fashioned values. One of them being a woman should always be a lady. And a lady should always behave in a respectable manner. That's what had her feeling so confused and bewildered, the very thoughts she was having about Damon went against her code of morals. Gabe was her man. He may not be perfect but he was her man and he deserved more respect than she was giving him.

Gabe was the second man she had ever slept with, and she had managed to keep him at bay for over five months, although not from his lack of effort. She had refused to make love with him until she was certain that was what they would be doing – making love. Her first sexual experience was with her first love, her college sweetheart. The man she believed she would spend the rest of her life with. He had ended up using her for her car and the little bit of money she made working part time at a local book store. The bastard left her for a white girl the second semester of her senior year. He told her that the white girl fit more into his long-range plans. She was better able to relate to him and his needs. That was the biggest slap in the face he could ever have given her. She could never understand how he even opened his mouth to say that a white woman could relate to him and his needs more than she. She may not have been the most down sister, having been raised by white people. Maybe she even spoke with a little twang in her voice, but never, not ever could a white woman take her place when it came to feeling her man's struggle. The whole experience turned her away from romance for a long time. She stayed by herself for the most part for the next two years until she met Gabriel Conrad.

He was in his last year of Law School and had big plans for the future. Gabe was one of the most intelligent men she had ever met. He possessed a strength and authority that made people listen to him. When she was with him she felt safe and protected. They had been together for almost three years before he proposed. It had been two years since and a wedding date still had not been set. After he proposed she moved into Gabe's, which was more like a house than a condominium. Gabe told her that he would have a bigger house built for her on the west side of town after they were married. Tara hoped that they would move forward with their plans by the spring of the following year. They had a long history of ups and downs, but through it all she had been faithful and to the best of her knowledge so had he. She looked at the slip of paper in her hand with Damon's number on it. She crumpled it and tossed it in the kitchen trashcan.

Tara was watching a court-T.V. show on the large screen in the living room when the phone rang. Her head was still throbbing and the ringing sent hot knives into her skull.

"Hello?"

"HEY BABY! HOW ARE YOU FEELING?"

Gabe's loud greeting almost made her drop the phone. "I'm fine but do you have to yell?"

What is Forever?

"OH I'M SORRY, DO YOU HAVE A HEADACHE?"

"Very funny, Gabe. Don't be an asshole, it doesn't suite you."

"I'm sorry baby," he chuckled, "but you know I had to mess with you at least a little. Besides, you did it to yourself. I didn't tell you to try and drink all the wine in the city."

"Look Gabe, I really appreciate what you did for me this morning but I'm not in the mood to be lectured."

"I'm not trying to lecture you, but maybe that's exactly what you need. It was very childish of you to go out and get drunk just because you were mad at me. What if you killed a kid or something? By the way, where is your car?"

"I took a cab because I'm too responsible to get behind the wheel after I've been drinking. And who the hell are you calling childish?" Her own voice was too loud for her head to take. "Look Gabe you're my man, not my father. I don't need you to chastise me. This headache is punishment enough, all right?"

"I can't believe your nerve. You come in drunk off your ass, smelling like a wino, but you don't want me to say anything about it? Girl, you must have bumped your head last night cause you sure have forgotten who you're talking to. You should know I'm not having no shit like that."

"You know what? I'm tired of you always flapping your lips about what you're gonna have and what you're not gonna have. You need to start worrying about me and what I want to have. One day you're gonna look up and wish you had."

"What's that supposed to mean? You trying to say I don't take care of your needs? Who else is gonna provide for

80

you like I do Tara, huh? You need to check your attitude. If you're not happy with me, leave. I can always get someone who will be. You need to remember that. You can be replaced."

She couldn't believe that he let those words come out of his mouth. "Gabe, you..." she stopped herself from continuing. "Just forget it. I'll talk to you later."

She placed the phone in the cradle and sat back in front of the television with her knees pulled up under her chin. She knew the tears were about to fall, and she didn't try to stop them. She went to the trashcan and pulled out Damon's number. He answered on the second ring.

"Hello?"

"Hi Damon."

"Tara? Hi. How are you doing?" His voice was full of concern.

"I'm still recovering, but I'll be all right. I just wanted to thank you for last night and to apologize for my behavior. That type of thing doesn't happen to me often."

"It's okay, Tara. You don't have to explain. I've been there myself."

"I just wanted to let you know that I had a lot going on yesterday. I was pretty upset and I drank way too much wine on an empty stomach. Well anyway, you were truly a blessing. I am very impressed and thankful for the way you took care of me. I mean in the condition I was in, you could have tried to take advantage. A lot of guys would have at least tried. It's nice to know that there are still good men in the world."

What is Forever?

"Trust me Tara, that's one thing you would never have to worry about from me. I have nothing but hate for any man who would use a woman like that." There was an unwavering conviction in his voice. He paused as if he were going to say something then changed his mind. "I just know guys who have done that kind of shit and it had really bad consequences on everyone involved. I'd never get involved in something like that."

They spoke for a few minutes. Before they hung up Damon told her that he hoped he would see her at the next poetry night. She told him that she wasn't sure, but she'd try to make it. When she finally hung up the phone, for the first time in over five years, she questioned the depth of her love for Gabe.

CHAPTER 4

"Why is Tara still calling you, Damon? We've been through this a thousand times. If there is nothing going on between the two of you, why is she still whining on your answering machine?"

"What are you talking about, Alexis? I haven't spoken to her in weeks. I told you that."

"Well then you need to listen to this." Alexis handed him the cordless phone, a look of anger and pain on her face. "I'm tired of this, Damon. She needs to get a life, and get out of mine."

Damon pressed the code to replay the message and listened. When it finished playing he hung up and looked at Alexis.

"Baby, I told you when we met that Tara and I are still friends. She's going through a rough time right now. There's nothing going on between us. I promised her that I'd try to be there for her. I know this is uncomfortable for you, but I need you to be patient. She's not as strong as you. Things not working out between us and then losing her mother have been hard on her. I'd like to help her through the pain. It's the least I can do after all she's done for me."

"Well why does she have to call you after eleven at night? I'm telling you, she's trying to get back with you by causing tension between us. Look Baby, I'm not trying to be unreasonable but you really do need to talk to her and let her know in no uncertain terms that it's over."

What is Forever?

"All right, Baby." There was defeat in his voice as he sat on the bed and kissed her lips. "I'll call her tomorrow and try to find out what's going on. I'll also tell her she shouldn't call late at night, but she already knows that our relationship is over. She just needs someone she can trust to talk to. I need you to trust me. I'll handle it. I don't want you to let Tara cause problems between us. After all, you're going to be the new Mrs. Damon Christian Black soon. I want our life together to always be as good as it is now."

Alexis decided not to pursue the issue further, but she knew she would be keeping an eye on Tara. She opened her arms and allowed Damon to crawl in between them. They fell asleep snuggled close together.

The next morning Alexis was awakened by Ebony pulling on her bare shoulder. When she realized who had awakened her she quickly pulled the covers over her bare breasts.

"Well good morning, Sweetie. How are you this morning?" She tried to hide her embarrassment.

"Good morning, Lexxus. I'm fine. You want to watch Saturday morning cartoons with me? Winnie the Pooh is coming on. I like pooh bear. That bear's sooo silly."

"Sure Sweetie, I'll watch Winnie the Pooh with you." Alexis yawned and stretched one arm high over her head while holding the blanket in place with the other. "Do you want me to wake your daddy so he can watch it with us?"

"Daddy never gets up for Saturday Cartoons. He just lays there and snores."

What is Forever?

"Well then I guess it will be just us girls and Pooh, huh? I'll tell you what. You go turn on the TV and I'll brush my teeth and be in there in a minute."

"Okay, but hurry up so you don't miss the song."

The little girl ran out of the room singing the Winnie the Pooh theme song. It was not familiar to Alexis. They must have changed it since she was a little girl. She got out of the bed and went to the bathroom to freshen up. She slipped on one of Damon's T-shirts and a pair of long bike pants she had left over a couple of weeks earlier. She pulled her wild hair back in a ponytail, then went into the kitchen and poured two big glasses of orange juice. Ebony remembered to say thank you when Alexis handed her the glass of juice and sat on the couch with her. She was just in time for the theme song. It was different from the song they played when she was a child. She had to admit that the new song was much better.

"Your boobies are bigger than my mommy's."

Alexis gagged on the juice she was drinking. She looked at the little girl next to her not knowing how to respond to her statement.

"Why are yours bigger?"

She took a moment to formulate her answer. "Well sweetie, everyone's made differently. Some people are taller than others, some have longer hair..."

"And some people have bigger boobies." Ebony finished. "Why don't boys have 'em?"

"Because boys and girls are different."

"Why?"

What is Forever?

"Ebony, it's not that I don't want to talk to you about this, but I think it might be better if you talk to your mom about those things."

"Why?"

Alexis was on the ropes. " I just think that those are the kind of questions a little girl should ask her mom."

"Daddy says you're gonna be my step mom."

"Yes Baby I am, but your mom might want to talk to you about those things herself." Alexis didn't want to start stepping on Keisha's toes already. She prayed the child would not have any more difficult questions.

Just then Damon walked into the room bare-chested wearing cotton pajama bottoms. "What's going on out here? Why didn't you guys wake me up? Hey, Winnie the Pooh's on." Damon plopped on the couch on the other side of Ebony. "What did I miss, Squirt?"

"Nothing. This one's been on before."

"Well I don't know about you ladies, but I'm as hungry as a bear. Anybody want some breakfast?"

"I want pancakes!" Ebony screamed.

"How did I know you were going to say that?"

Alexis could see in his eyes the love the man had for his child. She hoped that he would have that much love for the children they would have together. She wondered if some type of competition would develop for Damon's love.

"Cause we have pancakes every Saturday."

"Oh yeah that's correct, we do have pancakes every Saturday." He said with a terrible nutty professor imitation.

"Daddy's silly, isn't he Lexxus."

"He sure is honey. You have one silly daddy."

86

What is Forever?

After watching Winnie the Pooh, the three of them went into the kitchen and made pancakes. Alexis loved every minute of it. It had been a long time since she'd had that kind of family time. She didn't even get upset at the pancake flour and batter that Damon and Ebony seemed to paint the kitchen counters and floor with, even knowing she'd be the one with clean-up duty. If she let Damon and Ebony handle it, the kitchen would be in worse shape when they finished.

Alexis had grown up in Maryland, the older of two girls. Her mother was a teacher and her father a manual laborer. Alexis' father was a stern, hard-working man who believed there was no shame in any job as long as it was done well. Growing up she'd often felt that he was over-protective of her and her sister Arielle. He pushed them to excel academically, and they did.

Alexis had attended Spellman College and graduated Magna Cum Laude. Although they bumped heads frequently while she was growing up, she now realized that he'd always had their best interests at heart. He was a man who wanted the best for his daughters, but didn't want them to have to depend on a man to get the best. He had instilled self-reliance in them, and they both had grown to be independent women. Arielle was a doctor in Boston and Alexis owned a computer networking company in Charlotte.

Ruth, Alexis' mother, was the perfect counter-balance to her father's overwhelming personality. She was a small, quiet woman with a heart big enough to care for the world. Alexis had no memory of Ruth ever raising her voice in anger, but she was a strong woman who had earned the

What is Forever?

respect of all who knew her. She was the only person Alexis knew who could put her father in his place.

Alexis had many fond memories of her life with her parents and sister. Her parents saved all year so that they could go on a family vacation every summer. Some of the best times of her life were when they were on vacation at places like California, Jamaica or Mexico. They were a very close knit family that spent a lot of time together doing family activities: fishing, bowling, going on picnics and any other activity her parents could come up with that promoted good health and family values. Alexis never missed a Sunday of church for the first eighteen years of her life. She stopped going for a brief period after she went away to college. A period she thought of as her rebellious time. She wanted to stretch her wings and get away from the life she spent with her parents. It was during that time that she had her first beer, first cigarette and her first lover. It didn't take her long to find her way back to the things that her parents had taught her were right and true. She soon let go of the beer and the cigarettes. Her lover she kept a while longer.

Now that her family had been spread across the country they got together less frequently. Alexis communicated with her mother and sister through e-mails at least once a week. She had to write letters or call her father because he refused to learn how to use a computer. He believed they were just the latest invention to get people to spend more money.

"I have used pen and paper all of my life and that's what I'll use as long as I am able to pull breath," he had said more than once.

What is Forever?

Computer expert or no, she still loved him dearly. Seeing Damon with Ebony only served to remind her of that.

After breakfast Ebony went upstairs to her room to play. Damon went into the small office on the other side of the den to finish up some type of paperwork he had brought home from the television station where he worked. As Alexis set in to getting the kitchen cleaned up, she looked at the ring on her finger and admired the way it sparkled. She looked around the kitchen and thought of her future with Damon. When the phone rang she jumped. She knew before she picked up the receiver who would be on the other end. She picked up just as Damon answered the other extension. She held her breath when she heard Tara's voice. She started to hang up and respect his privacy, but hesitated. She was now his fiancé. He no longer had any privacy. She placed her hand over the mouthpiece and listened.

"Look Tara, I'm really sorry about all that you're going through right now. I know it's been rough on you."

"You don't know the half of it, Damon. Now the thermostat in my car is broken and the repairman wants five hundred to fix it. I just don't know what I'm going to do. Now with momma gone I don't have anyone to help me."

"You don't have five hundred? How much do you have?"

"I really don't have anything extra after I pay the rent and the car loan. I'm trying to stay positive but it seems like every time I take a step forward, I get knocked back two." She started to cry.

Alexis felt sick.

What is Forever?

"You've got to keep your head up, Tara. I know things are not going well for you right now, but you have to keep trying. Remember to pray and things will get better."

" I know that you're right. It's just hard sometimes." She took a deep breath, gathering herself. "Damon I don't mean to bother you with my problems. You are the only one I can talk to about these things. You always understood me, and you never judged me. I just want you to know I appreciate that."

"It's all right, Tara. We're still friends and I'd like to be there for you as much as I can, but you do have to understand that I have someone in my life now-"

"I know, I know. I don't want to cause trouble between you. It's just so hard sometimes. I mean you've gone on with your life and you're so happy. Believe me, I'm happy for you...it's just that sometimes I just feel like I'm never going to be happy again. Ever since we parted my life has just gone downhill."

Alexis' blood started to boil. What a load of shit Tara was shoveling. Why couldn't Damon see the woman was trying to get his sympathy? All she knew was that she could smell Tara's shit and she was gonna flush that bitch out of Damon's life for good.

"Damon, could we get together for a cup of coffee sometime? Oh I forgot, no coffee for you, but can we get together just to talk or something? I promise I won't talk about us, I just need someone to talk to about all this shit in my life."

What is Forever?

"I don't know if that would be a good idea Tara, but we'll see. Anyway I have to go. I'll get you the five hundred dollars as soon as I can."

"Damon I didn't call you for money, I was just telling you what was going on."

"I know Tara, that's why I don't mind doing it a bit. Besides after all you've done for me it's the least I can do. You were there for me when no one else was, and I'll be there for you."

"Won't your girlfriend get upset?"

"No, not at all. She's very sweet. She'll understand."

Alexis couldn't believe her ears. She slammed the phone into the cradle.

When Damon came into the room less than a minute later, Alexis' arms were folded over her chest. She could feel the steam pouring out of her ears.

"Why are you eavesdropping on my phone call?"

"What! I know you're not even about to trip over me listening to your phone call and you up there talking to that bitch."

"Wait a minute, Alexis. You don't have any reason to call her that. You don't even know her. Besides, it doesn't matter who I'm talking to, you have no right to listen in on my phone calls. That's disrespectful to me and I don't deserve it."

Alexis held up her ring finger as if she were giving him the bird. "This ring gives me every right to listen to anything you say to anybody. When you asked me to be your wife you put me into your business."

What is Forever?

"So you're saying that in order to have you for my wife, I give away all rights to my privacy?"

"Why do you need privacy, Damon? What's going on in your life that you need to hide from me?"

"I don't need to hide anything, but I don't feel the need to have you listen in on every phone call I make or to have to tell you every thought that goes through my mind. After all, I don't treat you like that. It's called trust. Any relationship or more importantly marriage has to be built on it. I trust you, so I don't feel the need to listen in on your conversations or to go through your things."

She hated to admit that he made a good point. So instead she asked him, "Why are you giving her money? Doesn't she have a job?"

"Why are you concerned about what I do with my money? I'm not asking you to give her any money."

"It's not like you're rolling in dough. Can you afford to give her that kind of money?"

"Look, just because I don't have my own company and don't make the kind of money you do doesn't...you know what, just forget it." Damon walked into the bedroom and emerged a few moments later with his workout gear on.

"And just where are you going? I think we're in the middle of a conversation."

"I'm so upset and disappointed with you right now that I really don't have anything to say. If you don't mind watching my daughter for a couple of hours I'm going over to Bear's."

His attitude caught her completely off guard. Why should she stay and keep his daughter while he ran over to his friend's house? And the way he'd said that: *his* daughter. If she was going to be Ebony's stepmother, then Ebony was going to be her daughter too. Of course she would watch her. There was no reason for him to ask her to baby-sit. Her head was swimming and she lost the will to fight. She flagged him off with her hand.

BAM! The door slammed shut. Damon was gone without a goodbye to her or Ebony. Most of the time he was the sweetest man on earth. He was loving, considerate and generous to a fault, but while his giving heart was one of the things Alexis loved most about her man, it was also one of the things that caused the most tension between them. Damon just didn't know how to say no. He'd literally give a stranger in the street his last dollar. When it came to his friends or the little family he had, Damon would do anything. She loved his kind heart, but she didn't appreciate when it got in the way of their relationship.

Now Tara was trying to work her way back into the picture. Alexis knew that Damon couldn't see that bitch's ulterior motives, but she could and she wasn't about to let that woman take the best thing that ever happened to her. Not without a fight.

Alexis had met Damon while on a business trip to the outer banks of North Carolina. Sonya, her partner and best friend, had convinced her to take a break from the job and spend some time at the beach. The two of them were laying out near the surf taking some well deserved R & R, when Bear almost fell on them while trying to catch a football that had been overthrown. He crashed awkwardly over their blanket and into the sand. Alexis jumped up, spitting sand from her lips.

"I'm sorry. Please excuse me ladies," the big man said after he managed to get up.

Alexis had read childish pick-up prank all over the near miss. "I'm sure it was an accident," she'd responded coldly.

"It really was." Bear was very contrite, but Alexis wasn't hearing it.

Sonya spoke up. "Really, don't worry about it. It's all good." She gave Alexis a look that told her to relax.

It was then that Damon had come running over, looking as edible as a Hershey bar. He was obviously the one who had thrown the wayward ball.

"I'm really sorry about that. The ball slipped."

"You guys really don't have to keep apologizing. No one was hurt." Sonya had always been a friendly, laid back person.

"Good. I would have felt terrible if Bear had landed on one of you." He laughed.

Alexis had already gone back to her book.

"Bear? Is that your name?" Sonya asked.

"No, but that's what everyone calls me. Even my parents."

Sonya continued talking to them. Alexis looked up from her book to find Damon's attention on her. He asked her, "What are you reading?"

As if you really care, she thought to herself. He probably hadn't picked up a book since college. She knew he had been to college because of the horseshoe brand on his chest. "It's

What is Forever?

a book called *The Color of Water*. Have you ever heard of it?"

"Actually I have. I read it when it first came out. Good book."

Interesting. She decided to put him to the test. "What are you reading now?"

He knelt next to the blanket. "I'm about half way through *Waiting in Vain* by Collin Channer. At first it was a little hard to read the dialect, but once you settle into the rhythm of his style the book is great."

She was impressed. She hadn't run into many men who liked to read. It was definitely her favorite hobby. Alexis found herself loosening up a little.

The four of them ended up having a great conversation. Damon invited them to dinner and they accepted. They had a grand time. Later that night she and Damon went for a long walk along the beach. They talked about everything. Alexis even found herself telling him about some personal things that she hadn't shared with her closest friends. There was something about him that just made her open up. Damon was a perfect gentleman and showed her the perfect evening.

The following day before he and Bear left, they exchanged numbers and promised to keep in touch. Alexis didn't expect him to follow through because they lived over an hour away from each other. When she returned home four days later there was a message from Damon waiting on her machine. They started doing the long distance dating thing, and it had progressed into the greatest relationship she'd ever had. She was not willing to risk losing him.

What is Forever?

Alexis and Ebony spent the morning together having a wonderful time. They went to the mall where they both tried on outfits and shoes, then stopped by the pizza shop in the food court. Alexis ate a stuffed vegetable slice and Ebony had extra cheese. They spent time in the arcade and in the book store. The more time Alexis spent with Ebony, the more she loved her. She felt like she had known the child far longer than she actually had. There were even a few moments while the child was trying on her new clothes that Alexis had allowed herself to forget that Ebony wasn't her biological child and really felt like they were mother and daughter.

By the time they returned home they were loaded down with bags filled with goodies from their girls' day out. Alexis found her anger had subsided. She hadn't forgotten the conversation she'd had with Damon, but she did have a chance to think about what he'd said and how he was feeling. Damon had the kind of personality that made him feel that he had to take care of the world's problems.

When they had first met, he'd told Alexis about Tara and the kind of person she was. Damon had called her fragile. He said she was too dependant on other people to solve her problems, and that when times got hard she tended to drink too much. He also said that she was very kind and intelligent. He had done all he could to assure her that his relationship with Tara was platonic.

Alexis knew that Damon was attracted to her because she was self-sufficient and early on in their relationship it was hard to make her jealous. She never worried about him going out with his friends, or if he noticed a woman passing by.

What is Forever?

She had never suffered from a lack of confidence. She felt there was no woman out there who could offer her man the love that she could, so why worry. She was always proud of the fact that she was never one of the women who felt the need to have a leash around her man's neck. Her motto was if you feed a man at home he won't eat out. If he did then he'd never get a home cooked meal again. As time had gone by she noticed that she had become a little more protective of him. She wanted to be the only one to cook for Damon, and that was that. She decided not to spend any more time worrying about Tara. If he wasn't sure about their relationship, he never would have bought her the ring.

Damon didn't get home until four-thirty that afternoon. When he walked in the door his best friend Bear was with him. Bear was six feet five inches tall, and weighed close to three hundred pounds. He was an intimidating figure, but his close friends knew his nickname should have been Teddy Bear because of his gentle and kind personality. Damon and Bear had been best friends since college, where they pledged Omega together. As usual when they were together, they were running their mouths as they came through the door.

"Bear, you crazy as you look. I'm telling you those damn music videos are half of the reason black folks are sliding backwards instead of moving forward. It don't make a bit of sense having all of those young sisters walking around damn near butt naked in those videos. What makes it worse is that most of the time they don't even have to be near a beach to have on a string bikini. What kind of message is that sending to our people? You wanna know? It's saying have sex. And it's not even encouraging responsibility."

"I understand what you're saying Damon, but shit! You can't tell me you don't like to look. They got some fine young sisters in 'em and I like to look. Hell, ain't nothing wrong with a brother looking."

They hadn't noticed Alexis and Ebony sitting on the living room floor watching television and coloring in one of the child's coloring books until Bear tripped over the little girl.

"Ow! Uncle Bear, you stepped on me."

The big man gently picked her up. She looked no bigger than a stuffed animal in his arms.

"I'm sorry Honey, I didn't see you sitting there. I was too busy talking to your crazy father. Hey Alexis, how you doing? Mmmmh, I think I smell something good cooking."

"Hey Bear," she responded with a smile.

Although she didn't find him attractive, Alexis had a deep love and respect for him. She knew that he and Damon were like brothers and that Bear would always have her man's back, no matter what. It made her feel good to know that Damon had a person in his life he could count on other than her. "I have dinner on the stove. A roast and baked chicken in the oven, some string beans and collards, mashed potatoes and sweet potatoes."

"Oh yeah that's what I'm talking about. A brother is hungry, too. Girl, why you cooking such a big meal on Saturday?"

Alexis chuckled. "So I won't have so much to cook tomorrow after church."

What is Forever?

Bear looked confused, which tickled her even more. "I cooked today for tomorrow. Tonight we're going to order Chinese takeout."

Bear looked like he just lost his best friend. Then suddenly he perked up. "Well I like Chinese food too."

"That's good. Let me give you the number so you can go home and order some."

"Now Alexis, you know you ain't right."

"You've had my man all day and I haven't complained a bit, but now it's time for him to spend some time with his family."

"Yeah, I heard he gave you the ring last night. Engaged less than twenty-four hours and a sister's trying to pull rank already." He turned towards Damon who was laughing. "Well Brother, I guess I'll only be seeing you in church from now on. Now Alexis, don't choke him with that collar."

"You know there ain't no collar around his neck. Damon comes and goes as he pleases. I don't have time to baby-sit a grown man. Tell him, Damon. I don't try to control you, do I?"

Damon pulled at his collar with his pointer finger and made coughing noises. "No Baby, ain't no collars on me."

They all burst out laughing. Ebony just shook her head at how silly they all were.

"Seriously though, I just wanted to spend a little time with them before I go back to Charlotte tomorrow night. I have an important meeting on Tuesday morning that I'll have to prepare for on Monday."

"Y'all engaged and you gonna keep living way down in Charlotte? When you gonna move up here?"

What is Forever?

She looked at Damon waiting for him to answer his friend's question.

"Don't look at me. He asked you. You know as far as I'm concerned you don't ever have to go back to Charlotte."

"What about my job?"

"Damn Alexis, ain't you the boss? Why can't you just move your office up here?" Bear asked.

Alexis didn't have an answer for him. After all, she had only been engaged for less than a day. She and Damon hadn't begun to talk about moving or wedding dates. It was true that she was the boss. She had five permanent employees and about that many independent contractors to manage, but the truth of the matter was she could work from almost anywhere as long as she could get into the office once or twice a week to check on things. Sonya was perfectly capable of managing the day to day affairs.

"That's all the more reason I need to spend some time with my man. We have some plans to make."

"That's cool. I was about to leave anyway. I just have two things to ask before I go. One, who's going to be the best man?"

"You know nobody's up for that job other than you, my brother." Damon said, giving Bear the secret handshake.

"That's what I thought. So question two is: can a brother get some of that grub after church tomorrow?"

"Oh, you know I got you covered on that one." Alexis shot back at him with a smile.

"Bear, I need to show you something before you get out of here. Ebony I want you to go upstairs and play."

What is Forever?

Bear put Ebony down and she ran up the stairs to her room. The two men were walking back towards Damon's office when the phone rang. Alexis knew it would be Tara. She hurried to answer it before Damon could. She had a few things she wanted to get off of her chest.

"Hello." She had attitude all up in her voice and she knew it.

"Hello, Alexis? This is Keisha. Can I speak to Damon?"

Keisha sounded strange, not warm and friendly like when Alexis met her. She sounded nervous and shaky.

"Sure Keisha, he's right here. Hold on a minute."

Damon turned around when he heard Keisha's name. He took the receiver from Alexis.

"Hey Keish, what's up?"

There was a brief pause and his face became stone serious.

"What? Oh, hell no! You just stay right there. I'll be right over."

He hung up the phone. "Yo Bear, let's roll. We got some business to take care of."

"What do you mean you have business to take care of? What did she say? Where are you going?" Damon's tone made Alexis worry. She didn't like the dangerous look on his face.

"Junior beat up Keisha. I can't go into it now, Baby. I got to get over there." He kissed her on the lips and gave her a halfhearted smile before heading out the door with Bear on his heels.

"Wait a minute, Damon. You can't just walk out like this. I'm coming with you." She moved to follow them.

What is Forever?

"No Baby, I need you to stay here with Ebony. I don't know what's going on over there, and I don't want y'all in any danger."

"Well then you can't go either. I don't want you in any danger. Tell Keisha to call the police. You don't have to run over there into God knows what kind of situation."

Damon's face was set in stone. He was not going to argue over it. "That's my daughter's mother, and I will never let any man beat on her." His tone was calm and determined.

Alexis knew she couldn't convince him not to go. When the front door closed behind them Alexis yelled up the staircase "Ebony Honey, let's go for a ride." The little girl came bounding down the stairs. Alexis opened the front door in time to see Bear complete a three point turn and speed down the street. Alexis hurried Ebony into her BMW. She fastened her small passenger's seatbelt as she backed the vehicle out of the driveway and down the block after her man. She tried to keep her distance as they weaved in and out of traffic, but was afraid to let them get too far ahead. She didn't know how to get to Keisha's house. For that matter, she wasn't even sure that Keisha had called from her home.

She had only followed the men for about fifteen minutes when she started to recognize landmarks from Keisha's neighborhood. It took another three minutes before the men turned onto Keisha's street. Alexis stopped at the corner and waited until she saw the men enter the house before she turned the corner and pulled up behind Bear's truck.

What is Forever?

"Why did you bring me home, Lexxus? I'm not supposed to come here 'til tomorrow."

"I know sweetie, we're just coming to visit for a minute." Alexis began to question her impulsive decision to follow Damon. What was she going to do now? Should she just go to the door and ring the bell? What would she say when they answered? She was about to start the car and go back to Damon's when she realized that she didn't know how to get back. She didn't want to get lost. "Ebony, do you know how to get to your daddy's house from here?"

The child gave Alexis a sorrowful look and a shrug of her shoulders that let her know that she didn't have a clue.

"Oh well." She said more to herself than to the child. "Let's go in." They got out of the car and walked to the front door. She could hear Damon speaking loudly, although she couldn't understand what he was saying. She hesitated for a moment before she pushed the doorbell.

Damon snatched the door open in what seemed like less than a second. His fist was clenched until he recognized Alexis at the door. A look of amazement was quickly replaced with irritation. "Why in the hell did you bring Ebony over here?"

She felt like a timid child when she said "I was worried. I wanted to see if I could help in some way."

He exhaled loudly and turned and walked away from the door. Alexis and Ebony slowly entered the living room. It was no longer pristine. The love seat had been turned over and several of the pictures on the bookshelf against the near wall had been knocked to the floor. There were pieces of

103

glass all over the floor. Alexis looked at the couch and saw Keisha at the same time that Ebony did. Her mouth fell open.

"MOMMY!" Ebony ran to her mother. She threw her arms around her mother's waist and buried her face in her mother's bosom. Keisha looked a mess. Her left eye was swollen shut and dried blood caked in the corner of her mouth. Her already full lower lip was swollen to the point of bursting. When she realized that her daughter was there and had seen her condition, tears streamed from her red eyes.

"Alexis, why in the hell did you bring her here?" She screamed and cried at the same time. "She doesn't need to see this. I can't believe you brought her here. Oh God, I don't want my baby to see this." She lowered her head and wept. Her shoulders shook violently.

"I'm so sorry, Keisha. I didn't... I didn't know you would be... like this." The last two words were uttered in a whisper. Guilt and sorrow for the woman overwhelmed her. She didn't try to stop the tears that came from her eyes. She heard Damon's voice, but couldn't look up.

"I can't believe you Alexis," he turned away from her and said "Keisha, where is that mother fucker? You need to stop trying to protect his punk ass."

"Protect him? Why the hell would I try to protect that bastard after he did this to me?" Keisha screamed loud enough to scare the child in her arms, but couldn't control herself. "I hate that mother fucker! I hate him! I hate him!" Her voice broke as the tears took over again.

Damon was not deterred. "Then why do you keep letting him back in the house after he does this kind of shit to you? Every time he says he won't do it again, you let him come back and then the next time he hurts you worse than the last. I'm telling you, I'm gonna break that nigga's neck and if you let him come back here to recuperate I'm gonna break your neck and then take my daughter out of here for good. How do I know when he gets tired of beating on you he won't try it on her? Then I'd have to kill him."

"Damon," Alexis said softly. She walked over to him, and put a hand on his shoulder. "She's been through a lot tonight. She doesn't need you coming down on her right now."

"She's right, Dog. Leave Keisha alone and let's go find that bitch ass nigga and teach him about putting his hands on women." It was the first time Bear had spoken since Alexis had gotten there.

Damon's posture softened a little. Alexis could tell he realized that he was being too hard on Keisha. "You're right, Bear. My business right now is with Junior." He turned and walked out the door without another word. Bear was right on his tail. Alexis was afraid for him but she knew there was no way she could stop him. She walked over and sat beside Keisha who was still sobbing and holding the weeping child tightly in her arms. All Alexis could do was to put her arms around the two of them and cry with them.

They'd been sitting on Keisha's couch for about ten minutes when Alexis remembered she had left the oven on. She'd been cooking on low, but she didn't want to leave the oven on for too long unattended. When she moved to leave she could see the fear of being alone in Keisha's eyes. She asked her fiancé's baby's momma if she wanted to come to Damon's and stay the night. Keisha didn't hesitate to accept the offer. They packed an overnight bag and left her house without cleaning up a thing. They were going to leave a note for Damon, but decided against it. Junior might come back and they didn't want him to know where Keisha was.

The three of them were riding back to Damon's in Alexis' car. Ebony was asleep in the back seat. Keisha sat quietly in the passenger seat, her head leaned against the window. She ran a hand over her wounds. She reminded Alexis of a blind person, reading something in each cut and bruise. Hopefully they were telling her that Junior couldn't love her and treat her like that.

They rode in silence except for the sound of the Smooth R&B and Classic Soul station. Keisha only spoke to give directions. It bothered Alexis a little that Keisha knew the way to her man's house when she didn't. She shrugged the thought off and drove on until *End of the Road* by Boys to Men came on the radio.

"That's my song," both women said in unison.

They both began to sing along and sway and snap there fingers to the beat. Alexis was happy that the song seemed to take Keisha's mind off of her problems even if only for a couple of minutes. She even saw her smile for a moment when it got to the good part.

"This used to be the jam," Alexis said.

"I know that's right, Girl. I remember back in college when this song came on everybody hit the floor." Her eyes grew dreamy. "Shoot, me and Da—" she cut off Damon's name, but Alexis knew what she'd been about to say. They rode the rest of the way in an awkward silence.

What is Forever?

Alexis carried Ebony into the house and started up the stairs to put her in bed. "Keisha, make yourself comfortable."

After she was sure that the child was sleeping peacefully, she returned downstairs and went into the kitchen to fix an ice pack. When she brought it to the couch Keisha was shaking her head back and forth and mumbling to herself.

"I brought some ice for your eye." Keisha put her head back against the couch and Alexis gently placed the bag over the purple flesh. "I don't mean to be nosy, but what happened?"

"Junior is a first class ass, that's all." She crossed her arms over her chest and stuck out her already swollen lip. Alexis had to prevent herself from laughing when she saw the woman make the same pouting motion her daughter had made earlier that day. "I mean, he had been out all day with his friends, which is what he does every weekend. By the time he got home he was half past drunk. I been getting fed up wit that shit so I told him about hisself. I told him he wasn't gonna keep going out every Friday and Saturday, coming home stinking and sloppy while I stayed there waiting for him. I told him he needed to spend some time with me, especially when Ebony was over here and we could spend that time together."

Alexis didn't see anything wrong with that. Keisha went on "He just started yelling and knocking shit off the tables."

"What did you do?"

"I cursed his drunk ass out. That's when he decided to use my head for a punching bag."

"Oh Keisha, I'm so sorry."

What is Forever?

"Look Alexis, I appreciate your help but I don't need you to feel sorry for me. I'm gonna be all right."

"I know you will, Keisha. I didn't mean I feel sorry for you. I'm just sorry you had to go through this. Has he done this to you before?"

"Never this bad. I mean, we've had our squabbles and he might've pushed me or grabbed me too hard, but he's never done anything like this." The tears were released again. She leaned over and cried into Alexis' shoulder.

Alexis put her arm around Keisha and rocked her gently. "You can't let him keep doing this to you. You have to leave him or one day he might kill you."

"I know. I should leave him, but I ain't got nowhere to go. I refuse to move back into my mother's house."

"But why, Honey? It has to be better there than with Junior. Did you buy the house together?"

"Buy? We ain't buying that house. We been renting it. If you really want to know the truth, I been renting it. The lease is in my name. He just lives there."

"Then why don't you put his ass out?"

"You just wouldn't understand, Alexis." She looked up into Alexis' eyes. "You wouldn't understand my life. You have a good man. I mean Junior tries, he's just never been nothing and he's never gonna be nothing. His future is easy to read. He'll work for the plant Monday through Friday and drink every weekend until he retires or drinks hisself to death. He'll always make enough money to get by, but never enough to do something special. Damon's different. He'll make a difference in this world. He has a way of touching people's lives so that they're never the same."

What is Forever?

Alexis was surprised that she didn't feel jealous or bothered by her comments. She knew that it was true. Damon was a very special man. He was the type of man who cared about everyone he met. He never judged people. He accepted them for who they were. Damon made friends with almost everyone. He had a way of dealing with people on their level. He could drink a forty with a thug on the corner, or discuss world politics with the President and be equally accepted by both. Damon would give money to a man on the street even if he knew the man would spend it on a bottle of wine.

"Keisha, can I ask you another question? Why did you and Damon break up?"

CHAPTER 5

Keisha sat in front of Dr. Ellison's big oak desk. She had put off making this appointment for as long as she could. Dr. Ellison had been her doctor for as long as Keisha could remember. He was probably her first crush. He was a tall, lean man with skin the color of coal. He was very handsome with sharp features that made him look like royalty. She figured he was in his mid fifties, but she couldn't be sure. In her mind he had never aged or changed in any way. That was one of the things she loved about him, he was consistent. She could always count on him to be the same. No matter how her life changed or spun out of control, Keisha could always count on the distinguished, avuncular man. Keisha remembered being enthralled by his African accent. His voice had an effect on her that she could never explain other than to say it touched her on the inside.

Over the years he had become much more than just her doctor. Dr. Ellison was and would always be her guardian angel. In fact he was more like the father she should have had. He was there cheering her on when she was on the High School track team. He had paid for a Geometry tutor and he sat in the front row at her high school graduation. He made more noise when she walked across that stage than any father in the building.

When she had felt like she was ready to lose her virginity she went and talked to him instead of her mother. It was he who told her how special she was, and that her virginity was a gift that should be saved for a special person at a special

110

What is Forever?

time in a special place. He taught her about STD's, teen pregnancy and the other dangers of sex. And it was because of Dr. Ellison that she waited another year before finally giving her special gift to James "Pee Wee" Morgan in the Gymnasium under the bleachers on the wrestling mats.

Keisha had been sixteen then. After it happened Dr. Ellison was the first person she called. She was too ashamed to look him in the eye and tell him, so she phoned. He'd had her come in, gave her an examination, and discussed birth control with her. He couldn't put her on the pill without telling her mother, so he gave her condoms and told her how important it was for her to always use them. He said that she was much too important to end up pregnant and living off the county. She felt much closer to him than to the sorry man who had impregnated her mother. It was very hard for her now to go to his office and tell him that she thought she was pregnant, but he was the only person who she felt she could count on to tell her what to do.

When she told him his facial expression never changed, but although he did his best to hide it she could see the disappointment in his eyes. After examining her and verifying her pregnancy they sat in his office. They were both silent for what seemed like an eternity. Keisha kept her head bowed. She was too conscience-stricken to look in his eyes.

Finally he cleared his throat. "So Keisha, what do you plan to do?"

Tears welled in her eyes as she shrugged her shoulders. She felt like she was a little girl who had fallen out of grace with her father.

111

What is Forever?

"I've told you a thousand times that if you want me to understand you, you must speak. I don't read sign language."

Keisha knew good and well that the man spoke at least four languages. He was probably very fluent in sign language, but she understood his point.

'I don't know, Doctor Ellison. I don't understand how this happened." She could see from his expression that was the wrong answer.

"So you are telling me that you don't understand how women get pregnant?"

'No, I mean of course I know how it happened. It's just that I--we took precautions. I did everything I was supposed to do to prevent this." Keisha knew, and she suspected that he knew as well, that this was not exactly a true statement.

If he did, he let it pass. "Look, my darling. It does not matter how it happened. What is important now is what are you going to do about this? Does the young man know?"

Keisha shook her head. Before he could admonish her again, she whispered: "No."

"Well I think your first step is to let him know that he is going to be a father."

Keisha snapped her head up, pleading with her eyes. "I can't tell him, Dr. Ellison. At least not until I decide what I'm going to do."

"I don't understand. This concerns him as well as you. Don't you think he has at least some say in the decision you make?"

"I know, it's just that I...I don't want to lose him." She could hear the defeat in her own voice. She knew what he would say next and that he would be right.

What is Forever?

"Keisha, if this boy is the man for you, there is no way that he will leave you. If he is the type of man you need in your life he will stand by you through this. A real man never runs out on his responsibilities. If he does that, then you know that you don't need him and the sooner you find out about him the better."

His voice became gentler. "Keisha, do you want to keep the baby?"

The question hit her like a prize fighter with a title shot. In all of her worry over being pregnant she had never considered the actual life growing in her womb. Once she thought of it as a small life, as a piece of Damon that she would always have, there was not a moment's hesitation.

"Yes, at this point there is nothing more important to me in the world than this child."

"Well then you've already made the difficult decision. Everything else will work out in the fullness of time." Hearing him use the saying that Damon used so often somehow reassured her that everything would be fine. "Keisha, just know that you will never be alone. You will always have God and me. On that you can depend."

Keisha's spirits were lifted by the time she left his office. She had decided she would tell Damon when they went out later that night. She only hoped that he would turn out to be the man she believed he was.

When Damon pulled up in front of the house in his seventy-seven Corolla it was about seven p.m. Keisha was looking out her bedroom window. She had the front door open before he could ring the door bell.

What is Forever?

"Hey Baby, what's up?" He pulled her close and kissed her deeply.

"Mmmm, nothing much." She replied when he finally released her. She didn't want to have this conversation on her front porch. Her next door neighbor, Ms. Emma, was always in her window waiting to catch the next bulletin to spread over the neighborhood grapevine. "You ready to go, Baby?" She tried to sound as if everything were normal. She didn't want anything in her voice to alarm him.

"Yeah, sure. Let's roll." He walked around the car and opened the door for her. She had been out with a lot of guys who did that on the first, maybe the second date, but after that a sister was on her own. Not Damon, though. He had opened every door they'd ever entered together for the last three months. That was just one of the little things about him that she loved so much. He always treated and made her feel like a lady.

"You wanna check out that new movie at the Multiplex? I heard it was pretty good."

"Nah, not tonight. I'd rather just spend a little time with you, chillin. Do you know someplace where we can go to be alone?"

Keisha watched the naughty smile spread across his face. Before he could suggest their favorite hotel she said. "I don't mean be alone like that. I mean be alone so that we can talk."

"You want to talk, huh? What's up?"

"Nothing Baby, I just feel like it would be nice to spend a little time talking to each other for a change."

"All right, that's cool. I know a spot where we can be alone and talk." He made a sharp U-turn and headed in the

114

opposite direction. It wasn't long before they entered the City Lake Park. It was a place where a lot of the college crowd hung out on Sunday afternoons. Instead of turning right to head down to the lake front where every one congregated, Damon went straight, seemingly away from the lake. After a few moments they came to the end of the paved road. A chain with a "Do Not Enter" sign hung between two wooden posts. Damon put the car in park and walked over to the chain where it met one of the posts. He fiddled with the screw that held it in place for a moment and the chain dropped to the ground. He got back into the car drove across the chain onto a small dirt path. He got out of the car and replaced the chain, then drove along the dirt path. It led up a hillside. He parked the car behind a large dirt mound.

"Damon, where in the world are we? I've lived in this town all my life and I've never been up here."

"Wait, you haven't seen the best of it yet." He got out of the car and went to the trunk. When he walked around to let Keisha out of the car he had an old green comforter with him. He held her hand as he led her from behind the mound. Keisha's breath was taken away. They were on a hill about one hundred feet above the lake. There were trees scattered all around them. The setting sun was reflected off the surface of the water as families of ducks and swans glided over it.

"Oh Damon, it's beautiful. I can't believe it's the same lake."

Damon spread the blanket on the ground and motioned for her to sit next to him. He placed his arms around her waist and rested his chin on her shoulder. "This is the closest you'll ever get to heaven while you're still breathing."

For a moment Keisha felt like she was in heaven. Then she remembered why they were here. Before that thought could completely surface, another sent cold chills through her body. "Damon, how do you know about this place?"

The question obviously caught him off guard. He stammered over his words. "Oh, come on Girl. I know what you're thinking and it's not even like that. Sometimes the brothers and I bring pledges up here when we need some privacy, if you know what I mean. I think I'm the only one who noticed how beautiful it is up here. When you said you wanted some quiet time with just us, I knew it would be the perfect spot."

It was a good explanation but she was not totally convinced. She decided to table the matter for the moment. She had much more important things to talk to him about. Keisha leaned back into his arms. She wanted to burn the image of this perfect moment in time into her memory forever. She had to hold on to it for as long as possible before her news for Damon brought this perfect fairy tale crashing down around her head.

"You all right, Baby?" He squeezed a little tighter.

"Mmmm." the strength of his arms comforted her. She took a deep breath. "Damon, there's something I need to talk to you about." She only hesitated for a moment. "I'm pregnant." She hadn't intended on blurting it out in that way. She'd gone over it in her mind before he'd picked her up and had planned to ease her way into giving him the news, but when she finally worked up the nerve to open her mouth the

116

words just spilled out. Once they were out she was physically unable to utter another sound. It was all she could do to keep breathing while she waited for his reaction. She felt his heart beat against her back. She thought she noticed it increase slightly, but couldn't be sure. She was afraid to turn around and look at him. She was afraid of what his eyes might reveal. She pressed her eyes shut instead.

A small chuckle came from Damon's throat. Keisha's eyes popped open but she was still afraid to turn around. His chuckle became a laugh. Keisha was completely mystified. She spun around to look at him, afraid that the news had driven him mad. He grabbed her by her shoulders and she could see that he was beaming.

"Are you serious? Oh my God, I can't believe it. I'm going to be a father!" He pulled her tight against his chest.

Keisha was stunned by his response. She had never imagined that he would be happy about this, let alone ecstatic. His joy was contagious. She felt a warm, full smile spread across her face.

"You mean you're not upset about it?"

"Upset! Are you kidding me? Hell no, I'm not upset, I'm a father and you're a mother. Keisha, do you know what this means? We are a family! Oh Keisha Baby, I love you so much. Thank you, Baby." He pulled her into his chest again. He held her so tightly he almost cut off her air. When he finally released her he was a little calmer. "So how far along are you?"

"Well as near as Dr. Ellison can tell, I'm about two months."

117

What is Forever?

"So this explains why you haven't been feeling well lately and why you've been a little moody."

She slapped his shoulder. "Moody? Me? I'm never moody." They both laughed.

Keisha and Damon stayed on the hill overlooking the lake for two hours. They made plans for their future together and promised their undying love. As the last rays of the sun went down past the horizon they made love.

Things went well between them for the next three weeks. Damon showered her with small gifts and fussed over her whenever he had the opportunity. He refused to allow her to put salt on her food, made her drink at least six glasses of water a day and complained when she didn't get to bed before ten-thirty at night. Keisha loved the attention. It all made her feel loved and important. What she loved most however was the way that he made love to her, always slow and gentle. He said he didn't want to be banging into his baby's head, so he always took his time. Keisha let herself enjoy his sweetness.

Trouble came at the beginning of her third month. Up until then Keisha had been fortunate when it came to morning sickness. Overnight after reaching month three she became sick at the sight of food. She found herself throwing up every morning and all throughout the day. She was constantly tired and irritable.

What made matters worse was the fact that she had just two weeks left until college midterms. Keisha just felt like that there was no way she could prepare for her exams while she was vomiting all over the place. She had already missed several classes because she was too sick to make herself go.

What is Forever?

She started to consider withdrawing from school for the semester. She knew that it would set her back, but she figured that withdrawing would be better than failing half her classes.

Although Damon had been trying to take care of her, he was spending a lot of time preparing for his midterms too. Keisha wanted to be understanding because she knew how important doing well in school was to Damon's future. He was applying for film school after graduation and he couldn't afford mediocre grades. She did her best to be patient with his increased absences, but she couldn't help feeling insecure whenever Damon wasn't with her. Her hormones were playing tricks on her mind, but she couldn't shake the roller coaster of emotions that had taken hold of her.

One afternoon Keisha sat in her room reading a baby name book. She heard the tap on her bedroom door as Rolanda walked in and closed it behind her. "What's up, big momma? How's that bun in your oven?"

Keisha smiled at her friend and rubbed her still flat belly. "We're cool. What's up with you?"

"Damn Keisha, you sure you're pregnant? You don't look like you've gained an ounce."

"Hell yeah, I'm sure. The way I been throwing up around here I better be pregnant. Dr. Ellison says that's why I'm not showing yet. I'm spending too much time vomiting everything I eat. He said I'll start to show somewhere around my fourth month, after the morning sickness goes away."

"Well you may feel bad, but you look damn good girl. Shit, my ass got fat as soon as Li'l Man was conceived. I still can't get rid of this baby fat."

What is Forever?

Rolanda had been overweight before she got pregnant, but Keisha didn't want to make her best friend feel bad. "I know that's right, Girl. I hope I can get rid of mine after it's all over."

"You better hope so if you wanna keep your man. Shit, that stank heifer already over there after him."

Keisha's stomach dropped. She ran out the room and doubled up over the toilet. When she finished she didn't bother to rinse her mouth. She went back to the room and closed the door.

"Ro, what the hell are you talking about? Who's after him?"

A look of innocence crossed Rolanda's face. "Girl, I didn't mean nuthin. I mean there ain't nuthin to it. It's just talk."

Keisha knew her friend wanted her to beg for whatever information she had. Normally she wouldn't give Rolanda the satisfaction, but this was different. If someone was threatening her relationship, her family, her happiness she had to know about it.

"Ro don't play with me! If you know something about Damon you better tell me."

"I don't know nuthin for sure." She paused, as if that was all she was going to say, but the look on Keisha's face let her know she'd better spill it. "My cousin Netta goes to school over there too. She said that her boyfriend wanna be a Que so he be around them all the time. He said he saw Damon wit some ho over there the other night all hugged up."

Keisha's heart began to beat wildly in her chest. "How did he know it was Damon?"

What is Forever?

"Girl, I told you! He be all up under dem Ques. He know all of em."

Keisha couldn't stop the tears from rolling down her cheeks. Damon had said he'd been studying late, and how important his grades were to him. That bastard, he wasn't no different than any other motha fucka out there. Here she was carrying his baby and he was out there trying to make another.

Rolanda put her arms around Keisha's shoulder. "I'm sorry to be the one to tell you this shit girl, but at least you know what's up."

Keisha put her head on Ro's shoulder and cried. "I can't believe he would do this to me. Do you know how I've changed my life for his ass? I've been sitting up in this house not going anywhere. Trying to watch everything I do and say."

"I know that's right. I ain't seen your ass in a while."

"Well you don't hafta worry about that no more, cause I'm not gonna sit around waiting for his ass while he out with some other bitch."

"Well Sista, it's good to have you back."

"That's right, Girl. It's good to be back"

"If you're serious about it, I think we should celebrate. You know the Kappa's are having a party tonight. I say we get real fly in our tightest, sexiest shit and have a good time."

Keisha paused. It had been quite a while since she had been out to a party. As a matter of fact, she hadn't been to a party without Damon since they had been together. She didn't know how Damon would feel about it with her being pregnant.

121

What is Forever?

"Oh come on now Keisha, I know you not just full of shit. I know he ain't got your nose so wide open he can fuck you over and then keep you on a chain. Damn he must really be swingin' wood."

"Hell no, Ro. I'm just trying to figure out what I'm gonna wear tonight. Shit."

They gave each other high fives. Keisha's stomach was still in knots, but she managed to smile. She wasn't sure what she was getting herself into, but she knew that one way or another, her life was truly about to change.

Keisha was ready to roll by ten. She had on a black Liz Clairborn mini with spaghetti straps. The dress ended well above her knees and showed off her long legs. Although it was getting cold out she decided not to wear stockings. She didn't want the waistband of pantyhose squeezing her midsection. She wore a black thong underneath to prevent unsightly panty lines. Rolanda showed up about ten-thirty in her souped up lime green eighty-nine Honda accord. The car was shining like it had just been driven off the lot. The way the tires glistened, Keisha figured Rolanda must have put an entire bottle of Armor All on each one. Keisha was out of the front door before she could turn the engine off.

"What's up, Girl? You ready to have some fun?"

"You know it." Keisha's party tone belied the insecurity she felt. She couldn't get rid of the feeling that she would be much better off if she just went back into the house.

"Here, Girl. You want a little of this?" Rolanda pulled out a pint of Gin from under the driver's seat. She took a hit then passed the bottle towards her partner.

What is Forever?

"I don't know if I should drink, Ro. You know, with the baby and everything."

"It's up to you. I ain't trying to put you under any peer pressure or anything, but you know Keeta's a CNA and she told me that you can drink up until your fourth month without harming the baby. So if you plan on getting your drink on before you have that rug rat you might as well do it now."

"Well in that case, pass the bottle. It's been a long while since I had a little drink anyway." Keisha took a long swig from the bottle. The fire water burned its way down into her stomach. When it got there she felt its warmth spread over her. It was the first thing that she had consumed that didn't make her nauseous. She wondered why the alcohol didn't make her ill as she took another long draw from the bottle and handed it back to Rolanda who took another swig.

"All right, Ro. Why we sitting here? Let's roll."

Rolanda put the stick in first gear. Her tires screeched as they pulled from the curb and were off.

The Kappa's house was located near the downtown historic district of the city. It was a large two story house that had been built in the early thirties. The Kappas had gotten the house for next to nothing, and had raised money to have it renovated. When the girls pulled up in front they could hear the music blaring from the street. There were people hanging out on the lawn and on the front porch. Keisha saw a few people she knew from class talking in a small group. She decided she would try to avoid them. She didn't want to have to answer any questions on why she hadn't been to class over the last few weeks.

What is Forever?

"Damn, Keish. Looks like this party's slammin."

"I know that's right, Girl. Let's get on up in here and see what kind of trouble we can find. But first let me hit that gin one more time."

"Be careful now, Keish. You know gin will make you sin." They both laughed and high-fived again.

When they got into the house the party was on full throttle. There were people in the living room and den. When they walked back to the kitchen they found a game of strip spades going on. Rolanda looked in the refrigerator and pulled out a couple of Heinekens. She handed one to Keisha after opening them with a bottle opener she found on the counter.

They made their way through the house bobbing their heads to the beat of the Roots. They found a seat in a quieter corner and busied themselves talking about the other women at the party. Who was too fat for what they were wearing, who's hair was fake and of course which girls were ho's. They sat on the couch sipping on their beer until Keisha thought she saw a familiar shaped head moving thru the crowd.

"Damn!"

"What's wrong, Girl?"

"Damn! I think I just saw Damon's ass over there."

"Oh shit! What you wanna do, Keish? You wanna bounce out a here?"

"Oh hell no! If that motha fucka gonna be here partying when he should be studying, then I ain't got no reason to leave."

What is Forever?

"Well it's your call, Honey. You just let me know what you wanna do. Mmmm-mm-Mmmm. Damn Keish, who's dat?" She pointed to a six-foot six-inch mountain of a man with a bald head. "Now that's what I call a man."

Keisha looked over to where Rolanda was staring. She was not particularly impressed with the guy, but she had seen him around campus. "I don't know his name but I've seen him around. I think he's on the football team."

"Well touch-down, I'd let him go for the extra point." Rolanda adjusted her already too low cut blouse and stared at the mammoth man until she caught his eyes. She gave him the most ridiculous come hither look that Keisha had ever seen. Somehow it worked. He worked his way over to where they were sitting.

"Hello, ladies. How y'all doing tonight?"

Keisha gave him a generic "fine" and turned her head to scan the room for Damon.

Rolanda on the other hand gave him a syrupy smile. "Oh I'm doing fine, but I'd be much better if someone asked me to dance."

Keisha couldn't help but to look at Rolanda sideways after hearing her weak Scarlet O'Hara wannabe southern bell impersonation.

"Well my name's Hill, and I'd love to dance with you." He took Rolanda by the hand and led her into the living room which was doubling as the dance floor.

Keisha noticed Ro was putting a little extra sway in her hefty hips. She smiled and sat back on the couch, a wave of loneliness overtaking her. She got off the couch and decided to see if the head she saw really was Damon. She didn't

125

think he'd be here. He had complained earlier about how much studying he had to do. Not to mention the fact that the Kappa's and Ques had a bit of a rivalry and she didn't think he'd support a Kappa function. She didn't have to walk far before she saw him. He was standing with Bear and Adrian, two of his frat brothers. There was a girl standing with them and as much as Keisha hated to admit it, the chick was beautiful. She had long reddish brown hair and a body that was banging. She had on too-tight blue jeans and a fitted v-neck sweater. The sister kept it simple but sexy. She was all smiles in their faces. Keisha couldn't tell who she was with because she was talking and flirting with all three of them and they seemed to be equally taken with her.

But Keisha knew women, and there was something about the way she looked at Damon. Keisha just knew the girl wanted him. Well she wasn't about to get him. Not if she had anything to say about it. Keisha was about to bum rush the show when she decided against it. She wasn't about to embarrass herself over any man. If he wanted that slut he could have her. She turned on her heels and walked back to the kitchen, grabbed another Heineken and returned to her spot on the couch. She downed the beer quickly. She was about to go to the kitchen for another when Chuck Tyler, a Kappa from her U.S. History class sat on the couch next to her.

"What's up, Keisha? What are you doing sitting over here in the corner by yourself?"

"Drinking beer," she said matter-of-factly.

"Well it looks like that one's empty. Do you want me to get you another?"

What is Forever?

She didn't know Chuck very well, but he'd always seemed like a nice enough guy. "Sure Chuck, that'd be nice of you."

"No problem, wait here. I'll be right back." He disappeared into the crowd headed for the kitchen. He was back in a couple of minutes with a cup of red punch in his hand. "Sorry Keisha, but there wasn't any more beer. This is what we call Crimson Tide, guaranteed to cure your every problem." He handed her the cup.

Keisha took a small sip from the cup. It tasted great, just like fruit punch. She couldn't taste any alcohol so she didn't take her time drinking it down. "Thanks Chuck, that was good. I thought it was gonna be full of alcohol and nasty but it tastes good."

"Yeah, it's our own special blend. So you never told me why you're sitting over here in the corner by yourself. Where's your boy?"

"I don't know. I don't keep him in my pocket." Keisha didn't feel like talking about Damon so she cut the topic short.

"That's fine Baby, I was just asking."

"Can I get another cup of that punch?"

He was gone a little longer than the first time. Eventually he came back with two more cups of the punch. He handed one to Keisha and began to sip on the other.

"You know I've had my eye on you for a while now." He was sitting close to her and because of the music he had to lean over and speak into her ear in order for her to understand him.

What is Forever?

"Is that right? Why haven't you ever said anything to me before now?" Keisha could feel her body relaxing and her head starting to swim. She could tell that she was slurring a bit. She readjusted herself and sat up a little straighter in an attempt to get her head together.

"I don't know. You was always up under home boy. This was my first opportunity to tell you how I was feeling."

She knew he was full of shit but she decided to let him continue to shoot his game. With Ro gone she didn't want to be sitting over in the corner by herself. If Chuck left she'd probably end up having to deal with someone worse in her face.

"Oh really? Well brothers need to learn how to go after what they want. You never know what a sister might say."

"I guess you have a point there. Look Keisha, I can barely hear you in here. Why don't we go upstairs to my room where we can talk for a minute, maybe get to know each other a little."

Keisha knew that would be a stupid thing for her to do, but she found herself getting up and walking towards the staircase behind Chuck. She felt like she was walking around in a dream. There was a blurry halo in her vision. She tried to shake her head to clear the cobwebs, but couldn't get the fog out of her mind.

She felt like she was watching herself from outside of her body. She could see the mistake she was making but was powerless to stop it. She and Chuck ascended the stairs and walked down the long hallway to the last room on the left. Keisha noticed pictures of famous African Americans lined the hallway. She saw the faces and she knew they were important people, but for the life of her she couldn't put a name with a single face.

Chuck's room was dimly lit and sparse. There was a full sized bed with a plain blue comforter neatly spread over it, and a wooden dresser and dark blue stuffed chair that reminded Keisha of part of her grandmother's living room set. Chuck sat on the chair, which left nowhere for her to sit other than the bed. She flopped down. The mattress was much too soft. The lack of light made her sleepy and that much more difficult to keep her wits about her. Chuck tried to make small talk for a few minutes before he slid from the chair to the bed beside her. He casually leaned back on his elbows and spoke in a non-threatening voice. Keisha heard him talking but had trouble processing whatever he was saying. It wasn't long before he began to kiss her on her neck. Soft little pecks at first in between his trivial conversation. It was apparent that talking was not the reason he had brought her to his room.

"Chuck, you need to stop. I don't know what you think is about to happen here, but I ain't going out like that." Her words were stronger than her will to resist. It wasn't that she was attracted to him, it was the fact that she was feeling betrayed by Damon mixed with the alcohol clouding her mind that prevented her from just getting off of that bed and walking out of the room.

"Come on now, Keisha. I know that you're feeling me or you wouldn't have come up here with me." He began to kiss her neck deeply, gently biting as he sucked on her flesh.

Despite herself she could feel her body react to the attention his lips were giving her. She was surprised at the soft moan that slipped from her lips. That was all the authorization Chuck needed to put his hand on her right breast and squeeze gently. In her mind she knew that she had to stop him before things went too far. Her body would just not obey the fading voice in her head. Chuck's hand slipped down to her thigh and began to creep up under her dress. Her head fell back and her resolve dissipated as his thumb touched the soft spot between her legs. Her head began to spin and her breathing became deep as he slipped a finger in her panties and played in her wetness. When he pulled his hand from between her legs she knew that it was soaked without opening her eyes to look at it. Chuck pulled the straps from her shoulder and pulled the top of her dress down to reveal her breasts. This time it was Chuck who moaned as he covered her left then right nipple with his saliva as he suckled on each.

Keisha was barely conscious by the time he pulled the thong from her rear end. She just hoped that he would put a rubber on and was relieved when she heard him open the little packet and curse softly as he tried to put it on. She was a little surprised that he wasn't bigger when he entered her. In fact she could barely tell he was there. Once it was truly too late to turn back she thought of Damon and a single tear fell from her eye and ran down the side of her face into her ear.

She felt the man moving on top of her and heard his heavy breathing, but her true consciousness had retreated somewhere deep inside her mind. She had become totally disconnected to what was happening to her body. She couldn't tell how long he was on top of her before she heard him moan noisily and suddenly roll off of her body.

"I'm going to the bathroom. I'll be right back."

She didn't move or speak when he got off the bed and walked to the door. She did notice that he cut off the light as he walked out of the room and closed the door. Sleep came quickly and deeply. She didn't stir until she felt Chuck climbing back on top of her and trying to insert himself inside of her. This time there were no tender kisses or soft caresses. It was not until she realized how much larger the penis was that she became aware that it was not Chuck on top of her. She opened her eyes to see that a much lighter-skinned man had penetrated her and was quickly pumping in and out of her. He was finished before she could truly grasp what had just happened. When he rolled off of her another man crawled on the bed and began to suck on her left nipple. She tried to scream to push his head away from her but the alcohol or whatever they had put in the punch made her arms too heavy to lift and had stolen her voice. She knew what was happening to her, but was powerless to move or even verbally protest.

It's okay, Baby," the next guy whispered. She recognized him. She knew she had seen him before, but just like the pictures in the halls she was unable to place him or his name. She only knew that he was also a Kappa. "It's okay Keisha, Im'a take care of you," he said in her ear as he too inserted himself into her overworked private areas. The realization that she was about to be violated yet again was too much for her. She looked into the man's face and blacked out.

What is Forever?

Keisha dreamed of being huddled in mire with a screaming baby clutched to her bosom. Out of nowhere hands reached up from the muddy dirt grabbing at her, ripping her clothes as they attempted to rend the child from her arms. Keisha screamed for help as she pulled the child closer, struggling to protect it. The number of hands multiplied. Her flesh was covered with their groping fingers. Sharp nails pierced her skin as blood streamed out of her wounds. She screamed louder, but as loud as her cries were the sound of child's wails drowned out her own. She began to sink into the mud. The more she struggled the faster she was sucked down as the demon hands pulled her under. Somehow Keisha knew that they were not after her, but after the baby. She was cognizant that if she gave the child to the hands she might be released. Something inside of her knew that to give up the child would mean to give up something more important than her own life. As she was pulled beneath the surface and everything went black she thrust the child over her head and out of the mire. If need be the demons could have her, but they would never have her child.

Abruptly the mud above her head was ripped open like dry rotted cloth and a blinding light showered over her. She didn't know what was happening to her, but she could hear that the child had stopped crying and in fact had begun to giggle as it was gently pulled free of her grip.

"Noooo, no, no, you can't have her. Please give me my baby, please don't take my baby."

She reached up, stretching her fingers as far as they would go. She felt the touch as she heard the voice. The warmth of the fingers touching her finger tips raced through her like electricity.

"Quiet child, everything is all right. Your child is safe and so are you."

She began to float out of the darkness that surrounded her, up into the light. She panicked, afraid that she was dead and the light was God calling her to heaven. Somehow she knew she wasn't dead. The voice was very familiar. At first she thought it was Doctor Ellison, but suddenly she realized it was Damon. She turned her head away from the light, filled with shame. He called to her.

"Keisha, it's me. It's all right Keisha, it's me, Damon."

She sat up with a start and was instantly aware of her surroundings and her nakedness. It was only a second later that she remembered why she was naked. He was there sitting on the edge of the bed with her right hand in his and his left hand on her shoulder. When she looked him in his eyes there was no way for her to hide her shame.

"Oh Damon..." the rest of what she said was indiscernible through her deep and hysterical weeping.

"Shhhhh.... Keish, it's all right. It's all right, I'm here. Everything's all right."

She heard his words but couldn't believe what he was saying. Couldn't he see what was going on, what had happened?

"Damon, why... how did you know I was here?" Her mind was still spinning. Emotions were twirling through her like a ballerina.

"We don't have to talk about that right now. We need to get you out of here, then we can talk." He sat her up and helped her get her dress on. He pulled her to her feet and grabbed her when she almost fell to the floor. "Keisha, I need you to try to straighten up for just a couple minutes so we can get out of here."

She could only manage to nod her head then lean it on his shoulder. Her legs were weak and she staggered so badly she knew that she wouldn't be able to walk three steps without his assistance. She let him support her weight as they walked out into the hallway. The music was blaring. The party was still in full swing. When they made it down the stairs Damon directed her towards the kitchen rather than the front door. He swiftly guided her through the crowd of people. When they got to kitchen she saw the back door. She could see people looking at them. Some of them were laughing, others whispering to each other. Keisha felt like all of them knew what she had done. The cool air felt good on her skin once they were outside. When she was safely in Damon's car she leaned her head against the window. Although she didn't make a sound, tears still streamed from her face. They hadn't traveled a block when she quickly rolled down the window and vomited. She was unable to get her whole head out of the window and she felt nasty as it poured down her chest and into her lap.

"Don't worry about it Keisha, I'll take care of you."

She tried to speak but her mouth wouldn't work. She leaned her head back and passed out for a second time. Damon took her to his dormitory. He stayed in the honors dorm which was the nicest on campus. His room was set up like a suite with a sitting room, a kitchenette, bathroom and bedroom. She didn't know how he had gotten her out of the

What is Forever?

car and up to his room. She didn't come to until she felt the cold water from the shower washing over her. Damon had apparently removed the dress and put her on the floor of the shower. When she looked at him he was in a pair of gym shorts leaning over her gently washing her. The water on his arms and chest made his muscles more noticeable and sexier than normal. Damn he's good looking, she thought.

"I'm such a fool." She meant to think that too, but she wasn't sure that she hadn't said it aloud. "Damon, I'm so sorry, I'm so sorry."

"Be quiet, Keisha." He said it quietly, but with the intensity of a smoldering volcano about to erupt.

He continued to swirl the soap around her neck and breast. When he reached her stomach he stopped, he took a deep breath then turned his head for a moment. She wasn't sure but she believed he wiped a tear from his eye. He began to lather her stomach. As he did, his touch got firmer. He began a scrubbing type motion as though he were attempting to remove a stain from the shower tile.

"Ouch, Damon! That hurts."

He pulled his hand away from her stomach so quickly she thought he had drawn it back to strike her. "I'm sorry." He finished washing her in silence.

Keisha slipped in and out of consciousness throughout the night. She awoke the next morning in his bed. It wasn't the first time she had spent the night in his room, but she was caught off guard by not being in her own bed. When she tried to lift her head a searing pain ran through her temples. She let her head drop back to the pillow, which sent another sharp pain through her head. Every time she moved she felt as if her brain rattled around in her skull. She lay there for what seemed like a day before she attempted to move again. She felt the pain again as she lifted her head, but this time she fought through it and finally rose to her feet. She pulled the comforter that had been over her around her shoulders and shuffled out to the living room. Damon was lying on the couch in the same shorts he'd worn the night before. His right hand was stuck in the waistband of his shorts as he watched television. She could tell that he wasn't really watching the game because he wasn't yelling and cursing at the screen. Damon was an avid football fan. It was the only thing she had seen him treat with as much passion as he treated her. His eyes were on the screen, but it was apparent to her that his mind was a thousand miles away.

She cleared her throat. He jumped when he saw her standing in the doorway of the bedroom. "Damn Keisha, I didn't see you there. You scared me."

"I'm sorry, I didn't mean to. But please do me a favor - don't talk so loud."

"Oh YOU MEAN LIKE THIS?" He teased in a loud voice.

"Damon, you're the devil." She smiled at him.

His smile disappeared as quickly as it had come when they made eye contact.

"So, what time is it anyway?" She asked, suddenly feeling out of place.

"It's about two thirty."

"Oh shit, are you kidding? I need to call my Momma. She's gonna kill me."

"I already did last night."

What is Forever?

"You called my Momma? What did she say?"

"I told her you weren't feeling well and you were gonna stay with me last night. She didn't seem too happy about it, but she didn't say anything out of the way."

"Well, I should probably call her anyway to let her know you didn't take advantage of her little girl." She regretted the words before they finished slipping from her lips. She relived the previous night in a flash.

"Humph" was all he said as he turned his head back toward the television.

"Do you mind if I sit with you?"

Damon sat up and swung his thick legs off of the couch to make room for her.

Keisha eased onto the couch next to him. She was afraid to make eye contact so she just looked at the floor while she rubbed her temples. "I think we should talk. I mean about last night. Damon I am so s—"

"Look Keisha, I'm not ready to talk about this. Even if I were, I wouldn't know what to say to you. I mean, I'm really not sure how all of this happened or what role you played in it. I only know that you have my baby inside you, and you not only disrespected yourself and me, but you disrespected my unborn child."

There was nothing he could have said to have made her feel smaller. He laid his head back against the sofa and exhaled. She could tell by the way he kept blinking that he was trying to keep himself from crying. When he continued there was anger in his voice.

"I mean, could I have been that wrong about you? Are you some kind of freak that just fucks anybody that asks you for some? I've been sitting here thinking about how you got mad at me because I hadn't tried to get with you like that. I thought it was cute at the time, but now I realize that you were really expecting some dick and there I was holding back on you. Well now, don't I feel stupid. I'm the only motha fucka around here stupid enough to fuck you and get your ass pregnant."

His words cut through her like razors. Each word he spoke tore pieces of her heart away from her. Deep inside, she felt that he must be right. Why else would she have put herself in that situation?

He wasn't done. "How in the world could you have done that to me? Haven't I been good to you? Haven't I tried to be the kind of man that you want?"

She turned on him with venom in her voice, moving quickly from prey to predator. "Oh yeah? You think you were being the kind of man that I want when you were out fucking with that bitch I saw you with last night?"

He stared at her in disbelief. Utter shock was all over his face.

"That's your fucking problem, Damon. You can dish it out but you can't take it. You thought I didn't know about your little freak on the side, didn't you? Well guess what, I do know. So you know what, Damon? It's your fault what happened last night. You made me do what I did."

Damon was in such a state of shock that for a moment he could not close his mouth. It took a full ten seconds before he could respond. "Keisha, what in the hell are you talking about? I haven't been with anyone other than you since

138

we've been together. Where in the world did you get some bullshit like that?"

His denial was like a counter-punch to her gut. She gasped at the thought that he might be innocent. He couldn't be innocent! If he wasn't messing around on her then that meant that the blame for what happened last night could only rest on her shoulders.

"You're full of shit. I got this information from a very reliable source. I know you been messing round with that girl. Why don't you be a man and admit it."

She could tell by the look on his face that he wasn't lying, but she couldn't bring herself to let go of her only excuse for behaving like a whore.

Damon looked in her eyes. His voice was unwavering. "I don't have any reason to lie to you. I have not been seeing anyone but you."

She heard the sentence, but the only thing that registered was that he had no reason to lie to her. Was she such a sorry ho that she was not worth lying to? It could only mean he no longer wanted her. She was running to the bathroom in a flash. She had expelled all the contents of her stomach the night before, so there was nothing more to vomit other than gastric juices and air.

When she finally finished dry-heaving, Damon handed her a towel and set out a new toothbrush and some toothpaste on the counter.

"Use these," he said. He turned without another word nor a pat on her back and walked out of the room.

When she walked back into the living room. Damon was putting her black dress into a plastic grocery bag. He walked into the bedroom and came back with a blue sweatsuit in his hand. He dropped it at her feet.

"Put this on so I can take you home."

Once they were in his car headed towards her house Keisha tried to talk about what had happened. "Damon, I really think we ought to talk about—"

"I told you I don't know what to say to you. At this point I don't know if I should be taking you home, or to the police or doing something to you that would get me thrown in jail. I don't know anything."

Keisha tried to speak, but the words stuck in her throat. She could see the tears that he desperately held back. She wanted to reach out to him, to comfort him but she knew she was the cause of his pain. What was worse, she had no answers for him. She remembered everything that had happened, and although she knew it had been wrong, she had not truly attempted to stop it.

He continued. "I only know that you have my child inside you. No matter what happened last night, no matter what kind of person you really are or what happens between us, that's my child in you and I will always love him and be there for him."

His lack of clarity for their future cut her to the core, but she made no attempt to push that issue. Damon said he'd always be there for his child, and deep within she knew it was true. For the time being that was enough for her.

CHAPTER 6

Alexis sat on the couch speechless, staring into Keisha's eyes. Damon had never told her the entire story. In fact he had given her very little information by comparison. He had only said that they realized they weren't right for each other and decided to part as friends.

Keisha's eyes were filled with red veins streaking across the whites. "And you know Alexis, he never once went back on that promise. He's been the best father in the world to that little girl. That's probably the only thing I ever did right in my life was getting pregnant by Damon." There was another awkward silence. "Anyway, I don't even know why I told you that story." Sniff. "I ain't never told anyone the details about what happened that night, not even Rolanda. Shit, we been friends forever, but I could never let myself talk about it out loud. I think about it almost every day, though."

Alexis wasn't sure how to proceed. She had never expected to hear such a tale. "So Keisha, what happened to those boys? Did you press charges?"

Keisha's eyes dropped to her lap. "No. Damon tried to get me to press charges, but I just couldn't. I mean, how am I gonna charge somebody with rape if I really ain't sure it was rape? I didn't want it, but I did put myself in that situation. I didn't want to ruin nobody's life for something that was just as much my fault. Plus the fact I didn't want my business all over campus. In the end that's what broke us up. I think he felt that if I didn't press charges then I must have been a

141

willing participant." She paused. "Sometimes I still wonder if I was."

Alexis had heard people say crazy things like that on Oprah, but she could not believe that real people could have such a misconception. "Keisha, you have to stop this. There is no way that what happened to you was your fault. You were the victim. Who gives a damn what happened to them. Their asses should still be rotting in jail."

"Do you know what Chuck is doing now?" She looked up and stared Alexis in the eye. "He works for a major corporation in Atlanta that helps thousands of poor minorities get decent housing. He's doing great things with his life. He's helping people. If I had pressed charges a lot of those people would be homeless or worse. I'm glad I didn't do anything. I'm just not worth all of that."

"Keisha." Alexis' voice was soft as she grabbed her hand. "You couldn't be more wrong. First of all, if he wasn't doing that job they would have hired someone else to do it. Secondly, you are important, and you are worth far more than you seem to know."

"That's funny, Damon used to say the same kinds of things. I even started to believe him, until I proved that theory wrong."

"Let me make you some herb tea. You need to try to relax." Alexis went to the kitchen and prepared two cups of Sleepy Time tea. By the time she got back to the couch Keisha was fast asleep. Alexis pulled an Afghan out of the hall closet and draped it over Keisha's sleeping form.

She left one cup of tea on the coffee table and took the other into the bedroom with her. She sat in the bed with her feet pulled under her as she thought about Keisha's story and her relationship with Damon. She had finished her tea and was just about to doze off when she heard the front door close. She shot up in bed and felt her heart race in her chest.

She walked to the bedroom door and quietly cracked it open. She watched as he walked over to the living room couch and stood over Keisha. He stood there for a good thirty seconds, seemingly studying her face. She saw him bend over and delicately adjust the covering that she had partially kicked off. Alexis jumped when he turned toward the bedroom. She quickly slipped back into the bed and turned her back to the door. She was feigning sleep when he entered the room. She made light breathing sounds. She could feel the heat from his body and recognized his scent as he stood over her, his eyes upon her. She listened to him walk around to her side of the bed. He knelt down and kissed her lightly on her forehead.

"I love you so much, Alexis." He whispered.

Her heart pulsed a little at the touch of his lips and the sound of his voice. She was relieved to have him home safely. "Baby, you're home." She pretended to have been awakened by his words. "Are you all right? What happened?"

"Shhhh. Everything's fine." He spoke softly. "We found him passed out in an alley over in the bottoms. Bear wanted to beat his ass and I almost let him. I just couldn't do it though, not in the condition he was in. We threw him in the back of the pickup and took his ass to the police station. We filed a report and they're holding him for drunk and disorderly, but he'll be out first thing in the morning.

143

What is Forever?

Keisha's gonna have to take out a warrant on him for what he did to her." He paused. "By the way, what's she doing here?"

"I just didn't feel right leaving her there. I was afraid he might go back there and beat her again, so I brought her here. I hope you don't mind. I just didn't know what else to do."

Damon kissed her on the lips. "Of course I don't mind, Baby. Just another thing I have to love about you, your compassion. I'm gonna take a shower and come to bed. I'm worn out."

A variety of emotions barraged Alexis after he walked into the bathroom. She felt jealous of his relationship with Keisha. She didn't feel threatened by their relationship. She believed the romance was long gone. There was something else however, something possibly worse. Alexis felt that there was something between them that was just for the two of them. They shared a very special place where she couldn't go.

She was also proud of the way he had handled the situation with Junior. Damon always did things in that fashion, with strength and honor. He was the kind of man who stood up against wrong and took action, but he never took advantage of a situation. He showed that tonight, through his restraint with Junior. Thinking about the day caused her to feel weary. She had Damon's baby's momma sleeping on the couch, and his ex-girlfriend scheming on how to steal him from her. She fingered the rock on her left ring finger and it made her feel a little happier. She decided to zero in on those feelings. After all, she and Damon would

What is Forever?

soon be married and all the scheming in the world wouldn't be enough to come between them. She closed her eyes and felt herself drifting off to sleep.

CHAPTER 7

Tara was excited. She was picking Damon up in a few minutes and they were going out together. She couldn't believe it. She'd dreamed of it but never thought the two of them would ever end up on a date. Of course this wasn't technically a date, but she'd take what she could get.

Over the last two months she and Damon's friendship had grown. They had met several times for lunch and she had gotten into the habit of calling him every afternoon before Gabe got home. Each day they would talk for an hour or more, sharing the highs and lows of their day or helping each other through personal problems. She had given him her shoulder to lean on when he had to drop out of film school so that he could get a job to help support his daughter Ebony.

About a week after the first poetry reading he'd revealed to her that he had a child. Initially after he told her about Ebony she'd assumed he was just another baby-making brother running away from responsibility. Too many men were playing games with women, confessing love and promising forever just to lay them down. When the girls turned up pregnant they were on the first thing smoking out of town. They'd do anything to get away from the women and their unborn babies. All too often those men mysteriously lost or forgot the mother's address so there could be no way of sending money for child support.

As with everything else, Damon was different than most men when it came to his daughter. Ebony was often with him

146

What is Forever?

when Tara phoned. Damon was always doing this or that for his little girl. He had found a friend who could give her free piano lessons, and he frequently took her to museums or children's plays. He loved to talk about how smart and curious she was. Damon believed his daughter was going to be a special person and he was determined to give her the tools she needed to do something special in the world.

When Tara had called him this afternoon, he'd seemed down in the dumps. Damon confided that he was feeling the role he played in his daughter's life was insignificant. What concerned him was the fact that his job as a studio operator at a local television station didn't pay very much. He barely made enough money to support himself, let alone provide any meaningful amount of money to Ebony. Damon hated not being able to give his daughter the monetary support she deserved.

"Tara, I'm telling you, sometimes I feel like a deadbeat dad."

Tara asked Damon how the baby's mother was treating the situation. Was she riding him about child support or threatening to take him down town? He told her that Keisha was very cool and understanding about his financial situation. That didn't allow him to excuse himself, however. Damon loved his daughter and had a responsibility to her.

Tara was touched by the man yet again. Men like Damon were few and far between.

"Damon, if you'd like I could give you some money to help you out. I just sold a rather large house and made a very nice commission on it."

What is Forever?

Tara thought the phone went dead after she made the offer. The line was silent. "Damon, are you there?"

"Yeah, I'm here."

"Did you hear what I said? I can give you a thousand dollars if you want it."

"Tara, I don't know what to say. I really appreciate the offer, but there's no way I could take that kind of money from you."

"But why, Damon? I'd understand you're not wanting to take it if it was going to put a strain on me, but really the market has been really good lately. Plus, with what Gabe brings home the only thing I do is bank my checks anyway. You are such a good person, and you've been such a good friend to me, please let me do this for you."

Damon paused for a long moment before he spoke. "The only way I can let you do this is if we consider it a loan. I might be able to pay you back early next year."

"If you want to pay me back that's fine, but you don't have to put a time limit on it. Pay me whenever you're able. There's one more thing I want you to do for me before I give you the money."

"Uh oh. Why do I feel like I should be afraid?"

"No need to be afraid, just be dressed and ready to roll around seven."

"Ready for what?"

"I told you I just made a big sell, and I want to celebrate."

"What about Gabe? You mad at him again? That's the only time you want to hang with me." Damon's voice was light as he teased.

What is Forever?

"For your information Mr. Smarty pants, Gabe left early yesterday for Atlanta on business. He'll be gone until tomorrow evening."

"Oh, so I'm your second choice since your perfect lawyer boyfriend is gone huh?"

"Look, Mr. Black. Are you going to help me celebrate or not?"

"Seven o'clock did you say?"

"Yes Damon, seven o'clock."

"Do I need a tux?"

She couldn't help but laugh. "Only if you've got one in your closet."

"Weeeell, as a matter of fact I do have the powder blue one I wore to my senior prom. I never took it back to the shop."

"That's cool," she said smiling, "you'll just have to sit at a different table and we can pass notes, cause I'm not going anywhere with a man in a powder blue tuxedo."

"Okay no tux, but don't think about getting me drunk and having your way with me."

"Oh shucks. That's just what I was thinking."

"Don't think about it, just do it."

They both laughed. "I'll pick you up at seven, Mr. Black."

"I'll be ready."

Tara felt like she was floating after she hung up the telephone. She attempted to keep her thoughts pure, but she couldn't keep her lust-filled ideas under control. It was about two in the afternoon and she had too much time on her hands before their date. She tried to busy herself around the house with cleaning. Even after the place was spotless she still had over three hours before she was supposed to pick him up. She tried to watch television but there was nothing on that kept her attention. Finally Tara decided she'd take a run before she and Damon got together. She hoped the exercise would take her mind out of the gutter. She reminded herself that she had always been faithful to Gabe and she wanted to continue being faithful.

So why *was* she going out with Damon? She told herself they were going out as friends, but she could always tell when she was lying to herself.

After she put on a pair of royal blue bike pants and a white Nike sweatshirt, she walked outside and began stretching. She hadn't been running since Monday and feeling her muscles pull and stretch felt good. She ran at a vigorous pace. She tried to think about Gabe and their still unscheduled wedding as she ran through the neighborhood. She contemplated what their marriage would be like. She tried to convince herself that once they were married things would get better. She couldn't help wishing that Gabe could be more like Damon. If he were, her life would be perfect.

By the time she got back to the condo it was five thirty. She had about an hour to shower, get dressed and leave to pick up Damon. Once her body was clean and dressed Tara looked at herself in the full length mirror.

Tara had started running for exercise about a year earlier. The running was definitely paying off. She really didn't need to lose any weight. She had always been on the thin side; she just wanted to tighten up her body. She flexed a leg as she looked in the mirror. It looked lean and strong. Tara studied the outline of her breasts. They were small but perky. She wasn't sure what running had to do with her breasts, but even they looked a little better tonight under her tight-fitting blouse. She twirled in front of the mirror once more, and then she was out the door.

She pulled up in front of Damon's apartment at seven on the dot. He was waiting on the front stoop. He had a bunch of daisies in his hand and he looked good. His shirt was a pretty shade of blue. His loose fitting khaki pants really suited him. Tara figured none of his clothes were brand name garments, but they hung on that great body of his just right.

He got in, handed her the flowers and kissed her on the cheek. "Congratulations Tara, I'm very happy for you." He smiled. "So where are we going?"

"You just sit back, relax and enjoy." She put the car in drive and sped away from the curb. They listened to a John Coltrane CD as they talked and laughed.

"I like this music. Who is it?"

"Mr. Black, please don't tell me you are not familiar with John Coltrane."

"We've never hung out, but I think I've seen him around." They both chuckled.

To be honest, although I've heard some jazz that I like, I'm really not very familiar with it. I could never go into a record store and ask for any particular artist or any thing like that."

"Well I guess we'll have to bring you up to speed. After all, jazz is the only form of music that is native to America, and it was created by black folk." The truth be told, Tara had only come to know jazz through Gabe. Everything she knew about it she had learned from him. She chose not to share that fact with Damon.

"I hate to disagree with you, but you seem to have forgotten at least one other form of music that is native to America."

"Oh really? And what would that be?"

"Hip Hop."

"Touché, Mr. Black. I stand corrected. Hip Hop was also created by our brothers."

"That is true, Ms. Johnson."

They rode along and Tara gave him an introductory course in Jazz. She told him about her favorite artists, and those that she respected but didn't really care for. It took about fifteen minutes before they pulled up in front of Bryan's steak house.

"Oh, you're Ms. Big Baller, huh? I hear this place is on the expensive side."

"Damon my dear, when dining with the best company, only the best meal will do." They both laughed at her perfect British accent. "I hope you're not a vegetarian. They serve the best steaks here."

Tara handed the keys to the parking attendant and they walked into the restaurant.

"This place is really nice." Damon was looking around at the decor which was simple yet sophisticated. "I guess this isn't one of the chain places that hang all of the old junk they can find on the walls to make 'atmosphere'." He made quotation marks with his fingers.

Tara giggled. "No, I guess this is the kind of place where less is more."

What is Forever?

They walked to the Maitre De's station.

"Good evening, Ms. Johnson."

"Hello, Michael. How are you?"

"Just trying to keep my head above water."

He spoke with a decidedly homosexual lilt to his voice. He looked Damon up and down before continuing. "Is Gabe joining you tonight?"

"No Michael, I'm afraid Gabe's out of town, but I'll tell him you asked about him."

"Please follow me."

Michael did a half pirouette and walked them to a secluded booth. Damon and Tara stole a quick glance at each other and struggled not to laugh.

They were seated and looked over the menu.

"So I guess you and your fiancé come here a lot?" Damon asked. "I mean, your knowing that guy by his first name and everything."

Tara snickered. "I've been here a few times, but that's not why I know his name."

She kept her eyes on the menu.

"So how do you know his name?"

"I don't know why you're so interested in how I know Michael. Oooh, I understand! If you like I can introduce you to him." She tried without success to hold back a giggle.

Damon, who had been taking a sip from his glass, nearly spit water all over the front of his shirt. "Oh, now I know you've lost your damn mind."

They both cracked up laughing. "Seriously, I know Michael because he's Gabe's cousin." She made the revelation without flinching.

153

What is Forever?

Once again, Damon choked on his water. "He's your fiancé's cousin?" Damon sputtered. "Why in the world would you bring me to a restaurant where Gabe's cousin works? Aren't you afraid he'll tell on you?"

"Why should I be afraid? We're just friends, right?" Tara sent up a quick prayer that he would realize it was a rhetorical question and not answer. "So there's no need for me to worry. Besides, Gabe hasn't spoken to Michael since he came out of the closet."

"Is he homophobic or something?"

"Not really, Gabe usually treats everyone the same – badly. I think his problem with Michael is that they were very close growing up. I think after sleeping together at each other's houses and changing together and all of that, he feels betrayed by Michael."

"Well even so I think you're taking a chance. Most men don't want to hear anything about 'he's just a friend.' You remember that song Biz Markie made. Plus you never know when Gabe and Cousin Michael might make up. This may be just the type of situation to bring about a reconciliation."

"I still have my foolproof ace-in-the-hole if Gabe hears about this dinner."

"Oh really, and what's that?"

"Gabe already knows that we're friends. I told him about you very shortly after we met." She looked back down at her menu as she said: "I also told him that you were gay."

When Damon choked on his water for the third time, Tara couldn't help but laugh.

After they ordered and ate their meals, they both sat back in their chairs feeling and looking stuffed. They were a little

154

What is Forever?

buzzed from the bottle of red wine they had consumed over dinner and conversation.

"That was delicious. Thank you so much, Tara. For everything."

She understood what he was saying. "It's no problem at all, Damon." She smiled. "I'm glad we did this. I really enjoyed your company. I just wish I didn't eat every morsel on my plate. I'm so full I'm miserable."

"I know that's right. Michael is going to have to roll me out of here if he wants this table for someone else."

"I'm sure he'll be happy to roll you anywhere you like, Sugar."

Damon threw his linen napkin at Tara's head. "All right now, that's enough with questioning my sexual orientation. Rest assured I'm all man."

"Mmm, I'm sure you are." She said under her breath.

Although she was certain she made the comment louder than she intended to, Damon pretended not to hear it.

"You know what, Tara? We need to work off some of this food."

"What'd you have in mind?"

"Well I know this little spot where the music is hot and the crowd is cool. You wanna go shake your money maker a little bit?"

She giggled. "I'd like that a lot. It's been a while since I shook my money maker."

Damon's spontaneity and light-heartedness was just the tip of a growing iceberg that attracted her to him.

They arrived at the Baby Grand at about nine-thirty, way too early for a crowd to have formed. They grabbed a small

What is Forever?

booth near the back of the club. Damon ordered a Corona
from the thin waitress. The girl looked much too young to be
working in a club. Tara guessed that she was no older than
seventeen.

Tara's distaste for a club allowing a minor to serve
alcohol did not deter her from ordering a Vodka tonic. She
was feeling a little high-strung about being with Damon and
wanted to take the edge off. The drink was mixed perfectly
and succeeded in relaxing her. The two of them talked and
laughed. He had another Corona and she sucked down
another Vodka tonic before they hit the dance floor.

There were only two other couples dancing on the floor.
Normally Tara was a little bashful about dancing on a floor
that wasn't packed. She always joked that she had picked up
her adoptive parents' sense of rhythm through osmosis. The
alcohol had her mellow, though. She closed her eyes and let
the driving beat of House Music take over her body. She
swayed her hips and rocked her shoulders, surprised at how
well she was able to keep the beat. She looked up at Damon
and smiled when she saw him staring at her intensely. His
gaze locked onto her eyes.

Damon moved in closer and put his hands on her hips.
He pulled her close to him. It wasn't long before she could
feel just how much he was enjoying the dance. The thought
that she was turning him on took Tara over the top.

"Carpe Diem," she thought to herself.

She slid her hands around his neck pulled his face close
and kissed him. She didn't worry about the fact that she was
engaged, or the possibility that someone who knew her
might be watching. She was totally lost in the moment. She

156

parted her lips and allowed his tongue to wash over her mouth.

The kiss only lasted a few seconds, but in that short period Tara saw a future with this man play through her mind. She could see her wedding and the birth of their children. Tara envisioned them retired together, sipping lemonade on the porch of a house where they raised their children and babysat their grand children. She became oblivious that there ever was a man named Gabe until Damon's lips parted from hers. She was jolted back to her present surroundings. Instinctively she pulled away from him. She was unnerved by the look of surprise on Damon's face.

"I'm sorry, Tara. I know that was inappropriate of me."

"No Damon, it's me who should apologize. I kissed you."

"I am perfectly aware that you have a man. It's not like me to try to sneak into the back door of a man's house while he's away. I guess it's time you took me home."

He put his arm around her waist and escorted her off the dance floor.

When she felt the strength of his arm around her, a wave of desire rose inside her once again. Her knees felt weak and her face felt flushed.

"Lord, what am I getting myself into?" She asked herself as she slipped her arm around him.

In the car, they rode for several minutes in silence.

Finally, Damon spoke. "Tara, I'm serious. I don't mean any disrespect to you or your man. I've tried to keep my feelings for you on a level of friendship. I never intended to cross the line."

"If any line has been crossed, we jumped over it together," she answered softly. "I don't want you to worry about it. I don't blame you, I blame myself. I can only guess what type of woman you think I am. Here I am engaged to Gabe, and I'm out kissing you." She turned pleading eyes on him. "Please believe that I have never done anything like this before, but to be honest with you, I am attracted to you. I guess I have been since we met. I've just been fooling myself that I only wanted to be your friend."

He remained quiet for a few moments. When he finally spoke he looked out the window avoiding her eyes. "I won't lie to you. I have feelings for you too, but I don't want to come between you and him. I've been hurt myself in the past, and I'm not trying to cause anyone else to suffer that kind of pain." He paused, as if he didn't want to continue. "Maybe we should just stop seeing each other."

Her heart skipped a beat. "No Damon, I don't want that to happen. Our friendship is too important to me. You're too important."

The thought of giving him up was almost too much for her. She was shocked at her reaction. She couldn't explain her feelings for him. On the one hand he was fast becoming the best friend she'd ever had. He was intoxicating to her. A perfect example of what a man should be. The kind of man she wanted to be *her* man.

On the other hand, Gabe was her fiancé. He was the man who had stuck by her side for all of these years. Sure Gabe had his faults, but he had been there for her when times were hard. She owed him.

"I don't like the idea either, but you and I both know where this will lead if we continue down this road. I know enough to know that these situations never lead to anyone's good."

They were silent for the rest of the ride. Both seemed to be lost in deep thought. When they pulled up in front of Damon's apartment, Tara put her hand on Damon's knee.

"Do you mind if I come in for a minute?"

CHAPTER 8

Keisha was gripped with fear. Junior had a gun pointed at Ebony. Just as he was about to pull the trigger she awoke, sitting straight up on Damon's couch. It took her a moment to recognize her surroundings. Pain brought back the memory of the night before. She fell back to a prone position and lifted the covers over her face. Her head throbbed.

Keisha felt lost and alone. What in the world was she going to do? She knew she couldn't go back to Junior, not after this. Staying on Damon's couch was not an option. He had a new life with a good woman, and she didn't want to cause problems for them.

Why didn't I keep him when he was mine?

She heard the bedroom door open and close. She remained silent as she heard the footsteps coming softly down the hall. It must be Alexis getting ready to fix breakfast. She closed her eyes and remained still as the footsteps came near and paused by the side of the couch. Keisha genuinely liked Alexis. She had shown last night what a good person she was and she had earned Keisha's respect, but right now she just couldn't deal with her. She had revealed some very intimate details about her life, and now she was a little embarrassed about having shared so much.

The footsteps continued past her into the kitchen. Keisha thought about how together Alexis seemed to be. She owned her own business, had beauty, intelligence and to top it off a good man by her side. A woman who had all that going for

What is Forever?

her still got up early on Sunday morning and cooked breakfast.

"Damn, I wish I could have that kind of life," she muttered quietly.

The pans made quiet clanks as Keisha listened to breakfast being prepared. She heard a dull thud and was surprised when she heard the deep voice.

"Shoot!"

She popped her head out from under the covers and looked toward the kitchen. It was Damon. Damon was looking at her while he hopped on one foot trying to grab the big toe of his other.

"Oh Keish, I'm sorry I woke you."

"I wasn't asleep. Just lying here thinking about my future."

He walked over to the couch. She sat up and slid her feet to the floor to give him room to sit. Her sore head and body protested at the movement.

"So what do you think about your future? What are you going to do?"

"Don't know. Right now I don't know a damn thing. I just seem to fuck up every time I make a decision. I wish somebody else would tell me what to do."

"I don't think that's what you need right now. I think you just need a little time to figure out your next step." He paused for a moment. "Well actually there is one thing that I will tell you that you need to do." His gaze was stern. "You need to go down to the police department and file charges against that sack of—"

What is Forever?

"Come on, Damon. Don't start with me already. I know I need to press charges. I just don't want to have to deal with that right now. At least let me wake up good before you start badgering me."

"You're right, I'm sorry. It's just that I can't stand the thought of him doing this to you. You deserve better than that."

"I know. I used to have better than that, but I blew it." She dropped her head to her hands.

He ignored her comment. "Keisha Jones, you have a lot more going for you than you're giving yourself credit for." He placed his pointer finger under her chin and lifted her head. "As a matter of fact, I think the only thing you're lacking is self confidence. I know that you have it in you to do anything you set your mind to. You just have to believe in yourself." He let his finger drop away. "Have you thought about going back to school?"

"Oh, hell no. I will never step foot back on that campus. You know I can't go back there."

"It's been almost five years since you were there. Everyone that was there is gone. Besides, that's not the only college in the world. You can go to another one and transfer the credits you've accumulated."

"I don't know, Damon. It's a lot for me to process right now, but I'll think about it."

"That's all I can ask you to do."

Keisha looked back at her knees. "Thank you for being such a good friend to me. I need to thank Alexis, too. Most women wouldn't be so understanding. You've got a good woman there, Boy. Don't blow it."

What is Forever?

Damon put his arm around her. She allowed her head to fall to her shoulder. A single tear escaped her eye. She quickly wiped it away.

"Thanks Keish, that means a lot to me. I really do love her, and I want our relationship to last forever."

"I know you do, and if you act right it will." She stopped herself from thinking about a time when he'd loved her and wanted their relationship to last. In her heart Keisha knew that her time with Damon was over and that she was lucky to still have him for a friend.

CHAPTER 9

Alexis stirred and reached across the bed for Damon. When she realized he wasn't there she awoke completely. She got out of bed and wrapped her powder blue dressing gown around her body. As she walked down the hall toward the living room she heard voices talking quietly. Alexis was surprised to see Damon's arm around Keisha.

"Is everything all right?" she asked, feeling uncomfortable about finding them in such a compromising position.

Damon looked like a kid caught with his hand in the cookie jar. "Good morning, Baby." He walked over and kissed her lips. "I guess I'm waking everybody up this morning. I was just getting ready to make us all some breakfast. Are you hungry?"

"Not yet. Right now I think I'd just like a cup of tea."

"Well I'm starving," Keisha informed them. "I'll bet that little eating machine upstairs is hungry too. I'll go wake her." Alexis noticed that Keisha's gaze remained pinned to the floor as she walked past her.

For some reason Alexis truly cared about Keisha and wanted the best for her. She had known more than a couple of girls who had been in her situation. Some of them eventually woke up and got rid of the no good men who thought a woman was only there to use as a punching bag. She knew others who went through life pretending like they were not in abusive relationships, telling themselves that the man would change or that it wasn't his fault. They just

164

couldn't admit that any man who put his hands on a woman was simply a coward. She watched Damon place strips of bacon into a large black frying pan, and thought about how lucky she truly was.

Her only complaints about him were that he was too nice, too giving of himself. His best qualities were the same things that sometimes drove her up the wall. Still, she'd rather spend her life with Damon than anyone else.

She walked past him to open the cabinet where he kept the mugs. He had already put the kettle on the stove and was heating water for her tea. She felt a soft smile spread over her lips. Before she could speak he did.

"Alexis, I know that my sitting on the couch with Keisha like that may have looked funny, but I promise you it was innocent."

She placed her hand on his shoulder and gently turned him towards her.

"I know there was nothing going on. I get a little jealous sometimes and I feel funny about your caring so much about Tara and Keisha, but I know that it's just the way you are. You feel the need to take care of the world. For the most part, I really admire that in you. Just make sure you don't allow others to take advantage of your kindness and turn it against you, against us." She kissed him on those perfect lips. "I want you to know that I trust you. I don't believe that you would ever do anything to intentionally hurt me. That's one of the things I love about you. I know you always have my good at heart."

What is Forever?

He slid his arms around her and spoke softly into her ear. "Don't worry Baby, I know where home is. There's nothing I want more than my home cooked meals."

"Well you need to check that bacon, you're about to burn it."

They both laughed as he turned the bacon over in the sizzling grease. Alexis made her tea and quietly watched as Damon finished preparing the meal.

Twenty minutes later the four of them were seated around the table eating quietly. "Keisha, would you like to come to church with us?" Alexis asked.

"I probably should, but I need to get back to the house and clean up all that mess."

"Ain't no probably to it. I know you haven't been to church in four years." Damon scoffed as he put a fork full of eggs into his mouth.

"Now how you supposed to know when the last time I been to church?"

"I'll bet a hundred bucks that you haven't been near a church since Ebony was christened. Now tell me I'm wrong."

"You wrong. I go past a church every day on my way to work."

Everyone at the table laughed.

"I understand you wanting to get your house together, Keisha. We'll just drop you by there on our way. But don't let the next time you go to church be our wedding." Alexis held out her left hand so that Keisha could get a look at the diamond. She could see the surprise on Keisha's face. Guilt

What is Forever?

made her face flush with warmth. Maybe she shouldn't have sprung the news in that manner.

"Oh my God! Girl, that ring is beautiful. Congratulations! I can't believe you got this cheap man to buy such a pretty ring."

Alexis could tell that her excitement for her was genuine, and it made her like Keisha more. "I know what you're saying Girl, I've never known a man who had a tighter hold on his wallet."

"Wait a minute now, this isn't gang up on Damon Day. I'm not cheap. Besides, if I was out spending my money on everything else, you'd have had to settle for a diamond you'd need a microscope to see."

Alexis leaned over and kissed him. "I know, Baby. You're just frugal."

Throughout the rest of breakfast the four of them ate and laughed like old friends. The air of the previous night's events lifted for a time. After breakfast Alexis, Damon and Ebony prepared for church.

Once they were in the car and on their way, a cloud seemed to hover over them. By the time they reached Keisha's house they were all silent. Alexis didn't feel right dropping Keisha off. "Are you sure you'll be all right?"

"I'll be fine. Junior is probably still sleeping off all that liquor down at county anyway. If he does come around, you know he'll have an arm full of flowers crying about how sorry he is."

Damon snorted. "I know you better tell him to take those flowers and stick them up his ass."

167

What is Forever?

"Damon! We are on our way to church. You could show a little respect for the Lord and your daughter," Alexis admonished him.

"Daddy, you shouldn't say bad words," Ebony chimed in.

"I know, Baby. You are absolutely right. I'm sorry. I'll be more careful." He placed his hand on her head and looked back at Keisha as she exited the car. "Keish, make sure you use your head. You don't have to settle for this mess."

"I know." She smiled. "Alexis, I really appreciate everything. You have really been an angel through all of this."

"Don't worry about it. If you need anything, please call me. I'll do anything I can to help out."

"I'll be okay, but if ya'll don't mind keeping Ebony one more night it would give me a chance to handle my business, if you know what I mean."

Alexis answered quickly. "We don't mind at all, Keisha. Take as long as you need."

Alexis watched as she walked toward the house. Anxiety boiled in her stomach. She imagined the woman taking a last walk to the gas chamber. Alexis promised herself that she would say a special prayer for Keisha when they reached the church.

CHAPTER 10

Alexis' spirit felt revived as she walked out of the New Zion A.M.E. church. Reverend Smith had spoken to her soul yet again. She was not a member of the church but she had been going with Damon whenever they spent weekends at his place. She really liked the old minister. He had a sweet avuncular air about him, but his eyes were deep and sharp. Since she and Damon had started dating she had learned that he and Damon were very close. Damon and Reverend Smith did a lot of work in the community together. He was Damon's mentor and father figure.

What she liked most about him was that he could preach. He had a way of mixing old time preaching with a modern thinking. While his sermons focused on spiritual life and keeping heaven as your goal, he always gave practical instructions for daily life.

More and more often Alexis found that Reverend Smith's sermons addressed issues she was dealing with. Today he had compared a relationship to a house. He told the congregation that love was the nail that held a relationship together but that the house also needed to have a foundation of faith in God and doors and windows of trust and to be beautified with passion to keep it strong and make it beautiful. He went on to say that there were natural things that would come along that could wear down a house. There was rain (apathy) and wind (jealousy) and lightning (people trying to come into your relationship). In case of a cataclysm you always had to have an insurance policy. The insurance was God. As long as you have your insurance your house is covered, and even if the worst happened your insurance could build your house back up bigger and better.

By the time he finished the sermon and went on to the alter call she grabbed Damon's hand and they went down to the altar to have Reverend Smith pray that their house would always remain strong. She also remembered to say a special prayer for Keisha's safety and happiness.

The sun felt warm against Alexis' face. She stood in front of the church believing that everything would work out fine for her and Damon.

"Damon, what time are y'all eating dinner?" She heard Bear's big voice.

Alexis scanned the crowd of parishioners who were greeting each other with smiles and handshakes until she spotted him making his way through the throng of people with his girlfriend Lola in tow.

"What's up, Alexis?" He greeted her with a tight hug. "You all right after all that drama last night? You remember Lola, don't you?"

Alexis looked at the short woman. "Sure. Hello, Lola. How have you been?" Alexis gave Lola a friendly hug.

Lola was just a few inches too tall to be considered a little person. She had heavy breasts and a big round behind. Her long flowing jet black hair spoke of a Native American ancestry, but the gold tooth in her mouth gave away her closer ghetto roots. She was an attractive woman, but that tooth would have to go.

What is Forever?

"Oh Girl, I'm just trying to make it. You know how hard it is for a sister these days. The man always trying to give us a hard time on the job."

It hadn't taken Alexis long to figure out that Lola was a wanna-be Assata Shukur/Angela Davis power to the people type person. That was cool with Alexis, but she figured the first thing Lola could do to help her people was to learn how to talk and use birth control. Damon had told her that Lola had five kids by at least 3 different men. She had worked a job at Wal-Mart but was fired after being caught giving merchandise away to her family members. She would have been prosecuted, but Damon had called in a favor and her case was dismissed. The other thing that really bothered Alexis about Lola was that she always had a negative attitude. No matter what the situation, the glass was always half empty with her. Alexis was in too good a mood to let Lola bring her down. She really hoped Bear wasn't bringing her to dinner.

"So what time y'all having dinner?" Lola asked Alexis. "Bear told me you can burn, Girl. So what y'all havin? I hope it ain't pork, cause I don't eat no pork. You know the man be puttin all kinds of shit in that pork cause he know black folks the main ones eatin it."

"Damn Baby, you need to watch your mouth. We're standing on the church steps."

Lola just sucked her teeth and rolled her eyes at Bear. "God knows my heart." She looked back at Alexis for an answer to what was on the menu.

"Lola honey, you know you just gonna have to wait and see what's for dinner. But I will tell you now that there will be plenty to eat that doesn't have pork in it. We should be ready to eat at about four-thirty."

Lola didn't appear to be satisfied with the answer, but didn't press Alexis.

Damon put his arm around her shoulder. "I guess we'll see you two in a little while. I need to get on home so I can take care of some business before dinner."

Once they were back in the car Alexis checked to make sure Ebony was properly buckled in and handed her the program from the service and a pen for her to draw with before turning to Damon. "What kind of business do you have to take care of before dinner?"

"Nothing really, I just need to run a few errands."

"Well, please don't let your errands take too long. I want to eat on time."

"No problem, Baby. I'm already hungry so you know I'm not trying to be late for that feast you cooked."

He had promised Tara he would give her money. That must be the business. She wanted to ask him, but decided against it. She didn't want to start another argument. She had promised herself that she was going to trust him. There was no reason for her to get upset. He was being the kind person he was born to be.

When they got back to his place, Alexis went into the bathroom to freshen up and change. When she came out, she found Damon sitting on the bed writing in one of the leather-backed journals that he kept. He had a small bookshelf filled with identical journals that he'd kept since he was in high school. There was only one journal that didn't match the others. It was a simple black and white composition book that sat first in the row of journals.

"Are you writing another poem? Is it about my beautiful eyes or my devastating smile?" She struck a silly pose, grinning from ear to ear and batting her eyes.

"No, but if you like I can write one about the silly grin on your face."

"No thank you. That's quite all right." She quickly responded after catching a glimpse of herself in the mirror over the dresser. "So what are you writing?"

"Just making a journal entry. I'll be done in a minute."

Alexis could tell by his response that he was making a private entry. She often wondered what secrets those books held. On occasion Damon would write a poem or his thoughts on a social or political situation and read to her from the books, but he'd told her early on in their relationship that the books were the one area of his life that was off limits even to her. After they married and lived a long happy life together, he'd assured her, she could read them after he died. At the time it was a joke, but Alexis had her engagement ring now. In fifty or sixty years she would convince him in his senility to let her read them before he passed. That way if there was anything in them that pissed her off she could make him pay for it while he was still alive. For now she left him to his work and went to the kitchen to begin pulling out the food she had prepared the night before. It wasn't long before he surfaced from the room.

He kissed the back of her neck. "I'm going to run those errands. I promise I won't be too long."

What is Forever?

"Dinner will be ready when you get back. Before you go, tell Ebony she can come down and help me if she wants to."

He kissed her softly on her forehead then looked her in the eye. "Alexis, I truly love you so much."

"Yeah, yeah. Only because I let you go out to see your other women." She tried to lighten up the strange mood he was in.

"Yeah, that too," he smiled, "but that's not all of it. You are just so perfect for me. I want our love to last forever."

"It will, Baby. I know because I love you that same way. I not only love you, I need to love you. It's hard to explain, but this...us...we are just so right together."

"Exactly. That's what I'm saying Alexis." He took her hands in his. "I was thinking; let's not wait to get married."

The comment caught her totally off guard. "What are you talking about?"

"I mean let's just do it. Let's get married tomorrow."

"Damon, we can't get married tomorrow! There's too much to plan, the guest list, reception halls and all of that. Not to mention our living arrangements. You know that closet of yours could never handle all of my stuff even if your stuff wasn't in it. Plus I have a business to worry about."

"Look Baby, as far as living conditions go, we can work through that as man and wife. And as for the guests, who cares. As long as you're there, that's all I'm worried about." He paused, as an awareness of an unwelcome possibility seemed to hit him. "Tell me honestly, are you sure you want to marry me?"

174

What is Forever?

"Oh Damon, that's the one thing in my life that I am totally sure of. But we have to be realistic about this. We owe something to our friends and family. Think about it. What about my family? They have only met you one time. What type of attitude do you think they'll have towards you if you marry me without even allowing them to witness the ceremony? Not to mention the fact that you haven't asked my father for my hand in marriage. He's a very traditional man. That would be like a slap in the face to him. Like most women, I have a vision for my wedding day. I know exactly the kind of dress I want to wear, the color of the bridesmaids dresses, everything. I know it probably sounds corny to you but I want a fairytale wedding, not one done at the end of a shotgun."

"Okay, okay. I see your point. I just don't want to wait to make you my wife." He paused again, his face showing as he searched for the answer to his problem.

Alexis couldn't understand why he was so desperate for the wedding to take place so quickly.

"I have the solution. I know what we can do to make this work out for everyone involved."

She listened intently.

"We can get married now, so that we don't have to go another day not being married..."

"Damon how is that "

"Let me finish, Baby. We get married now, but we don't tell anyone. We only need to get a couple of witnesses. After you're legally and spiritually my wife, we go through all the planning. We make a trip out to see your people, I ask your dad for your hand, and sometime in the future we do the whole big beautiful wedding thing. That way we don't have to wait, but you still get the fairytale wedding you've dreamed of."

Alexis was overcome with joy, fear and love. She couldn't believe what she was about to do. She heard her answer as it escaped her mouth but couldn't control it coming out. "Yes Damon, yes let's do it!" She threw her arms around his neck and kissed him passionately as he spun her around the kitchen.

"It will be perfect. I promise. Oh Baby, I'm so happy." He kissed her again. Alexis was not aware of how they ended up in the bedroom, but they had the most romantic hot midday sex she had ever experienced. When he climaxed inside her she felt it deep in her womb. They lay there, unable to move or speak until they heard the soft knock at the door.

"Daddy? Are you in there?"

"Oh God, it's Ebony." Alexis whispered, thoroughly embarrassed.

Damon held up his hand. "Yes Baby, we're in here. You up from your nap already?"

"Daddy can I come in? I couldn't sleep. I thought I heard someone yelling."

Alexis hid her head in her hands. She was mortified that the child had heard her yelling all the way upstairs. Hell, the neighbors probably heard too.

Damon seemed to be enjoying her discomfort. He sported a wide grin and could hardly contain his laugh when he answered. "Stay put, Baby. I'm coming right out." He slipped his bathrobe on and walked toward the door. Alexis jumped from the bed and ran into the bathroom like a track star. She heard Damon crack the door to allow his little girl into the room. She listened as they spoke.

"Is Alexis okay?"

"Yes Pumpkin, Alexis is fine."

"Then why was she yelling so loud?"

"We were just playing a game. I'm sorry we woke you from your nap."

"What kind of game? Can I play?"

"We were playing a game for grown ups. You won't be able to play that game for at least another thirty years."

Alexis snickered in the bathroom.

"You all right in there, Alexis?" Damon called to her. "Ebony was worried about you."

"Yes, I'm fine. I'm just going to grab a quick shower before I finish dinner." Alexis turned toward the shower and saw her pack of pills on the vanity. "Oh shit!" She realized she had missed taking her pills for the past two days.

"Alexis it's not nice to use bad language," Ebony yelled through the door.

"Sorry."

She heard Damon laugh. "Come on, Baby girl. Let's go see if we can help in the kitchen."

Alexis felt relieved when they walked out of the room. She picked up the small pack of pills and counted the tablets. Maybe she just couldn't remember taking them.

"Shit," she wailed again, more quietly this time. She had indeed missed taking two of her pills, not to mention the one she should have taken that morning.

177

What is Forever?

Alexis never missed taking her pills. It was one of the many things she was obsessive about. All of the drama of the weekend had thrown her out of her routine. She tried to recall her doctor's instructions on what to do if she missed a dose. She was pretty sure that if she missed one she should just double up the following day, but if she missed two in a row she was supposed to wait until her period came and start a new pack. She knew that her period was due in just a few days so she dropped the rest of the pack in trash and said a little prayer that Damon had not just fathered another child.

After bathing, she joined Damon and Ebony in the kitchen. They had all of the food warming on the stove and in the oven. All there was left for her to do was make her slamming strawberry pie and put the biscuits in the oven.

"Everything seems to be in order in here," Damon said. "If you don't mind I'm going to hurry up and run those errands."

She wasn't happy about it but she figured she might as well not make a fuss. "All right, but please don't be late coming back. You know I don't want to be left here alone with that Lola all up in my face getting on my nerves."

"All right Baby, I promise, I'll be back before they get here." He kissed her lips and headed for the door.

She couldn't help but wonder why he felt so responsible for Tara. It was something they would definitely need to discuss. She trusted Damon, but she wasn't so sure about Tara, and she was not about to let some woman come between her and her man.

CHAPTER 11

It didn't take long for Tara to feel comfortable in Damon's apartment. Within minutes she had her shoes off and was sipping on a Vodka and Seven Up as Damon put on Janet Jackson's latest CD. He sat next to her and they talked for an hour about everything under the sun. She was amazed at how much they truly had in common, and pleased at the way their differences didn't hinder the growing bond between them.

Tara wasn't sure when it happened or who initiated the kiss. She just felt the electricity that flowed between them as they kissed fervently on his couch. When she finally paused to take a breath, she found herself on his bed in her bra and panties. She remembered reaching for his hardness, wanting it, almost needing to be with him. She needed to go to the point of no return, so that she would never have to imagine what it would be like to have this man for her own again, even if only for a night.

The Vodka must have taken over at that point and sent her into a deep sleep. She awakened still in her panties with Damon lying in a spoon position behind her, his arms wrapped around her and his stiffness still there, poking her rump. She saw the sunlight streaming through the window. It didn't take long to comprehend her situation. She bolted upright in the bed. Damon was startled awake. She could still feel the moisture between her legs and she fleetingly allowed the idea of a quickie to cross her mind. Common sense told her that she needed to get home and get there fast.

179

What is Forever?

"Oh my God Damon, what time is it?"

Still groggy, he knocked the digital clock off of the night stand. He picked it up and stared at the large numbers for a full two seconds before he was able to decipher that it was six minutes after eight.

"Oh my God," she repeated. "I've got to get home. Gabe's gonna kill me."

The news of her impending demise seemed to lift Damon out of his fog. "Oh shit! You spent the night? Oh Tara, I'm so sorry. I was gonna wake you up after you had a chance to get a little rest and sober up some. I must have fallen asleep myself. It's my fault, Baby. What can I do?"

Tara didn't miss the fact that he'd called her Baby, but she didn't have the time to relish in the term of endearment. "Nothing, Damon. It's not your fault, it's mine. I'm the one who has to be home. I dropped the ball, not you." She tried to keep the irritability and anxiety she was feeling out of her voice as she rolled out of the bed and attempted to gather her belongings and put them all on at the same time. "Don't worry about it. Everything's under control." She carried her pumps in her hand as she dashed out of the room. "I'll call you a little later."

Gabe shouldn't be back until later this evening.

She looked over her shoulder and saw Damon standing in the doorway of his bedroom as she reached the front door. He had a look of bewilderment and confusion on his face. She noticed that he still sported the stiffy beneath his boxer shorts. On the drive home she thought about his hardness and wondered what his erection looked like without the boxers. She wished she was able to take care of it for him, but by now he had probably taken care of it himself. Just like she was going to handle her business once she got home.

By the time Tara reached her condo, her mind was far away from pleasuring herself. It was almost nine. She was one giant frazzled nerve. She avoided the answering machine and headed straight for the living room sofa. She knew that Gabe had called by then and she had no clue as to what she would tell him about her whereabouts overnight. And what about Michael? Who was to say that he wouldn't call Gabe and tell him that she had been to the restaurant with another man? What a stupid idea that had been. She was losing her damn mind. She slouched on the leather couch and dropped her head into her hands.

She closed her eyes and allowed her thoughts to wrap around each detail of the events of the previous night. Although she was terrified of facing Gabe, she was as giddy as a school girl about the fantastic night she'd spent with Damon. She couldn't believe that they hadn't made love.

When she was finally able to pull herself from the couch, she walked over the counter where the phone sat and looked at the answering machine. Sure enough, the message light was blinking. She pressed play.

"Hey Babe, it's me. It's about ten after seven. I guess you're out running errands or something. I just got out of a meeting and I'm headed back to the hotel to shower and change before dinner. We'll probably go over to Mr. Eisenburg's after that. He's having a party for the partners, and of course I'm expected to be there. I probably won't get in until late so I'll just call you in the morning. Hope you're having a good evening. Bye…" …beep.

What is Forever?

That was the only message on the machine. Tara hoped against hope that he had only called the one time. If she was lucky, he'd gotten caught up in the party and was too tired and drunk to have called by the time he got back to his room.

Tara was in bed nursing a slight hangover when she heard the front door shut. Gabe was home. Her stomach immediately began to somersault as it tied itself in knots. She tried to make herself relax. After all, Gabe didn't know anything about last night. Besides, nothing had really happened. All she had to do was keep her cool and everything would be fine. She pretended to sleep as he walked through the bedroom door. She felt his weight on the bed as he sat. She could feel the warmth of his skin when he leaned across the bed. She smelled the Scotch on his breath as he held his face close to hers. Tara was instantly turned off. His hand touched her forehead to brush a strand of hair out of her face.

"Baaaaby, are you asleep?" He slurred his words.

God, it was only three in the afternoon and he was already wasted. At least she waited until later in the day before drinking. Besides, she had serious issues on her mind. If it weren't for Gabe, she probably wouldn't drink nearly as much as she did.

She opened her eyes wide when Gabe ran his hand across her chest and roughly grabbed her right breast.

"Oh, so you *are* awake, huh?"

"I am now." She sat up and away from his groping hand.

"Hey baby, did you miss me?" It came out "mish me." Lord, he smelled awful.

182

What is Forever?

"I thought I did, but I want to know why you are coming up in here all drunk."

"Drunk! Who's drunk? I'm not drunk! I just have a little buzz that's all. You know how I hate planes. I had a couple of drinks to ease my nerves."

"Uh huh, whatever." Her fear of him learning about her recent activities melted in her anger and disgust.

Gabe darted his hand back to her breast as he lunged toward her neck. His mouth was extra juicy and he let what felt like a puddle of saliva drip onto her as he sucked greedily on her skin. Gabe had never been the best kisser, but he was in rare form. She winced as he chewed on her skin. She considered letting him get a quickie just to get him off of her neck. Then he pinched her nipple between his thumb and forefinger.

"OW!" She yelped as she pushed him away. He tumbled onto his back away from her. "Damn, Gabe that shit hurt! What the hell is the matter with you?"

"What's the matter with me? What's the matter with you! I thought you liked me to pinch your nipples."

"Not without any warning or warming up."

"I am warmed up, Baby."

It was then that Tara noticed that Gabe's pants were unzipped. His penis stood at attention ready for action.

"No you didn't come in here like this thinking you were going to get laid."

"What's wrong with you? Can't you see how bad I want you?"

"All I can see is how horny your nasty ass is. You might as well put that thing away or you can empty it yourself.

What is Forever?

You're not going to treat me like some hooker, here to get your rocks off." She got off the bed and stormed into the bathroom.

Gabe sat on the bed in silence. Tara was proud of herself. She knew Gabe was not accustomed to her standing up to him like that. Just one more thing she owed to Damon. He had taught her that she deserved to be treated like a lady. She deserved respect.

It didn't take Gabe long to recover from his shock. As she looked at the growing bruises on her neck in the vanity mirror, he began to bang violently on the bathroom door. He pounded so hard the door seemed to strain on its hinges.

"Tara! You better open this damn door right now! What the fuck is wrong with you? Open this damn door!"

Her stomach began to turn flips once again. She'd never seen him like this. He had a bad temper, but this time she began to fear for her own safety.

As suddenly as he had started banging on the door, the rumble of his fist on the wood stopped. Then Tara heard his voice much softer. "Tara Baby, look. I'm sorry. I didn't mean it. I've just had a bad day and I was really wanting to be with you, that's all. You've never rejected me like that before. I didn't know how to handle it, that's all. Come on Baby, open the door."

Tara felt a twinge of guilt. Here her fiancé was wanting to be with her, and she was withholding from him because her nose was wide open over another man. She took a step towards the door— BOOM! BOOM! BOOM! It felt like the entire house shook from the blows on the door. Tara fell backward and struck her head on the glass shower stall as the

184

door fell from it's hinges and almost landed on top of her. Gabe charged into the bathroom behind it. There was rage in his eyes.

"I told you to open the fucking door, bitch! Now look what you made me do." He snatched her from the floor like a rag doll. "You think I don't know why you don't want to sleep with me? Well guess what bitch, I know all about what your trifling ass has been up to." He pushed her through the door and toward the bed.

Terror ripped through her when she heard his accusation. "Gabe, wait! What are you talking about?"

"Shut up, whore!"

Gabe grabbed her roughly by the shoulders and shook her violently. Her head bobbed around like a spring-necked dashboard toy. Stars danced around her head as it whipped about. Gabe half carried, half dragged her toward the bed and flung her onto it. He was on her in an instant.

"Damn Tara, don't you know how connected I am? I know every move you make. I know that you can't fuck your man because you're out there fucking some other mother fucker. What did you think I was stupid? You think I didn't know about all the phone calls? The meetings? Bitch, I'm a divorce lawyer. I do this shit for a living. Did you think I don't know when my woman is fucking around? I was hoping if I didn't say anything, you would come to your senses on your own. I must have been wrong about that, cause I know what you did last night."

"Gabe please, it's not what you think. I never had sex with him." Guilt and panic intertwined and wrapped her up in a stranglehold.

What is Forever?

"Well I'll tell you what, if you're gonna give this pussy up like a hooker to someone else, you are damn sure gonna give it to me any way I want it."

Tara tried to push him off, but she was met with a backhanded slap that grazed her eye and turned her on her side. She balled as he turned her over and ripped her panties from her body. She felt shear pain rip through her when he inserted himself into her rear. Once long ago, near the beginning of their relationship they had attempted anal intercourse. He had begged her for a month before, and after a night of drinking she'd decided to try it. On that night he had been gentle and loving. He had purchased special lubrication to help her to be more comfortable. Even with all of his gentleness and the lube it had been too much for her. She'd told him then that she just couldn't do it. Now he was tearing into her with abandon. He had no sympathy for her comfort or feelings. If anything he was trying to make it hurt worse.

Tara knew that this was Gabe's way of punishing her for her sins. He wanted to hurt her as she had hurt him. Although the pain was almost unbearable, somewhere on the inside she felt that she deserved his cruelty. She withdrew into her self and let him do as he wanted. Fortunately for her, Gabe had always been quick on the draw. What seemed like hours to her was in reality only about two minutes.

When he was spent, his anger seemed to seep from him along with his semen. He rolled away from her. She felt his eyes on her back. When she looked at him the guilt in his eyes contradicted his cold tone. "I'll be back here tomorrow morning. Get your shit and be gone by then." With that he turned and walked from the room.

Tara lay on the bed for several minutes without moving. The burning ache in her rectum was nothing compared to the pain and confusion that seemed to pulse through every vein and artery coursing to and through her heart. Tears flowed freely down her face. Her shoulders heaved as she cried uncontrollably. Finally, Tara was able to pull herself to a sitting position on the bed. Her head and bum both throbbed. She attempted to pull herself together.

"Okay girl, what are you gonna do now?" She looked over to the clock and realized how little time had passed since Gabe had first come home. "You've gone from being engaged with a secure future to being homeless in less than an hour. Way to go, Tara."

She made her way into the bathroom and looked into the mirror. She was surprised that her face didn't look worse than it did. She was thankful that the blow had grazed the side of her head rather than striking her full in the face. The right corner of her lip was a little swollen and her right eye was blood red, but the area around it wasn't swollen or discolored.

For just a moment, Tara considered calling the police.

She chose not to. The whole situation was basically her fault. Gabe had never struck her before, and never would have if she hadn't been with Damon.

"Damon," she said out loud.

The sound of his name made her want to run to him. Instead she ran hot water into the tub. She took a box of Epsom salts from under the vanity and generously poured it into the steaming water. The water burned at her skin as she eased her body into it, but the burning felt good. Justified.

She sunk into the water until her head was submerged. She contemplated keeping her head under the water until all of the oxygen in her lungs was used up and she was forced to inhale the water, or perhaps she should get a razor from the drawer and pull it across her wrists. She imagined watching red streams of her blood flow from her wrists until the tub turned crimson. No. She would just fuck that up too, and then have to clean the blood stains from the tub.

By the time she was dressed and packed she still hadn't decided where she would go. She thought of the few friends she had and knew that she couldn't go to any of them. Jenny was the only person who she felt close enough to explain what had happened. Jenny was a feminist however, and she would demand that Tara go to the police or she would call some of her butch friends to "take care of" Gabe. She was angry with him, but she didn't want him hurt. She had already taken care of that.

She thought of Damon again. That's where she wanted to go, but she didn't feel like she had that type of relationship with him. She couldn't just show up on his doorstep and tell him that Gabe knew about them and had kicked her out. What if he said that it wasn't his problem and asked her why she'd come to him? What would she do if he turned her away after she had lost everything? What would she do then? Who would be there for her?

"Come on girl, get yourself together. You know Damon's not like that." She tried to convince herself, but uncertainty sat like a weight on her shoulders.

What is Forever?

She closed the suitcase and grabbed her keys. On the way to Damon's apartment she almost turned around several times. Her heart raced in her chest when she pulled up in front of his place. The anxiety she was feeling now was much different from the sexually charged feelings of anticipation she had felt when she had stopped in this very same spot the day before. Her hand shook as she knocked on the door.

Damon came to the door in a pair of basketball shorts and a blue tank top. He was dripping with sweat. "Tara, hey. What are you doing here?"

Maybe coming to him had been a bad idea. He seemed very surprised to see her and looked as though he were busy.

"I'm sorry if I caught you at a bad time. If you're busy I can come back later." She turned to walk away.

"Wait a minute, Tara. It's not a bad time at all. I was just working out." Damon grabbed her by the shoulder where Gabe had bruised it. She winced at his touch. Damon quickly pulled his hand away. "Hey, is everything all right?"

Tara turned back towards him and removed the sunglasses she had been wearing. When Damon saw her eye his face showed instant comprehension and dismay. "Oh Tara, I'm so sorry." He held out his arms and she walked into them. She wept on his shoulder.

CHAPTER 12

Keisha walked straight to her bedroom, right by all of the evidence of violence from the night before, and pulled every stitch of clothing off her body and stretched out on the bed. She was asleep before her head hit the pillow. She slept for over an hour before she woke abruptly after having another terrible dream.

"My God, what have I done to my life?"

She thought of Damon's advice to get rid of Junior and knew in her heart that it was sound. She made up her mind then and there that she was going to make some changes in her life.

"I deserve better than this. My baby deserves better than this."

Damon was right. She'd been punishing herself for way too long. It was definitely time to make a change. Keisha decided at that moment she would call over to the state university the following day and register for a few courses for the next semester.

She bathed and dressed in a loose fitting nylon sweat suit. She forced herself into the living room and took in the devastation for the first time. The room looked as though a hurricane had passed through. Without another moment of hesitation she began cleaning up. Each time she came across a special memento that had been broken she cursed Junior under her breath.

When she righted the small bookshelf that had been knocked over she found the hard covered edition of Zora

190

What is Forever?

Neal Hurston's *Their Eyes Were Watching God.* The cover had been ripped from the book. A single tear streaked her cheek before she wiped it away. Anger boiled up in her. It was one of the first gifts Damon had given to her. Before she'd met him she had spent very little time reading. He'd given her the book and told her that it was one of the greatest love stories ever written. It had taken her a while to get used to the dialogue, but by the time she finished the book she knew she had become hooked on reading. She had read that particular book three times.

"Dammit Junior, I hate your sorry ass."

"Now you know that ain't true, Baby."

Keisha spun around to find Junior standing in the doorway. A hot rage came over her. She lunged at him without saying a word.

Junior grabbed her by her wrist and easily held her at bay. He was tall and slim, almost skinny, but had a strong, wiry frame. If Keisha had to describe him in one word it was "hard." If she could use another it would be "dangerous." Originally those were the things that attracted her to him. Now she realized they were her worst mistakes.

Keisha had met Jermaine Thomas Watkins "Junior" about a year after her baby was born. Up until that time she had been waiting for Damon to come back to her. When she finally accepted that he was not coming back she had opened herself to seeing other men. None of them measured up to Damon.

Then she met Junior and no, he could never be considered Damon's equal, but that was just what he had going for him. Junior was the exact opposite of Damon.

What is Forever?

There was nothing about him that reminded her of her baby's father. Junior was tall and lean, and as opposed to Damon's smooth dark skin, Junior's was red. He had hard, striated muscles that always looked like they were being flexed. He had no high school diploma, let alone a college degree. Junior made no concern regarding the future. He was content to live in the present. He reveled in it. He believed that no one could see what would happen tomorrow, so why waste time worrying about it.

At first she wouldn't give the thug the time of day, but his persistence wore her down. He got her number from Rolanda, and called her nonstop. He somehow discovered where she lived and kept dropping by her momma's house bringing presents for the baby and her, telling her how much he wanted to be with her and if given the chance he would always be there for her and her baby.

After a few months of his persistence, she finally gave in and went out on a date with him. It wasn't long before they were living together. At first everything was cool. Junior gave up the street life, got a job at the mill and generally provided a good life for them. But after a few months, he started to hang out with his old friends again. He began to come home drunk and high more frequently. Eventually he began staying out all night.

That was when he first hit her. One Saturday morning he showed up around seven o'clock in the morning after staying out all night. Keisha had been livid. She was waiting in the living room when he came in. She lit into him, cussing him out with her finger in his face and her nose no more than an inch from his. He had warned her to give him some space.

What is Forever?

His head was killing him and he didn't want to hear her shit. Keisha ignored his warning and continued her verbal assault. She was totally caught off guard by the backhand that sent her sailing across the room. She was hurt more by the fact that he didn't even have the decency to apologize. Junior had the nerve to tell her that it was her fault that he hit her and that if she would have just left him alone for a little while he would have discussed his whereabouts in a rational way.

She knew she should have left him after that, but she couldn't help feeling like she owed him another chance. They agreed to put the incident in the past and once again he attempted to walk the straight and narrow. Every few months he would slip back into his old ways and they would get into more and more violent confrontations.

Keisha was fed up. There would be no sweet talk or making up. Junior's ass was gone.

"Come on now Baby, I am not in the mood for round two. It's time for making up."

His words shocked her so completely that they took the fight out of her. When he released her wrist she backed calmly away from him. "What are you doing here?"

"I just came by to tell you how sorry I am. I know I was wrong and I just wanted to make up." He leaned down and picked up the bouquet of roses he'd dropped when she went after him. He held the flowers out to her. "See? I even brought you your favorite flowers."

"You can take those flowers and—" she caught herself and contained her anger. "You know what? I'm not going there. There really is no need for me to. It's over, Junior. You need to get your stuff and leave."

What is Forever?

"Come on now Baby, what are you talking about?" He took a step toward her.

Keisha instinctively took two steps back.

"Keisha come on, you don't have to be scared of me. I know you've heard it before, but I swear Baby, I'm not gonna put my hands on you that way again. I've learned from my mistake. That's why I'm here. I want us to get past all our problems and move on."

Keisha couldn't believe her ears. She wasn't the slightest bit moved by his words. How had she ever believed anything he'd said? For the first time since she'd known him, she saw him for what he truly was: a no good, trifling bastard. She wanted to tell him exactly how she felt, but decided to handle the situation as calmly as possible.

"I don't want to hear any more of your excuses. Like I said, it's over. You need to get your shit and go before I call Damon to make you leave."

She knew instantly that using Damon's name had been a mistake.

Junior lunged at her with the speed of a snake. He had her by the shoulders. Keisha shuddered at the look of hatred in his eyes. "I ought to beat your sorry ass again. I knew that nigga was the reason you been actin all funny. You still fuckin him, ain't you?"

"No Junior, it ain't nothing like that." Her words were barely audible. Fear had all but stolen her voice.

Something inside Junior had snapped. His voice was calm and deadly. Keisha felt real terror blossom in her chest.

"You ain't gotta lie. I know you still kickin it with him or at least wish you was." He pushed her onto the couch. "See,

What is Forever?

that's what I'm talking about. That's what's wrong with this relationship." He paced in front of her. "Damon." He said the name more to himself than her. Junior looked her in the eye. "I'm sick and damn tired of Damon. That bitch ass nigga has been coming between us since the beginning. I only been putting up with his ass cause he was your baby's daddy, but that shit is over. Here I been asking you to have a baby for me and it's always been no. We need to wait another year. You think I don't know why you don't wanna have my baby, Keisha? You think I ain't good enough to be a father? You think Damon the only one good enough to have a baby by you? I tell you what, that nigga ain't shit! I'm the one been taking care of that motherfucka's brat for two years and he ain't done shit but spend money and pick her up every once in a while. I'm the man who been taking care of both your sorry asses." His anger was inflamed again by his own words. "I'm a tell you what. You're my woman and you always gonna be my woman. If I gotta take that motha fucka out for you to keep your mind on me, then that's what I'm a do!"

He turned on his heel and headed toward the bedroom. Keisha knew he was going to get the gun he kept on the top shelf in the closet. She ran behind him. She had to stop him, do anything it took; she couldn't allow Junior to hurt Damon.

She ran into the room and jumped on his back screaming and swinging her fists. She never saw the blow, only the stars it delivered. She felt herself sail through the air before she completely lost consciousness. When she came to her senses, Junior and the gun were gone.

CHAPTER 13

It had been almost a week since Tara had moved out of Gabe's condo. She hadn't been to work, she barely ate anything and she looked a mess. It was all she could do to make sure her body was bathed and her teeth brushed. Tara was confused to say the least. She couldn't untangle her guilt and anger for Gabe from her attraction for Damon. She also couldn't figure out exactly what was going on between Damon and her. The events that had led her to being at his place were brought on from the attraction that they shared, but since she had been there they had not discussed the passionate night they had shared, nor did Damon make any attempts to pick up where they had left off.

Damon had been very sweet to her, always a gentleman. Tara couldn't figure him out. There were times when she was sure that there were sparks between them. They would sit and talk about everything. Other times he seemed distant.

After she had shown up on his door step that day, he had held her there on the front step for a long time. He'd asked her what happened and she'd told him she and Gabe had an argument. She told him she didn't want to go into details and he didn't press for any. He just held her and rocked her gently in his arms until her tears subsided. Then he walked her into the apartment and to his bedroom. Her stomach quivered when he tenderly laid her on the bed and covered her with the flannel comforter that he kept folded at the foot of his bed. When Damon got into the bed and snuggled up behind her she felt at peace.

196

What is Forever?

Tara wanted to live in that moment forever. She had finally found a place, a person who made her feel safe. Someone who could take care of her and make everything all right. Her body was sore and her mood wasn't sexual, but part of her still wanted to be with Damon in spite of everything that had happened. She wanted him to take away the bad memories of Gabe's abuse, and she wanted to give him something to say thank you for the feeling he was giving her. Lying in Damon's arms she felt something that she hadn't felt in a long time. She felt loved and at ease. He'd stroked her hair until she fell asleep.

Damon had hardly touched her since then. In fact, he was rarely there. He seemed to always be at work or at the library. When he was there he spent most of his time in front of the television or cooking. Damon was a great cook but her appetite was almost non-existent.

Friday afternoon she found herself perched on his old couch in front of the television when he came in from work.

When he noticed her sitting there he smiled tenderly. "How are you feeling today?"

"Other than this splitting headache, not too bad."

They shared an uneasy laugh. She had attempted to make light of her condition, but she was feeling pretty bad. She couldn't decide if she felt worse physically or emotionally.

"Are you hungry? I make the best chili this side of the Mason Dixon."

The thought of putting food in her mouth almost made her sick to her stomach. "No, thank you. I'm fine."

197

What is Forever?

There was an awkward silence. She wanted to tell him exactly what had transpired between her and Gabe, but she was just too emotionally drained. She needed something else to occupy her mind other than her troubles.

"What are you watching?" He nodded at the television.

"It's one of those documentaries on starving children in Africa. You know, the ones where they show all of those beautiful children who were born without a chance. Every time I watch one of these shows it makes me want to send my next paycheck."

"I heard that those things are scams. I mean, yes the children are really starving, but the people who are responsible for disbursing the money put most of it in their pockets."

She felt her face turn red.

"Have you ever sent money to any of those organizations?"

"Yes, as a matter of fact I have." She felt a need to defend herself. "I know a lot of people think they're scams, but when I look at those kids I just can't help wanting to do something for them." Tara knew he must be thinking that she was naïve, but she didn't know how to explain to make him understand.

"Aren't you afraid that your money isn't being used properly? I mean, I feel for those kids too, it's just that I don't want to give my hard earned money to someone who doesn't deserve it."

"I just can't believe that anyone would do that to those children. A person would have to be totally heartless.

Besides, I've seen you give money to winos when you know they're just going to go out and buy a bottle with it."

Damon took a breath. He seemed to carefully formulate his words in his mind before they came out of his lips. "I understand what you're saying, and of course it makes sense, but I believe in a higher power. I believe that if I give a wino a couple of dollars to get something to eat and he buys booze with it, well that's on him. I've done my duty as a Christian. Besides, I drink. So who am I to judge his getting his drink on if he wants to?"

Tara was confused. "I don't see what the difference is. Even if I give the money and it's misused, my intentions were good."

"I guess you have a point. It's just the fact that a wino needs the money either way. Some fat cat up in a big office somewhere stealing from those children when he already has enough money to feed all of them...well that just goes against my conscience. But I suppose you're right. If you or I give to those kids or anything or anyone else with good intentions and with faith, then God will make sure that somehow that contribution will be a blessing to those people. I believe that God Is. I also believe that He can make a way out of no way."

"Well excuse me, Reverend Black. I didn't realize you were preparing for the ministry."

"I won't be giving sermons anytime soon, I just believe what I believe and my beliefs have always carried me through. But you better watch out or I'll lay hands on you when you're not looking." They both laughed.

What is Forever?

Tara motioned for Damon to come sit next to her. "Can I ask you a question?"

"Sure, you can ask me anything. We'll just have to see if I want to answer."

She giggled and played with the chipped nail polish on her index finger. "I was just wondering...I mean..." She took a deep breath. "Why didn't you make love to me the other night?"

The surprised look on his face made her more uncomfortable. There was a pause before he stood up, took two steps away from the couch then turned to face her.

"I don't really know how to answer that, Tara. I mean it's kind of hard to explain."

"Is it because of your religious beliefs? I mean I know that sex before marriage is a sin, I've just never met anyone who was able to resist."

"No," he laughed. "I wish that I was strong enough to resist because of that, but I'm not that strong yet." Damon sat back down on the couch, this time very close to her. She could feel the hairs on her arms rise as he looked her in her eyes. "Tara, one reason I didn't let it go any further than it did was the fact that you were obviously intoxicated. I wouldn't want to feel like I was taking advantage of you."

"I can understand that. I appreciate your having so much respect for me. But what about since then? I've been here for a week and you haven't tried anything."

It was his turn to blush. He cleared his throat before he spoke. "I'm just not sure if I want to go there with you."

Tara was certain that Damon's words were a catalyst that caused some chemical reaction in the universe that instantaneously sucked every molecule of oxygen out of the room. She willed herself not to hyperventilate and was barely able to mutter, "Excuse me?" She had never felt so vulnerable and self-conscious.

"I didn't mean it like that. It's not that there's anything wrong with you. It's actually the opposite."

"What's that supposed to mean? Is it me or is it you? Why don't you make up your mind?" She was getting frustrated.

"I told you, it's hard to explain. At least let me try to get it out."

She didn't say anything more. She wanted to hear what he had to say. She wanted, needed him to have a good reason for not wanting to make love to her. She wouldn't be able to handle it if he just wasn't interested in her, not after all she'd been through with Gabe.

"Tara, I really care about you. You're sweet, kind and absolutely beautiful. I love the way we relate to each other and the friendship we've formed."

Oh, no. Not the friendship line.

Damon continued. "I have to admit and I guess it's obvious that I'm physically attracted to you. You have to believe that I wanted to go through with it that night. You have no idea how much I wanted to do it." He paused again, choosing his words carefully. "But to be honest Tara, there are a lot of issues wrapped up in all of this. You have a man and I don't want any drama in my life right now. Not to mention the fact that we really don't know one another like that. I mean, yes we are friends and everything, I really enjoy spending time with you, but I don't know what you want from me and you don't know what I might want from you. I like sex, no I love sex Tara, and I have thought about sex with you on more than one occasion. But I respect you too much to just take you to bed and not know for sure that I want you to be my girlfriend. I can tell that you're the type of person who wants sex to mean more than just sex. I just don't want to start something I'm not ready to finish."

He had her nailed, but her pride prevented her from accepting the truth in his words. She had just lost her fiancé because of him. "What are you talking about finishing? I have a man, Damon. What makes you think that I wanted something more from you than just a roll in the hay? You're right, you don't know me. I never asked you to be my boyfriend. We were just hanging out and I was thinking about giving you some before I got married. Don't read more into it than that."

She walked out of the room before he could see the tears in her eyes. She didn't want him to know that everything she'd said was a load of shit. She did want to be his girlfriend. Hell she wanted to be his wife. When she reached the bedroom she slammed the door harder than she'd intended. She threw herself on the bed. She was lost in the storm that was her life. Here she was in the apartment of a man she wanted to love, and who obviously didn't want her. She had thrown away the security of a man who would have taken care of her. Now she was the one place were she never wanted to be…alone.

CHAPTER 14

Alexis was looking out of the window when she saw Damon pull into the driveway. She glanced at the clock; he had made it back twenty minutes early. She knew he would keep his word and be back before dinner. Although there had been some close calls, he had never let her down. When Damon walked in the door she planted a big kiss on his lips.

"Mmm, now that's what I like to find waiting for me when I get home."

"Well I guess in just a few days you can look forward to a whole lot of that."

"Yeah, well I guess this whole marriage thing was a good idea." He pulled her close and kissed her lips again.

She loved the feeling of being in his arms and wanted it to last forever.

"So is dinner ready? I'm about to starve."

"I took the pie out of the oven ten minutes ago. Everything else is ready."

"Good, then call Ebony so we can eat."

"You know we have to wait for Bear and his ghetto kitten to get here."

"Why? They can eat whenever they get here. We don't have to wait for them."

"Damon! Now you know that's not right. How are you going to invite guests over for Sunday dinner and not wait for them before you start eating? You know better than that."

"Bear ain't no guest. He stays over here more than he stays at his own place."

"That may be true, but he has his girlfriend with him today and that makes it different."

"All right, have it your way. I was trying to help you out. I wanted you to get a head start on the food. By the time those two get started there won't be anything left for us. You know how Bear eats, and I'm telling you he ain't nothing compared to that Lola."

Alexis couldn't help but laugh. "Okay big daddy, if they don't get here by four-thirty on the dot you can start eating."

"Now that's what I'm talking about. Bear has never arrived anywhere on time."

It was a quarter after four and the feeling between she and Damon was light and loving. Alexis didn't want to spoil the moment, but she couldn't resist asking him what had happened with Tara. "So did you get your errands finished?"

"Yeah, everything is cool. Reverend Smith can't do it tomorrow but he said he's free on Friday."

That news made Alexis very happy. She kissed him and squeezed him close. "So what did she say about all of this?"

Alexis noticed that he let out a small sigh before responding. "What did she say about what, Baby?"

It was her turn to get a little aggravated. "What did she say when you told her you were getting married? Did she accept it? Did she cry? What happened?"

"Nothing happened, Alexis. I didn't even tell her yet."

Now she was truly annoyed. "What do you mean you didn't tell her? Why not? I thought that's why you went over there."

What is Forever?

"Don't start badgering me about this, all right? I went over there to let her borrow a little money. She has a lot on her plate right now and I didn't want to upset her more."

"You didn't want to upset her? I thought you were supposed to be just friends. Why would telling her you're getting married upset her? You know Damon, I'm getting really sick and tired of your trifling ex-girlfriends. Why are you running over there to give her money anyway? Doesn't she have a job? I mean, damn. How are we supposed to be moving forward with the rest of our lives when you're still running behind Tara?"

"Alexis, you don't know what the hell you're talking about. I really don't want to get into this right now. Why is it that every time things are chill between us, you have to start with me?"

She was already regretting bringing Tara up, but she had come this far with it and wanted to get all of her issues with Tara out on the table. "Why do you always do that? Every time I want to talk about something that's important to me you just try to shut down the conversation. Well it's not gonna happen this time. I want to know what's going on with the two of you. Tell me the truth Damon, are you still sleeping with her?"

"See? Now I know you've lost your damn mind. Why in the world would I ask you to marry me then celebrate by going out and screwing another woman? Damn Baby, you know that doesn't even make sense!"

"Then what is it, Damon? What is the hold she has on you?"

What is Forever?

"She doesn't have any damn hold on me. And for your information, I have never even slept with Tara. She's my friend. *Just* my friend."

Alexis wanted to believe what he was saying but it just didn't add up. If Tara was just a friend, why would she be upset that they were getting married? "Come on Damon, I'm not stupid. You expect me to believe that you never slept with her, but she won't accept that we are engaged? Stupid is not written on my forehead. You've got to come better than that."

"I'm serious. I have never slept with Tara. Or let me say I have never had sex with Tara. As far as my relationship with her, it's too hard to explain and you wouldn't understand anyway."

"No, Damon. You are not going to start the rest of our life together like this. If you want me to be your wife you are gonna have to learn to open up to me. At least let me try to understand. If you truly love me and want to marry me, then you have got to trust me."

The look on his face let her know that she had him.

"All right then, Baby. Sit down and I will try to explain it to you. But you have to promise not to judge this situation. I just want you to know how things are between me and Tara."

Alexis sat on the couch. She was feeling a little anxious, almost scared to unearth what he had apparently buried a long time ago.

"It's really no big mystery or major thing. The reason why I try to help Tara when she needs it is because I feel responsible for her situation. It's really just that simple. I owe her, and as long as I do, I have to be there for her. If you know anything about me you know that I pay my debts."

"I don't understand. What do you owe her? And when will your debt be paid? I'm trying to have an open mind about this, and you're right I do know that you are that kind of person, but "

Bam! Bam! Bam! The door rattled on the hinges before it swung open and Bear's huge body filled it. "Coming in and I'm ready to eat." Bear and Lola strode into the house.

"Heeeey, what's up, big daddy!" Damon greeted his best friend. They embraced and gave each other their secret handshake. They acted like they hadn't just seen each other a few hours before.

Shit. Alexis knew Damon was happy to get this reprieve from their conversation. She also knew she would have to wait before she got any more answers about Tara. She shifted into hostess mode and sauntered over to Lola with a wide smile on her face as though she were truly happy to see her.

"Hey, Girl. What's going on?"

Alexis was surprised when Lola handed her a bottle of White Zinfandel. Personally Alexis was partial to Chardonnay, but it was a very nice gesture. Alexis figured Lola to be more of a malt liquor type of girl.

"I thought since ya'll was providing the food, we could at least bring some refreshments. Bear only wanted to buy beer, but I told him that we women needed to have something ladylike to drink. You know what I'm saying, Girl?"

Alexis saw that Bear was holding a six pack of Corona in his enormous hand. "That's right, Girl." Alexis imitated

207

What is Forever?

Lola. They both laughed. "Here Bear, let me take that beer and put it in the refrigerator."

"I love your place, Damon. This is so nice." Lola was checking out the decor.

"Thanks." Damon replied.

"It just needs a woman's touch to make it a little more homey." Lola winked at Alexis.

"Well now that you mention it, that's exactly what it's about to get." He informed them. "Alexis has just agreed to marry me."

"Dog, you forgot that we already knew y'all was engaged? Y'all need to find someone else to tell and stop flaunting it in front of Lola before she starts to get ideas."

Lola playfully swatted at his big arm. "I don't need them to get no ideas about you. I already got my six month plan going." Everyone cracked up laughing.

Once Damon quieted his laugh he continued. "Well, you knew we were engaged, but you didn't know that we are going to get married this week."

Bear's mouth dropped open. For the first time since Alexis had met him, Bear was speechless. Lola wasn't. She screamed louder than Alexis had when Damon gave her the engagement ring. She jumped up and down like she was on a pogo stick. "Oh my God, Oh my God, I can't believe it! I am so happy for ya'll! Oh my God!"

Ebony bounded down the steps with a frightened look on her face. She ran to her daddy and threw her arms around his waist. "Daddy, what's wrong? Why is everybody yelling?"

Alexis could tell that last night's events had more of an effect on the child than she originally thought. She had a pang of guilt for taking her over to her mother's house instead of waiting like Damon told her to.

Damon scooped her up in his arms and swung her around. Her face instantly lit up with joy.

"It's all right, Baby. Everybody is just happy, that's all."

"Why's everybody so happy, Daddy?"

"Because, baby girl, Alexis and I are getting married on Friday."

Ebony clapped her hands. "Yeah!"

Alexis figured she really just wanted to be a part of the celebration more than she truly cared that they were getting married on Friday.

"Well since we have so much to celebrate, why don't we eat." Bear had finally found his voice. He walked over to Alexis and whispered in her ear. "But before we do, I just want you to know how good I think you are for him. I'm glad you're going to be a member of our crazy ass family." He hugged her gently.

That touched Alexis deeply. For the first time since she had moved out of her parent's house, she felt like she was home.

CHAPTER 15

Keisha was frantic. She checked the closet shelf again, ripped all of the shoe boxes and sweaters down. She had to be sure that the .38 Smith and Wesson was gone. She rummaged through the wreckage but couldn't find it. She knew that Junior had taken it and she dreaded what he would do with it when he found Damon. She had to get to Damon first.

She was out of the house and zooming down the street in her old Ford Escort before she had processed her actions. She had broken practically every traffic law in the book by the time she screeched to a halt in front of Damon's condo. She felt like Dirty Harry when she burst through the front door to find Damon, Alexis, Ebony, Bear and a woman she didn't know sitting at the dinning room table laughing and eating pie.

For a moment, time stood still. Abruptly everyone stopped laughing and all eyes were on her. For an instant Keisha felt like she had shown up for school without clothes, but she quickly snapped out of her embarrassment when she remembered why she was there. When she saw the worried look in her daughter's eyes she forced herself not to blurt out what she had come to say. She attempted to look composed. "Hey y'all. I'm sorry to interrupt your supper, but Damon can I talk to you for just a second?"

"Hey Keisha. Is everything all right?" Alexis asked with genuine concern.

"Yeah, Alexis. Everything is fine," she managed to get out while keeping her eyes on Ebony. She hoped Alexis picked up on the fact that she didn't want to alert her baby girl by the inflection in her voice.

"Sure Keisha, hold on one second." Damon's voice was cool, but she could tell that he had picked up on her fear. He excused himself from the table. "Come on in my office."

She followed him into the bedroom that had been converted into his home office. After he closed the door behind them she started blurting out what had taken place between she and Junior. By the time she got out the fact that Junior was looking for him with a gun she felt totally exhausted.

Damon remained extremely calm for a man who had just been told that his life was in danger. The only emotion that ruined his cool demeanor was the anger that burned in his eyes.

"Damon, did you hear what I said? He's looking for you and he got a gun."

"I heard what you said Keisha, but to be honest I'm not too worried about Junior."

"What in the hell do you mean you're not worried? You see what he did to me? I'm telling you Damon, he's done lost his damn mind."

Damon delicately ran his thumb over the corner of her eye where Junior had struck her. He had a pained expression on his face. "Yeah Keish, I see what he did to you. And I'm gonna make sure he doesn't do it again. That's why I'm not afraid of him. Junior's a coward who beats on his woman to make himself feel strong, but he's not strong. He's weak and he knows it. He doesn't have to worry about trying to find me; I'm going to find him."

Keisha was more frightened now than when she had come. The last thing she'd wanted was for Damon to put himself in harm's way over her. "Damon, please. That's not what I want you to do. You have something special with Alexis and I truly believe that ya'll are gonna make it. It would tear me apart if something happened to you because of me. I'm just not worth that."

A tear rolled from the corner of his eye. He quickly wiped it away. It was only the second time she had seen him cry. It disturbed her now as much as it had the first time. Maybe more.

"Keisha, sit down for a minute, okay?"

She did as he asked without saying a word.

"There's something I've been meaning to say to you for a while now. Something I should have said a very long time ago." He cleared his throat and blinked away what she couldn't believe were more tears. "Keisha, what happened to you at that party...I know, and I need to make sure you know that it was not your fault."

His words put a lump in her throat, and transported her back to that night. "Damon I don't want to talk about it." She had done all she could to forget that what had happened to her was more than just a bad dream. She had tried to bury the shame of all of it. She couldn't bear to bring it up now, especially not with him.

"I understand that, but I really need to finish."

She dropped her eyes to her lap and remained quiet.

What is Forever?

"Keisha, I am so very sorry. I was wrong, I was very wrong." She was amazed to hear his voice catch on a deep sob. She could hear the strain in his voice as he tried to force the words out while holding back his tears.

"You were hurt, you were violated and I wasn't there for you. I was so caught up in my pride, in my hurt that I totally ignored yours. You will never know how ashamed of myself I am for that."

"No Damon, it wasn't like that. I never should have put myself in that position. I can't believe how stupid I was. I had no business drinking while I was pregnant. I mean, do you have any idea what could have happened to our baby? Just because I was stupid." Thinking about the fact that she could have given Ebony serious birth defects nearly pushed her over the edge. She wanted to cry but there were simply no tears left in her to shed.

"Keisha, please don't. You've had to bear the weight of that night on your shoulders alone. I should have been a better man, a better person. You should have had counseling. You should have had a shoulder to lean on. You should have had me, but all I did was turn my back on you."

"You were there for me. You saved me. If I had stayed in that room there's no telling what could have happened to me, but you came and got me out of there. I'm grateful for that."

"No Keisha, you don't understand. Do you know why I found you that night?"

Dread entered her heart. She was afraid of what he might say next. She didn't want to hear what she thought was coming.

What is Forever?

He must have read her thoughts on her face. "No, I wasn't up there looking to get laid. My friend Bobby heard that they had some girl up there. He went up to get in on the action and when he saw it was you he came to get me."

Keisha shuddered when she remembered. It was Bobby who had told her it would be all right that night as he took his turn at her. He'd said her name. He'd been the last face she'd seen before blacking out. He must never have told Damon the truth: that he only went to get him after he'd had his turn.

"Before I knew it was you, I thought it was funny. Just the guys having fun. After I found out who they had up there I was embarrassed that my friends would know what went down that night. I turned my back on you and that was wrong. I owed you more than that."

"I guess we both made our mistakes, but you don't owe me anything. What you gave me was the most valuable thing in my life. You gave me a beautiful daughter, who's smart like her father and beautiful like her momma. You've never let her down. The fact of the matter is that you never let me down either. At least not the way I see it."

She was relieved to see him start to regain his composure. "I just feel responsible for you're situation. If I had been stronger..."

She stood up and walked next to him by the window. She wanted to throw her arms around him and thank him for being such a good friend and father. Instead, she placed her hand on his shoulder. She was touched by his confession.

"You once told me everything happens for a reason. I've come to believe that's true. You may not have been meant to

214

be my man, but I'm so thankful that you were meant to always be my friend and my daughter's father."

He smiled at her through what was left of his tears. "I just want you to understand that you are worthwhile, and you don't have to settle for less. I want you to have a man in your life that will love and honor you. Junior is just not that man. It's been coming for a long time and Junior and I need to handle our business."

She was still afraid, but she knew there was nothing she would be able to do to stop him. "All I'm going to ask you to do is to be careful. Please, promise me you'll be careful. Ebony needs her daddy."

"Don't worry, Keish. Everything will work out in the fullness of time." He started walking toward the door then turned back to face her. He had suddenly turned a little sheepish. "By the way, I wanted to tell you about my wedding plans."

"Have you set a date already?"

"As a matter of fact, yeah, we have set a date." He grinned. "We're doing it on Friday."

Her stomach churned, but she put a smile on her face. "So soon? What's the rush? You knock Alexis up too?" She was joking, but she hoped she wasn't on to something. She wanted to hold on to a piece of Damon for a while longer.

"No way. I want to have more kids one day, but not quite yet. We just decided that we love each other and there's really no reason to wait."

"I guess I can understand that. I'm really happy for ya'll." She hoped that her true feelings weren't written across her face.

What is Forever?

"I really hope you can be there."

"Oh don't worry, I'll be there. Alexis might need help holding you down if you get cold feet." They shared a small laugh. Then an awkward moment of silence. "Well let me get outta here. I need to take Patches out before he makes another lake in my laundry room. Do you want me to take baby girl with me?"

"No, that's all right. I'll drop her in the morning about ten."

"I'll see you later." Keisha walked past him to the door, placed her hand on the knob, then turned around. "Damon remember, be careful. You have a daughter, and in a few days a wife. They both need to have you around, and so do I."

"Do me a favor. Don't say anything to Alexis about Junior. I don't want her to worry."

Keisha nodded and walked out without another word.

In the dining room Alexis was busy clearing off the table. She turned as Keisha paused in the doorway.

"Damon told me you're going to be a bride this week. I want you to know that I am truly happy for you."

'Thanks, Keisha. I just hope we can pull everything together before Friday."

"You know you will. We women can do anything we set our minds to. Damon deserves the best. He really is a good man, and I think you're just what he needs." She gave Alexis a warm smile and Alexis returned the same. "So where's my baby girl?"

"She's in the living room with Bear and Lola watching television."

What is Forever?

"We'll I'm going to go in here and tell her good-bye. I'll see you later."

"All right Keisha, take care."

Keisha found Ebony and Bear on the floor in front of the television. The little girl was sitting on Bear's round stomach trying to explain to him why the Rug Rats could talk even though they were babies. When Ebony saw her she bounced off of the big man and ran into her open arms.

"Mommy, Mommy."

"Hey there, Baby. You doing okay?" Keisha gave her a tight squeeze.

"I'm fine, Mommy. You doin' all right?" The child had genuine concern on her face. Too much concern for a child so young. Keisha knew that she had played a major role in putting that worry in her baby's eyes. She was not going to allow anything in her life that would put that kind of pain and worry into her child's heart again.

"Oh my beautiful, Baby. I'm fine."

"Hey Keish. You doing all right?" Bear had finally managed to get his massive frame off of the floor.

"Bear, you don't know how right I am. Matter of fact, I'm fantastic, and I'm going to be even better. There are just a few things I need to take care of and everything else will be gravy."

Bear chuckled. "Cool, cause you know how much I like gravy." He rubbed his belly. "Sounds like you have a plan." He said with a big smile and a knowing look. "You do your thing."

What is Forever?

"Don't worry Bear, I am. I gonna do my thing." She turned her attention back to Ebony. "Baby, you're going to spend one more night with daddy and Alexis. Okay?"

"But Mommy I wanna come home wiff you." She pouted.

"Not tonight, Baby. Mommy has a lot to do tonight. I won't be able to spend any time with you. So you just stay here tonight and when you get home tomorrow we'll have a great day."

"Okay Mommy."

Keisha knew her baby was disappointed, but she also knew she was about to make some changes to her life that would be good for them both.

CHAPTER 16

"What do you mean my checking account is overdrawn?" Tara held the cordless phone in one hand and a fistful of Insufficient Funds notices in the other. "I have over three thousand dollars in that account!" Tara was livid.

"I'm sorry Ms. Johnson, but all of the available funds were withdrawn from your account two weeks ago." The bank representative was apologetic but was not giving in.

It had to have been Gabe. It was just like him to take everything. He knew that she would put the account in the red because she would think there was still money in it. He wasn't just going to kick her to the curb, he was going punish her.

"Well thank you for your time. I'll just go by my local branch to straighten this out later."

Things were going from bad to worse by the minute. Ever since Damon had told her that he didn't want to pursue a relationship with her she just couldn't get herself together. She was still staying with him, but now she was sleeping on his couch.

She had gone into such a deep depression after everything that went down that she was unable to go to work for two weeks. When she finally did return she couldn't concentrate. She hadn't even come close to selling a house for two months.

Today was no exception. Her bad news this morning left her unable to do more than stare blankly at her computer screen. It wasn't much of a surprise when her boss called her into her office. Mrs. Manuel was a decent woman, but she didn't play when it came to business and her purse. Tara knew before the older woman opened her mouth that she was going to be fired.

She wasn't exactly right. Instead, Mrs. Manuel told her that she should take a leave of absence.

"You need to take some time to get yourself together. You don't even look like yourself."

Couldn't the woman see that her life was falling apart around her? If she could get herself together, she would. She went home feeling more lost than ever.

Now she was stuck with no job, no real home and no money. She had been making her car payments, but the checks were being returned. The repo man was probably out looking for her Saab right now.

"God, I need a drink." Tara looked at her watch and saw that it was five minutes before noon. "Damn." She couldn't justify drinking before noon.

She sat on the couch and watched the clock until both hands were on the twelve.

"Alrighty then. It's happy hour time."

Tara walked into the kitchen and looked in the cabinet were Damon kept his liquor. About a month ago it had been pretty well stocked. Not with the expensive spirits she had been accustomed to while she lived with Gabe, but he had collected a nice little stash of your basic stuff: E&J, Bacardi, Smirnoff and even a pint of Courvoisier. Mostly it was there for parties or events. He wasn't much of drinker; he just liked the idea of being able to offer company something when they came by.

What is Forever?

In the time that she had been there, Tara had all but decimated his stash. She went through the brown alcohol first. They didn't seem to affect her quite as much. Once she had killed the last of the E&J she went to work on the Smirnoff.

Now when she opened the cabinet, she found that there was only a little more than a corner left in the bottle. She poured it into a glass and added two ice cubes. She mixed a splash of orange juice with it and finished the screwdriver in one gulp. It warmed her insides. She felt the tension relax just a little.

"That's a little better. Maybe now I can figure out what I'm going to do."

She was hungry. She opened the refrigerator and found it pretty bare. Then she remembered that Damon had left fifty bucks on the counter and asked her to pick up a few things while he was at work.

She hit herself in the head with the palm of her hand.

"Damn, I must be getting senile. I almost forgot I told Damon I'd go to the store."

She knew she looked a mess, but didn't bother to comb her hair or brush her teeth before she grabbed her pocketbook and keys off the side table by the couch. She walked behind the apartment building where she had parked her car.

When she turned the ignition the low fuel light came on. Her car was about to run out of gas and she didn't have a dime other than the money she was supposed to buy groceries with.

What is Forever?

"He'll understand I had to put a few dollars in my tank in order to get to the store."

There was a Hess gas station and convenience store around the corner. She stopped and put seven dollars worth of gas in her car. When she went to the counter to pay for it she decided she needed to get a snack. Her stomach was cramping she was so hungry. She ended up getting two bags of Doritos and a Slim Jim. By the time she got to the grocery store she only had about forty dollars left.

The first aisle she went to was the wine aisle where she found a good bottle of Chardonnay for only eight bucks. A buy like that she just couldn't pass up. She ended up buying twenty dollars worth of food and spent the rest on chips and snack foods.

When she got back to the apartment the first thing she did was to open the wine and pour herself a large glass.

"Damn, it's nice to finally have something decent to drink around here."

She finished the glass and poured herself another. It didn't take long for the wine to go to her head. She was buzzing nicely when she decided that she had been in the house moping long enough. She needed a change of pace.

Thirty minutes later she found herself in front of Gabe's condo. She knew she should just keep going, but she couldn't bring herself to drive away. Gabe was responsible for her account being overdrawn, and she wanted her money. It was only about three o'clock; he would still be at his office.

She parked in the driveway and walked right up to the front door. She tried her key and was surprised to find that it still worked. A knot of apprehension rolled up in her stomach as she walked up the stairs and into the living room. It was her first time back in the house since Gabe had kicked her out. She felt homesick. She missed the smell of the place, the way the daylight filled the rooms through the large picture windows. This had been her home. She appreciated Damon's being there for her, but his apartment was like a cracker box compared to this.

Tara walked through the house, letting her hands brush over various objects as she inspected the premises. She walked up to the master bedroom. She went into Gabe's closet and found what she was looking for at the back behind a stack of shoe boxes. The small safe was bolted to the floor and locked as it always was. It only took a moment for her to locate the old brown robe that hung in the midst of Gabe's many designer suits. She fished in the right pocket and pulled out the key to the safe.

Her hands trembled as she inserted the key into the lock. When she opened the case she was not surprised to see a stack of cash. There had to be at least twenty thousand dollars there, along with Gabe's more valuable jewelry and some important paperwork. She grabbed the stack of money, carefully counted out three thousand and stuffed it into her purse. She started to put the rest back, then changed her mind and peeled off another grand to cover the bank fees and other expenses. Her heart was pounding in her chest as the adrenaline flowed through her body. She felt giddy. For the first time she was about to get the best of Gabe.

She closed the safe and put the key back in its proper place. It could be months or years before Gabe realized that

223

there was money missing. He'd had that same stack of money there for years. He never spent it, hardly looked at it. He had always told her that the money was only for dire emergencies.

"Well buddy, I'd say that my life is an emergency right now."

Back in her car she quickly sped away from the scene of the crime. Her victory had her feeling quite satisfied. She was so engrossed in her victory that she didn't realize when she ran a stop sign. She was only four blocks away from Damon's apartment when the flashing blue lights in her rear view mirror brought her back to reality. She was nervous when the officer walked up to her window.

"Ma'am may I see your license and registration."

"Of course, Officer." She opened her purse and panicked at the sight of the money she had stuffed into it. If the cop saw all of that cash he would be suspicious. She turned back further from the window to inhibit the cop's view of her bag. She rummaged through the money and found her wallet and license. She took a deep breath in an attempt to keep her cool. "Is there a problem?"

He took her license and registration and looked it over. "Well Ms. Johnson, you failed to stop for a duly posted stop sign back there."

Tara was shocked. "Officer, I am so sorry! I didn't even realize. I've had a terrible day and my mind must have been somewhere else. I'm so very sorry."

The officer's face was totally absent of sympathy. "I'm sorry too, Ms. Johnson, but we do have traffic laws that are designed to keep people safe. What if there had been another vehicle going through that intersection, or someone's child? Sorry wouldn't be good enough then, now would it Ma'am?"

"You're absolutely right," she conceded. She opened her mouth to say she was sorry again, but he had just told her that sorry wouldn't cut it. She swallowed the apology.

"Please just sit tight for a moment, I'll be right back." He swaggered back to his car.

If she hadn't been scared shitless she probably would have laughed. After about five minutes that felt like five hours, John Wayne made his way back to her window.

"You don't have any outstanding warrants, so I decided to give you a break this time. You need to be more careful in the future."

As he handed her license back, Tara let out a sigh of relief. The officer gripped the license before she could pull it from his hand.

"Ma'am, have you been drinking?"

Tara felt her heart miss two beats. Beads of perspiration dampened her forehead in an instant. How should she answer? If she said yes, maybe she could explain that her destination was right down the street. He might cut her a break. If she said no, he might feel insulted and cart her ass off to jail for lying. She was about to admit to having had just a glass of wine when she remembered that Gabe had told her to never admit it to a cop if you had even one drink. It gave him reasonable cause to investigate you. Gabe always said if you got caught drinking and driving it was the cop's job to prove that.

"No officer, I haven't." She attempted to sound offended by his question.

What is Forever?

"Step out of the car Miss."

"Why? I haven't done anything." Tara started to panic.

"You ran that stop sign back there, for one thing. I also think you just told me a bold-faced lie."

Tara knew right then that she was going to jail.

CHAPTER 17

After Bear and Lola left, Damon went upstairs to give Ebony a bath and put her to bed. Alexis took a hot shower and relaxed on the bed. She flipped on the television. By the time Damon came into the room she was well engrossed in an episode of her favorite Legal Show. He flopped down on the bed, clearly exhausted. She wanted to finish their conversation about Tara, as well as ask him what he and Keisha had discussed in his office, but she could tell that he was just too drained to get into it. Truth be told, so was she.

"So is this a good episode?" he asked her.

"Are you kidding? It's always a good episode!" Discussion of the day's events could wait until the following day. Alexis wanted to spend a normal evening with her man. She put her head on his chest. The only drama that would go on tonight would have to be on the television.

When she awoke the following morning the television was still on and she was still lying across Damon's chest. Alexis stretched lazily. She felt very well rested and full of energy. She was excited about the prospects of the day. They would spend it together and finish planning their wedding, which was only four days away. Oh yeah, this was going to be the best Monday ever. It should be after all, because it was truly the first day of the rest of her life with Damon.

She kissed him on the lips and giggled when he stirred. "Wake up sleepy head. You can't stay in the bed all day today. You've got a wedding to plan."

What is Forever?

He pulled her close. "Oh yeah? Am I supposed to be marrying someone?" He planted a big kiss on her lips.

"Not if you keep playing," she joked, "and by the way, this ain't TV. You can't be trying to talk all up in a sister's face before you brush your teeth." She hit him in the face with a pillow.

"Oh I know you're not talking, dragon lady." He tossed the pillow back at her.

"I may be a dragon lady, but you know you love it."

"Yeah, I do."

The rest of the morning was uneventful. The three of them went about getting up and dressed and having breakfast. They had a good time. Alexis felt like they were already a family. What would it be like to have her own child by Damon? She touched her stomach and remembered the missed pills. She wanted to have a family, but the time didn't feel right yet.

By ten o'clock they were in the car headed for Keisha's house. The three of them were in good spirits. When they pulled up in front of the house Keisha walked out onto the front stoop. She waved at them, a big smile on her face.

Alexis noted that the bruising to her face looked much better. "Someone seems to be in a good mood," she observed.

Ebony had the gate opened and was halfway across the lawn before Damon or Alexis were even out of the car.

"Mommy!" She launched herself into her mother's arms.

The love between mother and child was visible. It showed on their faces and seemed to fill the air around them. Alexis felt a twinge of jealousy. Although she and Ebony

228

had enjoyed a great time together that morning, it was no comparison to that bond.

"Hey Keish," Damon called as he made his way over. "You doing all right?" He reached them halfway between the car and the front door, where Keisha stood holding Ebony in her arms. For a moment Alexis imagined what they would have been like as a family. If a decision or two had been made differently, Damon and Keisha might have married and been working on their second child by now. She wondered if it would have been better that way. The way Damon loved his daughter; maybe it would have been better for her if they had made it work.

Alexis pushed the thoughts out of her mind.

"Hey Lexis," Keisha called. "You ready for the big day?" She winked.

"I'm working on it." Alexis smiled back.

Damon and Keisha spoke briefly, and then he was back to the car and they were headed off to the register of deeds to apply for their marriage license.

The office was downtown and in a busy area. They circled the block twice trying to find a parking space. Damon ended up parking the car two blocks from the building. As they walked, Damon cleared his throat.

"You know, I never finished explaining my relationship with Tara to you."

"I know, but I've been thinking about it and I'm not sure that you need to. I mean, we're about to get married. You told me that nothing is going on that I should be worried about, so I trust you with that. If it's a subject you're not comfortable discussing, then we won't discuss it."

229

What is Forever?

"I really appreciate that, but I don't want us to have anything left unsettled between us. I don't want to have secrets. I want to feel comfortable sharing everything with you. Let's sit down over here for a minute."

He pulled her over to a bench and sat down, drawing her down beside him. He looked into her eyes. "There are a couple of reasons why I've tried to be there for Tara. First of all, a couple of years ago while I was still in Film School and had nothing, she was the only person who was there for me. She supported me financially, emotionally, any way I needed her to. Secondly, I owe her because she lost everything because of me. She lost her fiancé, her money and her mind.

CHAPTER 18

By the time the guard called Tara's name she was a mess. They had taken her wristwatch so she wasn't sure how much time had passed, but it had to have been hours. They'd made her put on a nasty orange jumpsuit and flip flops. The guards refused to let her keep her own shoes. They had laces and could be used for suicide, they informed her. The idea of ending it all appealed to her.

"Johnson!" The manly looking guard called again.

"I'm here," Tara answered.

"You made bail."

The woman reminded Tara of a mutated gymnast. She was short, squat and walked like she had just bench-pressed a few hundred pounds. Her hair was extremely short and spiked up with gel. The brown uniform hid any indication that she was actually female. Her face did little to divulge her gender either. It was pale, pimply and completely void of make up.

"Unless you wanna stay here with your new friend." The guard gestured toward Tara's cell mate.

Tara took a quick peek at the old woman. She was asleep on the metal counter that was supposed to pass as a cot. She was obviously a street person who liked to get her drink on. She had cussed Tara out thoroughly for ten minutes before she had turned her wrath on the invisible "bitch" that had apparently accompanied her into the cell and who was more or less responsible for the woman's being arrested. She had admonished the imaginary friend for "swinging at a damn cop." She had paced around raising cane for some time before she sat on the cold hard cot, vomited, and passed out. She still laid there now, in the vile puddle, semi-conscious and muttering to herself from time to time. Tara fought the urge to retch.

"I'm ready to go." Tara's voice was weak.

Her head was pounding and she felt completely drained. As she walked through the maze that was the County Detention Center, she noticed that her hands were shaking. She felt like the walls and rows of cells would come crashing down on her at any moment. The feelings got worse as she stopped at the counter to pick up her personal effects. She was beyond uneasy. Anxiety plagued her as the deputy counted off the huge sum of money that had been in her pocketbook. Tara said a silent prayer that there wouldn't be any questions about the money. She should have felt relief when none came, but she didn't. All she felt was the increasing sense that the world was caving in on her.

Once the deputy was sure that everything was correct, she had Tara sign the appropriate documents. She only felt slightly relieved when she saw Damon waiting for her in the lobby. She was silent as she walked next to him out the door. Outside, the sun glared off the rust of his car. She had never been so happy to see that ragged little thing. At that moment she would have gladly ridden a donkey to get away from this place.

Her car had been impounded. The finance company had probably already laid claim to it, so she wrote it off.

She waited for Damon to blow up about having to come get her out of jail. Lord knows if it had been Gabe, he would have started in on her before they could have gotten out of the jailhouse. Damon, as usual, was quiet and did not push the issue.

"You all right?"

She knew he was trying to be kind, but the question simply made her mad. He had spurned her, her life was in shambles and she was just released from jail. Hell, did he think she was all right?

"I'm fine."

"I'm sorry it took me so long to get down here to get you out," he apologized. "It took me a while to get someone to cover me at work. Then I had to make a few calls in order to get the money for your bail."

"Look Damon, don't worry about it okay?" She was exasperated. She knew it wasn't his fault that she had been arrested, but she didn't feel like talking about it. "And don't worry about the money. I'll pay you back every cent."

"I don't care about the money, Tara. Hell, I owe you more than I paid today anyway."

"Whatever." Tara couldn't believe how nasty she was being. Damon was being so patient with her. She just couldn't help it.

They drove along in silence for a while.

"Damon, can we stop at the grocery store? I've got to get some female supplies."

"Sure. We need some bread anyway."

Bread was on the list of things she was supposed to have picked up earlier. She wondered if he was trying to make an offhanded insult. He pulled up in front of the Food Lion.

What is Forever?

"I'll be right back." She jumped out of the car and ran into the store.

Her stomach had been cramping for the last hour. She knew that she better pick up some tampons before her period started. It didn't take her long to locate the feminine hygiene aisle. Her first instinct was to buy a cheaper brand. Then she remembered the money she had in her pocketbook. Tara grabbed the biggest box she could find.

Then she had another idea. She put the box back, went to the front of the store and got a shopping cart. She went back to recover the box of tampons and also put a box of the best panty liners they had in the cart. She then proceeded to the fresh meat section and picked out two of the biggest, thickest T-bones she could find. Tara went up and down each aisle of the grocery store. She picked up any and everything that she wanted. On the way to the checkout she picked up a couple of gallon jugs of her favorite wine. By the time she walked out of the store the shopping cart was overflowing with groceries. She enjoyed the look of surprise on Damon's face when he saw her haul. He jumped out of the car to help her with the bags.

"Damn Girl, that's a lot of pads." The little car was barely able to hold all of the groceries.

She chuckled. Her shopping excursion had picked up her spirits. For the first time since she had been staying with Damon she was able to provide something instead of just taxing his limited resources.

"I may be a jailbird, but we're going to eat good tonight, Baby." She could feel the happiness in her voice, and she

234

liked it. Only her seatbelt was preventing her from floating out of the window.

Damon seemed confused by the sudden change in her disposition. "So is Food Lion giving away free groceries today, or do they pay people for spending the day in jail?"

"Ha, ha. You are so funny, Mr. Black." She teased. "For your information I got that trouble at the bank worked out. I figured it was time for me to help out with some things."

By the time they got back to his apartment they were joking and laughing. Tara's mind was almost completely off of the day's earlier events. Damon was a little hesitant to join Tara in a glass of wine after she had just gotten out for driving while intoxicated, but she convinced him that she was not going to leave the house again that night and that she just wanted to have a glass to celebrate her freedom. They opened the first bottle of wine and toasted to the liberation of Tara the political prisoner.

Tara had begun to prepare the steaks and every thing was going well. She was starting to feel that romantic vibe between she and Damon again when the telephone rang.

"Hello?" Damon answered the phone. "Sure, no problem. Hold on for a minute." He held the phone toward her. "It's a man he says he's your uncle."

She hesitated before taking the receiver. She only had one uncle, and she hadn't heard from him in over ten years. As a matter of fact the only relative of hers that she kept in touch with was her mother, and they hadn't spoken since shortly after she moved out of Gabe's condo.

"Hello?"

"Well hey, Baby. How ya doing?" Gabe.

What is Forever?

He spoke in a low congenial tone. Instantly she was reduced to a nervous wreck.

"How did you get this number?" She took a long sip of her wine.

"Come on, Tara. You know how resourceful I am. There's nothing I can't do or find if I put my mind to it."

"So I guess you're a great private eye. What do you want, Gabe?" She was trying to be tough, but Gabe would see through the facade. He'd always had the ability to look straight through her and find any weakness she had.

"I heard what happened today and I just wanted to call and make sure you were all right."

Always smooth, always cool. That was Gabe's way of doing business. He wanted something from her, she just couldn't figure out what.

"I'm fine Gabe, bye."

Before she could get the phone away from her ear to hang up he continued. "I know that you've been by the house."

Tara froze.

"Tara, there's nothing that concerns you that I don't know about. Don't you know that by now?" He sighed. "I don't want to argue with you. I just wanted you to know that I miss you. I was hoping we could get together and talk."

Silence. Her tongue had declared a mutiny.

"I know you can't be happy with your new little boyfriend. I've done some checking and he could never measure up to your standards. He could never give you the kind of life you want."

What is Forever?

Tara felt a wave of anger lap at her fear. It wasn't much, but it was enough to free her from her thrall. "Look, I don't know where you're getting your information, but Damon is twice the man you'll ever be." She looked up to where Damon was standing in the living room. He had been pretending not to be listening to her conversation, but now he turned around and faced her. Their eyes met for a moment. She turned toward the stove to avoid his gaze. She didn't want to deal with the questions in his eyes.

"Sell it to someone who will buy that shit, all right? I know you better than anyone on this earth. I can hear in your voice that you aren't happy. You haven't been since you left."

"I didn't leave, remember? Your sorry ass kicked me out!"

"That's because you were a cheating whore." His voice was as cold and bitter as a Chicago wind. "Like I said, I'm not trying to argue with you. I was trying to give you a chance to get your shit together. I don't have to chase you, Tara. I can get any woman I want."

"Then why the hell are you bothering me?"

"Because I thought you were smarter than you obviously are. I thought maybe you had served enough time in that hell you're living in. I thought that you were ready to get your shit together, stop being a slut and apologize. Then, maybe, I would take your ass back."

"You're a bastard."

"I may be a bastard, but you're a stupid bitch."

"Fuck you."

What is Forever?

"Before you hang up, I have one last thing to share with you." He paused, and Tara felt a shiver run up her spine. "I have surveillance cameras in the condo. You better have my money in my hand before Friday or I'm calling the police."

Click – the phone went dead in her hand.

With numb hands, she put it back on the hook. She felt the tears on her face before she knew she was crying. She tried to concentrate on the food she was cooking, but her vision was blurry. Her mind was moving in so many different directions that she was unable to focus. Once again she was on a roller-coaster from hell, and it seemed the only way she could go was straight down.

"Tara, don't worry about him." Damon had come into the kitchen and was standing behind her. "I don't know what he said, but I know that he's just trying to get to you. You've got to be strong. If you fall apart then he wins. Don't let him win."

She knew he was right, but she couldn't help feeling defeated. "You just don't understand. He's so mean. He's always been like that. He's horrible! Not just nasty, he's vile! He's wicked! And he's smart, he's so damn smart! How can I fight that? He's got everything. I have nothing. You just don't know!" She was blubbering, almost ranting but she couldn't stop herself. "He knows he has me right were he wants me! I can't fight him! I don't know how!" A sob hitched in her throat. "I've never known how."

Tara felt something inside break. The weight of everything she had been through was too heavy for her to carry anymore.

238

What is Forever?

She was aware that she had fallen to the floor and that she was sobbing uncontrollably. She felt Damon's arms around her. She heard him when he told her that he loved her and that he was there for her. She couldn't fight back the tears or the sobs that were choking her. All she could do was hold on to him, cling to her only lifeline. She must be dying. She felt herself falling into a place that frightened her, slipping into darkness.

When she came to, sunlight streamed through a window onto her face. Its brightness made her wince. She licked her lips. They were chapped and her mouth was incredibly dry. Her head throbbed. She was groggy, but she noticed the odd smell of the room. Something bitter, like cleaning fluid, or a doctor's office. No! It was a hospital! Her eyes flew open, squinting against the sunlight, taking in the white walls, white lights, white sheets. A hospital. She had always hated the smell of hospitals. What had happened to her?

"Oh God I wish I were dead."

"Tara, please don't say that." Tara was caught totally off guard when she heard her mother's voice.

"Mommy?" Tara looked to her right. Her mother was seated on her bedside. She wrapped her arms around her mother's neck. "Oh Mommy, I missed you so much!" Tears streamed down both of their faces as they embraced. They held on to each other for a long time. Tara pulled back first. She looked into her mother's face. Time had not been kind to her. She could count each wrinkle that had formed on her face since the last time she'd seen her. Tara was saddened by the gray hair that showed at the roots of her blonde hair. It had been such a long time since she had seen her mother. "What are you doing here?"

"I called her."

Tara hadn't noticed Damon sitting in a chair on the other side of the room. He looked tired. His eyes were red and his clothes disheveled.

"I didn't know what else to do. You were so upset, and you wouldn't talk to me. I got your address book and found your mother's number. We decided I should bring you here..."

Tara was touched by his concern.

"I came as soon as I could," her mother added.

"But I don't understand. Why am I in the hospital?"

"Baby, you've had a breakdown," Jane Johnson had never been one to fumble over words, "but don't worry. You're going to be just fine." Her crystal blue eyes sparkled with confidence.

It didn't really come as a surprise. In a way it was a relief to put a finger on the cause of her emotional distress. She'd felt so close to the edge. Maybe now she could find her way back.

Tara remained in the hospital for three days. By then the doctor had diagnosed her with Anxiety and Bipolar Disorder. He placed her on several medications and informed her that she would need to continue to be treated by a psychiatrist. Her mother thought it would be best if Tara returned to New York with her for a while in order to get herself together, and the doctor agreed. Tara was too doped up to put up much of a fight.

What is Forever?

The three of them stayed in Damon's small apartment until Tara's court date. The Judge was a kind looking, grandfatherly man who took pity on Tara. After she told him her story, presented him with doctor's notes and explained that she was going to New York to receive further treatment, he dismissed the charges.

Damon took them to the airport. They all made small talk on the way. Airport security wouldn't allow Damon to walk them to the gate. Tara had to say her goodbyes at the metal detector.

"I just want to thank you for everything you've done for me."

"Please Tara, don't even say that. I feel like I'm responsible for all that you've been through."

"No Damon, if it wasn't for you I wouldn't be here today. I wouldn't have this chance to get myself together."

"Well anyway," he looked into her eyes, "I just want you to know that I do love you Tara. I'm just sorry that I was too selfish to give us a chance to explore what we could have had."

"You're talking like I'm never coming back. I'm just going to take some time to work on me. When I get myself together you can believe I'll be back and you'll have the opportunity to explore all you want."

He pulled her close and kissed her softly. "I'll be here. You just concentrate on getting better."

As Tara boarded the plane, Damon's words echoed in her mind. He did love her. She knew then that she would do whatever she had to in order to get better so that they could be together.

CHAPTER 19

"She went to New York to live with her mother. I didn't hear from her for over a year. By the time she called, you and I had already been dating over three months, and I was in love with you." Damon's face showed shame.

Alexis was not certain that he should feel any differently.

"So what about the promise you made her that you would be here when she got better?"

"When I said it to her I meant it." His face looked tortured. "I guess things just weren't meant for us. I think I never allowed myself to go there with Tara for several reasons. First of all, there was Keisha. I'd given my heart to her and felt betrayed. For a long time I just wasn't willing to put myself in that position again." He sighed deeply. "Besides, when I first met Tara I knew she had a man. I wasn't trying to have a relationship with her. I never expected things to go as far as they did."

"Oh, I guess you was just gonna hit it and run, huh?" Alexis wouldn't have believed that Damon was capable of such behavior, but here he was telling her all about it.

"I didn't mean it that way. When I met her she needed a friend. That was the only plan that I had going into it. I just wanted to be her friend. As we got closer I developed feelings for her. To this day I can't really tell you what those feelings were. I was afraid of getting hurt. I tried to shut down and push her away before I could find out. It was only after everything that happened that I realized that if I was

242

ever truly going to be happy, I'd have to be willing to open myself up. I only learned that because of Tara."

"But I'm the person who reaped the benefits of that revelation?"

He paused, his face filled with uncertainty. "I guess so." When he continued it was with more conviction. "When she came back I was honest with her. I told her that I still cared about her, but that I was in love with you. I promised her that I would always be her friend, but that was all that I had to offer her."

Alexis didn't know how to take his disclosure. She had been so upset with Tara for trying to take Damon from her, when from Tara's point of view it must have been the other way around. She felt guilty. However, the reality of the situation did not evade her. Tara'd had her shot with Damon. Alexis knew that she could not hold herself responsible for their relationship not working out.

The truth about Tara did have an affect on the way she viewed Damon. It didn't change her love in the slightest but, she realized, Damon was human just like everyone else. He had made mistakes. She also realized that all of the things Damon had been through had helped to make him into the man that he had become. The man she loved.

"Damon, I can't scold you about your past. We all have one, but we are standing outside the office of the register of deeds about to apply for a marriage license. I love you more than I thought could be possible, but before we go any further there are some things that I need to know."

"Of course. I understand you have questions. I want to start our life together with total honesty."

What is Forever?

"First of all, do you love her?"

He didn't hesitate or lose eye contact for a second. "Yes. It makes me feel guilty to say it, but I do love her. Just not in a romantic way. I feel responsible for her."

Alexis had never respected him more. He had promised her honesty and he was delivering.

"Will your feelings for her affect our love? Will they affect our marriage?"

"No, Baby. I promise you that I will never let that happen. I truly want to be a friend to Tara, help her to get on with her life, but not at the expense of our relationship. If you say that to keep us together I can never speak to her again, then I'm willing to make that sacrifice."

Alexis knew that there was no way she would stand in the way of him being the man he was. One of the things that she loved most about him was his capacity for good. She knew that he could never live with himself if she forced him to abandon Tara. Still, her momma didn't raise any fools.

"I think that you know me better than to think I would ask you not to follow your conscience, but if I have to learn to deal with Tara then there are a few things that I feel need to be done." Damon nodded, so she continued. "First of all, she is going to have to respect me and our relationship. No more midnight calls. Secondly, I want to meet her. I think that if you are going to ask this of me I deserve to see for myself what is going on between you."

She watched him closely to see if he showed any signs of hesitation. He didn't.

"I don't have a problem with either of those things. As a matter of fact, I've always wanted you to meet her. I know that it may be strange for you at first, but once you meet her you'll see there's nothing for you to worry about."

"Wait a minute, Mister. There's one more thing."

"All right. What is it?"

"I want you to tell me that you love me and nothing can come between us."

He chuckled. "Baby, I love you with all of my heart and nothing will ever come between us."

They kissed passionately, there in front of the register of deeds. Alexis knew in her heart that their love would live forever.

"So, Mr. Black, shall we go in there and get our license?"

"Let's."

They walked into the building and found the counter for marriage licenses. Alexis was surprised at how simple the process was. She'd always heard that there had to be blood tests and waiting periods. She was happy to find that neither was true anymore. She and Damon showed their birth certificates, filled out the paperwork and paid the ten dollar fee. They were given the license right there on the spot.

Alexis felt exhilarated as they walked out of the building. She and Damon were really going to be married in just four more days. At that moment she felt as though nothing could go wrong in her life. They walked arm-in-arm, smiling like kids cutting school. As they passed an alley between a pawn shop and a Chinese Takeout, Damon stopped in his tracks.

"I don't believe it." The joy in his face was replaced with something darker.

Alexis turned to see what Damon was looking at. Three thugs were standing in the alley sharing a joint.

What is Forever?

"Damon, what is it? What's wrong, Baby?"

"See the tall skinny dude? That's Junior." He started down the alley without another word.

Alexis' heart sank but she took off after him. "Damon, what are you doing? Don't go down there. Just leave him alone."

He stopped and turned to face her. "I want you to go wait at the car. I need to have a word with this guy."

"Why Damon? Why do you need to have anything to do with him? Keisha's done with him. You don't have to get involved. Come on Baby, just let it go."

"Alexis you've got to trust me on this. This guy is around my daughter every day. It's time I had a talk with him just to let him know how I feel. Besides, he's supposed to be looking for me anyway."

By that time Junior noticed them. "Oh hell no, just the mother fucker I been looking for." Junior and his boys were walking toward them.

"That's funny because I've been looking for you too, Junior."

"Well I guess you found me, huh?"

"You know I'm not the type to beat around the bush, so I'm going to put it straight. I want you out of Keisha's house and away from my daughter."

Junior had been trying to posture for his boys but Damon's bluntness caught him by surprise. It didn't take long for him to come back.

"Hold on, mother fucker. Who the hell you think you are to tell me to leave my house?" Junior stepped right up to Damon's face. His boys stood right behind him.

What is Forever?

"Look Bro, you need to step back out my face. I don't wanna bust your ass, but believe me I will." His eyes flicked to the other two men. "This is between me and Junior. I know y'all don't want no part of this, so I think you need to go on about your business."

Alexis was surprised when the two large men looked at each other and began to walk away.

"Hey Man, we don't have nothing to do with it."

"I don't even be trying to get no situations like this." The smaller man said.

Junior seemed to loose a little of his bravado when he realized his friends didn't have his back.

"I don't see why you trying to come between me and Keisha. You sitting here with your own woman and now you wanna try and control what goes on in my house. Man, fuck that shit."

"No Junior, fuck you. I been trying to stay out of what goes on between you and Keisha. Technically that's not my business, but what goes on around my daughter *is* my business."

"Ain't nobody doing nothing to your kid, Man. Shit, if you that worried about it, all you got to do is come get the little bitch and never bring her ass back to my house."

Damon didn't say another word. He just hit Junior with a straight right punch to the mouth. Junior tumbled to the ground holding his face.

"Don't you ever disrespect my daughter again. That's your problem Junior, you don't have any respect. I don't give a damn about you, but Ebony is my child. You mess with her, you mess with me." He backed off a step. "You just make sure you get your stuff out of Keisha's house before the day is over." Damon turned to walk away. "Come on Baby, let's go."

As Damon turned toward her, Alexis saw Junior climb up from the ground. He reached into his pocket. Something bulged against the fabric and suddenly she knew that he was about to pull out a gun. "Damon, look out!"

Damon spun around to find Junior holding a gun less than a foot from his face. He didn't seem fazed in the slightest. "Oh, so now you're a big man, huh Junior? What you gonna do, shoot me in the back?"

Alexis was so frightened she was afraid she might faint.

"No, I'm gonna blow your fucking face off, Bitch."

"Then what you waiting for?" Damon took a step closer to the gun.

Alexis felt her heart beating like tribal drums. She knew it would burst from her chest at any moment. She watched Damon as he stared into Junior's eyes.

"Come on big man, you gonna pull a gun on me then shoot me. You know better than to pull a gun on a man if you're not willing to pull the trigger."

The next five seconds seemed to drag into an eternity. Alexis saw doubt creep across Junior's face. She saw the gun shake in his hand. His finger flexed on the trigger. She could see the muscles twitch. She felt her mouth open to scream and her body drop to the ground as Damon stepped to his left and grabbed Junior's gun hand with his left hand. He pushed the gun away from his face as it went off. Somehow Damon twisted the gun toward Junior and forced it from his grip.

What is Forever?

Alexis watched as Damon struck the taller man across the jaw with the weapon. Junior crumpled to the ground.

He was conscious, but in serious pain as Damon stood over him with the gun in his hand.

"I ought to end your sorry ass right here and now!" Damon's chest heaved as he breathed.

Alexis could almost see the adrenaline coursing through his body. She knew by the look on his face that he was considering putting a bullet into Junior's skull.

"Damon, please." It was all she could manage to get out.

He turned towards her and their eyes met.

"Come on Baby, you know he's not worth it."

His eyes softened a little. He turned back toward Junior who was still writhing on the ground half conscious, holding his jaw and moaning. "You are so lucky that my girl wants you to live. Make sure you are out of Keisha's place today."

Alexis heard the sirens headed in their direction. Someone must have heard the gunshot and called the police. Moments later three squad cars blocked off the alley. A tall officer approached them with his gun drawn. When he got closer he peered at them, then lowered his weapon just a fraction.

"Damon, is that you?"

"Hey James," Damon responded. He bent over, his hands on his knees.

"What the hell is going on here?"

"I had an altercation with my Baby's momma's boyfriend, here. He pulled a gun on me and I managed to disarm him." Damon gestured toward Junior who was still on the ground, but who seemed to be coming out of his daze. Damon handed the gun to the officer.

By that time four other officers had made their way down the alley. James told one of them to handcuff Junior and put him in a squad car.

"You all right?" He asked Damon. "Were you hit?"

"No, I'm fine. He's just a punk. All talk no balls."

James laughed. "Well you're lucky your ass didn't catch a bullet."

"No worries man. You know my ass is made of steel." They both chuckled. "By the way James, this is my fiancée Alexis. Alexis this is one of my frat brothers, James."

"Nice to meet you, James. Damon can't seem to go anywhere without running into someone he knows, but I can't believe he could run into a friend even in this situation.

"Well Damon's a good man. He's saved my butt on more than one occasion." James gave him an apologetic smile. "Bro, I'm still gonna need you to come down to the station so we can file a report on this. I'll try to make sure it doesn't take too long."

"No problem. Can I drive myself or do I need to get in the back of one of your cars?"

"I don't think that will be necessary. Just follow me back."

The police station was only about five minutes away from the scene of the incident. James was true to his word. Damon wasn't charged with anything, they simply took statements from both him and Alexis. Against Damon's wishes the police charged Junior with attempted murder and locked him up. James told them that charges had been filed against Junior for a domestic assault earlier that day.

Alexis was happy that Keisha had summoned the courage to take steps to get Junior out of her life. She could tell by Damon's smile that he was equally glad.

Once they were back in the car Damon stuck the key in the ignition but stopped before turning it. His head dropped to the steering wheel.

"Baby, are you all right?" Although she knew better she was suddenly afraid that Junior's bullet had not missed.

It was an agonizing three seconds before he lifted his head from the steering wheel and let it fall backward to the headrest. His eyes were open and glassy.

"Damon—"

"Yeah Baby, I'm fine. But do you know how close I just came to being killed?" He turned to her. "How close I came to possibly getting *you* killed? I have got to start thinking before I just go jumping into things with both feet."

His words frightened her. She wasn't the only one. Damon was shaking too.

"Were you afraid?" Alexis had only made it through the ordeal because of his strength. It had never occurred to her that he might be scared, or that he didn't know what he was doing. After all, he was Damon.

"Scared? I was scared shitless." He let out a nervous laugh. "I've never had a gun so close to my face that I could read the serial number."

"Oh, my baby." She leaned over and squeezed him for all she was worth. "I couldn't even tell. It didn't seem like you doubted yourself for a moment."

"Two years of drama at State. I'm a pretty good actor." He grinned weakly.

They sat together in silence for a few minutes until they were both feeling a little steadier. Finally, Damon started the car and pulled away from the curb.

"How did you take the gun from him like that?" Alexis asked as they rode. "You looked like Jackie Chan or something."

"I took a few self defense classes back in college too. I guess I picked up more than I thought I had. But I'll tell you what; I never want to be in that position again. Life is too fragile. Every moment we have with the people we love should be cherished."

"You are so right, Baby. I cherish you and our life together more and more every moment. Matter of fact I'm gonna call my mom and dad just as soon as we get back to the house."

"So you don't want to go over to Tara's now?"

She really only felt like going back to his place and chilling out with him, but she didn't want to put off the inevitable any longer. "Okay, I suppose there's no time like the present. Yeah let's go and get it over with."

"Whatever you say. Let me just call and let her know we're on our way." He pulled out the cell phone and dialed the number from memory. He apparently called it pretty regularly. "Hey Tara. You doing all right? Yeah, I'm fine. Look Tara, Alexis and I are not too far from your place and I wanted to bring her by so that the two of you could meet."

What is Forever?

He paused while she responded. Alexis studied his face to get an idea of how she was reacting to the request. She couldn't tell.

"Yeah, that will be great. She's not picky; anything will be fine I'm sure. Well you know that's what I like."

Alexis definitely didn't like the sound of that.

"We should be there in about twenty minutes. Okay, cool, see you then."

"I'm not picky about what? What did she say?"

"She said that she just ordered a pizza and wanted to know what you like to drink so she could run out to the store. I told her you're not picky about that kind of thing."

"And what does she know that you like?"

"Coronas." He brushed his hand over her cheek. "Baby, are you going to be all right with this?"

She felt pretty weird about going over to Tara's house to have lunch, but she might as well go with the flow. Besides, meeting over food and a beer might help ease the tension. "Sure baby, I'll be fine."

"Alexis, you are the strongest most together person I've ever known. I want to be just like you when I grow up." His smiled warmed her and eased her fear.

"If you grow up."

"Yeah, that's what I meant." They both laughed.

CHAPTER 20

Keisha had begun putting her life in order. When she had returned home the previous evening she'd gone straight to the laundry room where Patches sat whimpering. Guilt filled her heart when she looked down at the little ball of fur. The bowl she'd left him was empty, and the water had spilled. He'd pooped near the washing machine, and a yellow puddle spread over one corner of the linoleum floor. Normally Keisha would have had his hide for such an infraction, but this wasn't his fault. He had been neglected over the last few days because of her issues with Junior.

She had also not been there for her daughter. But Keisha was determined that those days were behind her. She opened the gate and the dog came bounding out into her arms. He licked her face to show her how happy he was to see her. He obviously wasn't holding a grudge. He was just looking for a little love.

"Hey there, baby boy."

He smelled terrible, but Keisha didn't pay it any mind. She got the dog food from the cabinet and poured Patches an extra large helping.

After he was fed she took him for a long, vigorous walk. She knew that he would enjoy the exercise after being in the cramped space for so long. It felt pretty good to her, too. The weather was brisk for early spring, but she liked it. The cool air on her face seemed to clean the cobwebs from her brain.

What is Forever?

As they walked, Keisha took time to look back over the last few years of her life. She thought about the time she'd spent in a relationship with Damon. During that period she had grown in so many ways. She had begun to like, and more importantly respect herself. After the relationship ended she'd found herself back were she had started. Why?

It was true that Damon had been the stimulus for her growth, but she didn't need him to continue growing. Hadn't he told her many times how intelligent and worthwhile she was? Why had she had so much trouble believing it? Why had she wasted so much time with Junior's sorry ass? As the realization of her true potential rolled over her, she wanted to kick herself. There was a great big world out there. She didn't have to live like she had been. The truth of the matter was that she had somehow been punishing herself because she hadn't been able to keep Damon. Maybe Junior was right, she was holding on to him. She wouldn't have hesitated to get rid of Junior if Damon had wanted to come back to her.

As she walked back to her own front door, Keisha came to some life-altering realizations. Damon had taken her to the door of happiness but she didn't need him to walk through it. She loved Damon and she always would, but he had gone on with his life. It was time that she went on with hers.

The first thing she was going to do was go into her house and clean up. She packed all of Junior's clothes in big trash bags and set them on the back porch. By the time she finished it was late, but she wasn't tired. She was filthy however, so she took a long hot bath. Afterward she decided she'd do some reading to help her relax. She reached to pick

What is Forever?

up *Their Eyes Were Watching God*, but thought better of it. She had read that book. It was time to move on to new material. She found a book by BeBe More Campbell that she had been intending to read. She curled up in bed and read until she fell asleep.

Keisha woke up very early the following morning. She fed and walked Patches, and was back home before six-thirty. It was time to get ready to go. She carefully picked out her outfit. She wanted to look good. She fixed her hair in a modest style and applied just enough make-up to look professional. She called into work and left a message on her Supervisor's voicemail that she was sick and wouldn't be in. By seven-thirty she had grabbed her keys and was headed out the door.

Keisha arrived at her destination fifteen minutes later. She was nervous and had some reservations about what she was going to do, but it had to done. She couldn't risk Damon's safety. She walked up to the counter.

"I'd like to press charges against my ex-boyfriend."

By the time she left the magistrate's office, Keisha no longer had any doubts that pressing charges against Junior was the right thing to do. Not only had she insured Damon's safety, she also felt a weight had been lifted off her shoulders. She was back home and feeling good by the time Damon and Alexis showed up with Ebony.

She was very happy to have her little girl back home. She always missed her when she went to her father's house. She was happy that Damon was the type of man to make sure he played a large role in his child's life, but there was always a feeling of relief when he brought her home. Although Ebony being away the extra night had given her time for some soul searching, she was happy when she felt the child back in her arms.

Keisha realized that as a mother she held the most important position in the world. She had never truly understood that before. It was her responsibility to insure that her child was brought up well. She had to make sure that Ebony grew up knowing that she was a gifted and worthy individual. She would make sure that Ebony would be full of self confidence. She would always let her daughter know that she was loved that it's good, no *vital* to love one's self.

Keisha had one more errand to run. After they put Ebony's things away, Keisha took her daughter by the hand. "Come on, Baby. Mommy has to go register for school."

"But Mommy, you're too old to go to school."

"That's not true, Baby. You're never too old to learn new things."

CHAPTER 21

Tara clicked "shut down" on the computer's menu. She had been surfing the net all morning, trying to get a feel for the market. She had been back in town for over three months. It was about time she started getting ready to get back to work. At least that's what her shrink told her.

Tara didn't feel like she was totally ready to get back out in the world. When she first got back to town she thought she would be ready. That was when she thought Damon was still waiting for her. Even though she had lost her mother and was forced to start from scratch, she knew that everything would be fine once she and Damon were together.

She was shattered when she finally tracked him down and found out that he was seeing someone else. Not only was his romantic life moving along, it seemed that ever since she left things had gone really well for him. He had gotten a promotion at the television station. He was directing and producing local shows. He had finally gotten rid of that rust bucket he called a car and moved into a condominium. Things were really looking up for him. To top it all off he had someone he loved to share his good fortune. There had been shame in his voice when he told her that he was in love with another woman.

The news had driven her to the brink of another breakdown. She had been so upset with him. He'd told her that he would wait for her. He promised to be there for her. But just like every thing else in her life her sunshine had turned to shit.

What is Forever?

In her heart she knew that she couldn't hold him solely responsible. After all he didn't hear a word from her for over a year. While she was in the loony bin, as she liked to call it, her doctors would only let her have contact with immediate family. Her mother was the only one that fit into that category. When she got out and started therapy and AA she was given strict instructions not to contact him. They seemed to think that he was a contributing factor to her illness. The counselors told her that he had played games with her. That he never really cared about her. She had tried to explain to them that Damon was the only thing in her life that was good. The only person that she could count on. They were convinced that she needed a clean break from her life in North Carolina. Tara knew better but she went along with what they told her because her mother told her to. After her mother died and what little estate she had was sorted out, Tara sold whatever she couldn't carry and hopped on the first flight she could get.

Now she was back in the only place were she had ever felt at home. She was back in therapy and wanted more than anything to get her life on track. Sure, she would love for Damon to come to his senses and be with her, but if he didn't she knew that life must go on. Besides it wasn't as though he had dropped completely out of her life. As always, Damon had kept his promise, at least in part. He had assured her he would be there for her and he had. He helped her find a car and an apartment she could afford. Since her return he had always been willing to listen to her problems and say something to make her feel better. He had even stopped by the previous day to loan her money since what little her

259

What is Forever?

mother left was gone. When she saw him all of her old feelings surfaced. All she wanted was to have things back the way they once were. The way she wanted them to be again.

"I've got to snap out of this funk."

Tara looked at the clock. It was two o'clock in the afternoon and she hadn't eaten all day. She decided to order a pizza, she just didn't feel like cooking. She called the local pizza parlor and ordered a large veggie lover's. Whatever she didn't finish she would eat later for dinner.

She turned on her CD player and put in *Kinda Blue* by Miles Davis. She was laid out on her couch lost in the music when the telephone rang. She didn't want to answer it but she was afraid that it was the pizza place calling back to confirm the order. She answered on the fourth ring. A streak of electricity traveled down her spine when she heard Damon's voice. Her stomach sank when he told her he wanted to bring Alexis by so that they could meet. She wanted to tell him that he was out of his freaking mind. Why in the hell should she want to meet his new woman? But she could never take that attitude with him. After all, what she really wanted for Damon was his happiness. If he found that with someone else she would at least try to be happy for him.

So she told him sure, it would be fine to bring her over, and that she had just ordered something to eat. She wanted to kick herself when she even went as far as to offer to run out and get some beer. She was very hesitant about that prospect. Tara had fallen off the wagon after Damon had first told her about his new girlfriend. She had managed to keep her drinking under control so far since then, but she didn't know how long that would last the way things were going.

What is Forever?

As soon as she hung up the phone she ran into the bathroom to freshen up and put on some decent clothes. There was no way she was going to meet this woman for the first time in sweats and no make up. Oh yeah, she was going to look fabulous when they walked through that door. He'd have to see what he'd given up and she'd be forced to see her competition. It only took her ten minutes to get dressed in a great fitting pair of blue jeans and a stretchy midriff top that emphasized her breasts and showed off her belly ring. She chose to forgo the bra just to add a little spice to the outfit. She brushed her long silky hair and let it hang down around her shoulders. She admired herself in the mirror. Tara had pulled off the exact look she wanted and in record time. She looked great, but not like she was trying to look great.

She had flung her purse over her shoulder so she could run across the street to the convenience store when she was startled by a knock on her door.

"Damn, they got here quick. All right Girl, keep it together. Breathe deep." Tara took a couple of quick breaths and put the warmest smile she could muster on her lips before she opened the door.

"Well Hello-" Tara's heart skipped two beats when she saw Gabe standing in the doorway.

"Well hello, Baby. How have you been?"

"Gabe, what the hell are you doing here?" *How the hell had he found her?*

"Come on now, Tara. I told you a long time ago there's nothing that I can't find out if I want to." He strolled right by her into the living room. He had a smug look on his face as he looked around the room, then made himself comfortable

261

on the couch. "Listening to Miles, huh? At least you hung on to a little of what I tried to teach you."

"Gabe, I'm busy. I don't have time for your games right now."

He turned toward her and looked dead into her eyes. "No games, Tara. I came to collect my property."

If he had come for the money that she got from his safe, he was going to be upset. That money was long gone.

"I don't know what you're talking about. I don't have anything of yours."

He stood up. "Of course you do. I came for you. I want my fiancée back."

Something in his eyes told her that he was serious. Even after all of the time that had passed, Gabe still scared her.

"I invested a lot of time and money into you. You owe me another chance."

"I don't owe you shit."

"I know that we've had our problems and misunderstandings in the past, but we can put all of that behind us."

Although she was afraid, she refused to let it show. "Misunderstandings? You mean like when you violated me? Was that a misunderstanding?"

"Look Baby, we both made mistakes. He who is without sin can cast the first stone. Besides, wasn't I the person who was there for you? Every other man in your life only wanted you for your looks. They just wanted to get into your pants. To use you. I'm the one who loves you."

Something was different about him. His usual confidence was missing. He just wasn't as alert or together as he had always been. For the first time since she'd opened the door, Tara noticed that he was dressed rather shabbily. Gabe was normally a clothes hound. He had always prided himself on his style.

"Tara, please don't act like this. I need you." He paused. "I'm in trouble."

She was unfazed by his revelation. "What the hell are you talking about? What kind of trouble?"

"I'm under investigation. They've accused me of commingling funds and a ton of other improprieties. Please don't turn your back on me. I need you."

Tara wondered if Gabe was up to his old tricks in an attempt to win her sympathy. In the past he had always known how to use her soft heart against her. He was trying to make her feel guilty. He'd always been able to convince her to do anything he wanted, and she had always put what he wanted first. She'd thought if she took care of him, he would take care of her. Therapy had helped her to know differently. She wouldn't let his words work their magic this time. She was stronger now than he gave her credit for.

When he saw that she was not giving in, he changed his tactics. His voice became demeaning.

"I know you're not still waiting on what's his name, Damon? Well I happen to know that he is seriously dating someone new. From what I hear, she's a hottie. He did you just like I knew he would. He fucked you, then fucked you over." His tone softened again. "But like I said Baby, that's all in the past. I'm here to make a fresh start."

"Stop calling me baby. I'm not your fucking baby." She was starting to lose her composure. "And not that it's any of

your business, but just so you know I never slept with
Damon. He's the only person who's ever been there for me
and never asked anything in return. You just wanted me to
be some kind of trophy. You were never there for me."

There was fire in his voice as he moved close to her. She
could smell the Scotch on his breath.

"I'm not gonna argue with your stupid ass. You're gonna
be mine again, and that's all there is to it." He grabbed her
roughly by the arms and tried to kiss her.

The touch and taste of his wet lips revolted her. Tara
tried to push away and managed to free one arm.

"Get the fuck off of me!"

In an attempt to get her back in his grasp he reached for
her and ripped her shirt, exposing her left breast. Tara could
see that he was captivated with her flesh. Fear gripped her as
images of his last assault rose fresh in her memory.

"So what are you going to do, take it again?" She hoped
that she sounded brave.

Gabe hesitated, giving her just enough time to plant her
knee squarely between his thighs. There was a slight delay
before she saw the pain register in his face. Then he went
down.

Tara bolted for her bedroom. She reached under her
mattress and pulled out the small twenty-two caliber gun that
her mother had kept under her mattress for so many years
after Tara's father died. She ran back into the living room
where Gabe was still prone on the carpet. Tara pointed the
gun at his chest. She was finally going to be free of Gabe
once and for all.

CHAPTER 22

Alexis was trying to keep herself from feeling nervous as they pulled up in front of the apartment building. What did she have to be nervous about? Damon was her man. Tara was the one who was being interviewed. If Alexis had the slightest doubts about her intentions, she would have Damon put an end to his relationship with Tara.

They walked towards the building. The apartments were definitely not high-end. They reminded Alexis of a cheap motel. She had followed Damon halfway up the steps to the second level when there was a loud scream.

"That's Tara!" Damon double-timed it up the remaining steps and into an apartment where the door was ajar.

Alexis definitely did not like the way he ran to her when he heard the noise. She quickened her pace to follow. Her chin hit her chest when she stepped into the apartment. She was not prepared for what she saw. A woman who she presumed must be Tara was pointing a gun at a man who was sprawled on the floor holding his balls. The look on Damon's face verified that he was equally shocked by the scene. Alexis was also taken aback by Tara's beauty. Alexis hated to admit it, but the girl looked good even with her clothes torn and anger clouding her face.

"Tara, what the hell is going on?" Damon sounded as confused as she felt.

Tara never took her eyes off the man on the floor. "Nothing much, Damon. Just taking care of a little

265

unfinished business. I'm gonna get this son of a bitch out of my life once and for all."

The man on the floor turned to look at him. "So you're the great Damon, huh? I would say it's nice to meet you, but considering the circumstances somehow it wouldn't sound sincere."

"Gabe, shut up! Just shut the hell up."

Alexis could tell that Tara was getting increasingly agitated. The gun shook in her hands.

"Come on now, Baby. Don't act like this. We have company." His voice held only the slightest trace of nervousness.

Alexis couldn't believe his attitude. He must be as crazy as Tara was.

"I'd suggest you shut your trap, man." Damon took a step toward Tara. "Come on now Tara, you don't want to do anything you'll regret. Put the gun down." He held out one hand like the hostage negotiators do on television.

"That's just it, Damon. The only thing I'd regret is if I don't finally send this bastard to hell where he belongs."

Gabe moved to get up from the floor. She jerked the gun toward him and her finger tensed on the trigger. Gabe froze where he was. He finally seemed to realize that she was totally serious.

"Wait a minute, Tara. What are you doing? This is me. Think about all we've been through together. Think about all the things that I've done for you."

"That's exactly what I'm thinking about. You never loved me. You wanted to own me. I sold you my love in exchange for what I thought was security, but all you ever

266

did was treat me like shit. Well it's over. Do you understand that? It's over." As an after thought she added, "And so are you."

Damon stepped between them. Alexis felt her heart drop all the way to her feet. He held his hand out to her. "Listen Tara, you can't do this. If you do, he still wins."

"How? He'll be dead," she retorted.

"So will you." Tara's eyes blinked. Damon took a step closer to her. "He'd rather be dead than see you happy. If you do this, he'll win."

He took another step as Gabe rose to a knee. "Just give me the gun. He doesn't have to have power over you. He's pathetic."

Alexis stood frozen in the door way. She felt like she was watching some melodramatic old movie on television, but inside she was totally aware of the seriousness of the drama that was unfolding in front of her. This was the second time a person with a gun had threatened to end a life in front of her today.

"I can't let him keep doing this to me." Tara's voice was tortured.

Alexis watched a tear fall from her cheek and hit the floor.

"That's true Tara, but this is not the way to end it." She seemed to be giving in to his words. "Give me the gun."

"Tell me that if I give you this gun everything will be all right." She was almost pleading with him. "Tell me he won't hurt me again."

What is Forever?

"He won't, Sweetheart." Damon stepped closer. His hand closed over the weapon. "I promise you he will never hurt you again."

Alexis looked at Gabe. Pure hatred burned in his eyes. Alexis had only been in his presence for a few minutes and she was afraid of him. She knew in that instant that he was a very dangerous man.

"Give me the gun, Tara." He didn't ask that last time. He told her what to do and she obeyed. Damon pulled the gun from her and set it on the coffee table. She fell into his arms. Deep sobs emanated from deep inside of her.

Even in this situation Alexis didn't like seeing another woman in Damon's arms. He led her to a chair and sat her in it. From where she was standing Alexis could see the entire room. She saw Gabe slip toward the table and pick up the gun. She yelled a warning as Gabe leveled it at Tara. Alexis saw Damon swing around to face him. Gabe's voice was crystal clear in Alexis' ears as he spoke.

"I can't believe you pulled a gun on me. I am so sick and tired of this man coming between us." He pointed the gun at Damon. Damon didn't flinch. "I ought to put a hole in his fucking head and get him out of our business for good."

Alexis' heart dropped.

"No Gabe, please no." Tara pleaded. "I'm the one who hurt you. Kill me. Don't hurt Damon."

Alexis couldn't comprehend that another woman could love Damon like that.

Gabe turned the gun back on Tara. He was obviously out of his mind. "See? That's exactly what I'm talking about!" Spittle flew from his lips. "You would sacrifice your life for him? Why can't you love me like that?" The gun was back on Damon. "That's why I hate him. Why I want him dead." His eyes were flat and cold. "But just like with everything else, I always give you what you want."

Alexis saw everything. She saw Gabe point the gun back at Tara. She saw him pull the trigger. She even thought she saw the bullet leave the barrel of the gun. Alexis screamed when she saw Damon dive in front of the bullet.

She was running to him then, running to get in front of that bullet before it hit its target, but she wasn't fast enough. She watched helplessly as the bullet entered her man's chest. She saw the pain register on his face and watched him slump to the floor.

Alexis dove to the floor on top of him. She wanted to shield his body from any other assault. Tara went on the attack. She ran toward Gabe, nails bared and ready to plunge into his eyes. Gabe took aim and pulled the trigger. There wasn't even a click. The old gun had jammed. Tara was on him in an instant scratching, beating and biting him. He was a bloody mess by the time he managed to pull himself away from her and run out the door.

Alexis held Damon's head in her hands. She looked deeply into his eyes as he looked into hers. His lips didn't move but she could hear everything he was saying with his eyes. She spoke to him in the same fashion. They were trying to communicate everything they felt, everything that had gone unsaid, before it was too late.

Alexis saw his bright eyes dim as his spirit left his body. She could swear she felt him kiss her goodbye as he passed on.

CHAPTER 23

Tara sat on the floor in shock. She had blood on her hands. She couldn't be sure if it was Damon's, or from the damage she had inflicted on Gabe's face. He had gotten away. She had tried her best to kill him, but somehow he got away. She wanted to kill him, like he had killed...

Damon! Oh God, Damon! No. It wasn't fair. Couldn't be real. Alexis was still cradling his head in her arms. She was moaning like an old woman. It was so unfair. She wanted to push the woman away so that she could hold his lifeless body, but she knew that Alexis was the woman that he had chosen. Tara sat there for an awkward moment not knowing what to do.

"It's your fault," Alexis whispered.

It took a moment for Tara to realize she was being addressed.

"It's your fault. If it wasn't for your crazy ass and your crazy ass man, he would still be alive."

The words burned holes in Tara's heart. It was true.

"Alexis...I am so sorry." She wanted to cry. She had always been a crier, but now no tears would come. "I would never cause Damon harm. I'd rather die myself. I told Gabe not to hurt him." Her voice was strained. "He jumped in front of me. It was supposed to be me."

Alexis looked at Tara for the first time. "You're right. It was supposed to be you. But you knew he'd never allow you to be hurt. He'd never allow..." Tears choked off her voice.

What is Forever?

She lay her forehead on his and her shoulders shook. "Damon. I can't believe you're gone."

Police came rushing into the room with guns drawn. "Don't move! Stay were you are!"

Tara found the way they came swarming into the room almost comical. Where were they when it counted? She was too weak to move anyway.

One of the officers knelt beside her and put his hand on her shoulder. "What happened here?"

Another tow-headed cop knelt next to Damon and put two fingers on his throat. "No pulse. Looks like he got it right in the heart."

If looks could kill, the look Alexis gave him would have burned him to cinders. "Her crazy ass boyfriend killed my fiancé."

Her fiancé? Tara's heart shattered. For the first time she noticed the diamond ring on Alexis' finger. It was true. He had truly chosen her. A third cop walked over to the body. Tara could see tears welling in his eyes.

"Oh my God, Damon." He was obviously shaken very deeply. He too knelt next to Alexis. He gently removed Damon from her arms and pulled her into his. "Alexis, I am so sorry. He told me how much he loved you."

"He's gone, James." Her voice was barely a whimper. "We're supposed to get married in four days." She buried her face in his shoulder.

Tara couldn't take anymore. She got up and walked into her bedroom.

What is Forever?

"Miss, I need to find out what happened here," the first officer called after her. "I need to speak with you." She ignored him and closed the door.

Tara didn't know how much time had passed when she heard a knock on the door. She was sitting on her bed rocking. She looked at the door when she heard another small knock.

"Leave me alone!"

The door cracked open. "Tara, it's me Alexis." Her voice was gentle.

She pushed the door open and eased into the room. She walked silently to the bed and sat next to her. They both sat in silence looking at their fists in their laps.

"Tara they need to speak with you. I told them what happened, but you're also a witness. They need any information you can give them so they can catch Gabe. He has to pay for what he's done."

"I know."

Alexis took a deep breath. "You really loved Damon, didn't you?"

"Yes."

"We both did." She sniffed. "I want to apologize for what I said before."

"No. You were right. He's dead because of me."

Alexis didn't respond, she just put her arm around Tara and led her into the living room.

CHAPTER 24

The phone rang, waking Keisha from the first restful sleep she'd had in days. She could barely make out what time it was through the goo that had built up in her eyes. One in the morning! She didn't need to look at the caller ID. Only one fool would be calling her this time of night. She snatched the telephone from its cradle and pressed the talk button.

"Junior, why in the world are you calling me this time of night?"

"It's me." A woman's voice came over the line.

"Me who? It's too late at night for you to be playing games—"

"He's dead."

Keisha was stopped in the midst of her tirade. Suddenly she was fully awake. The voice on the other end began to sob. Keisha felt her heart go cold.

"Alexis? Is that you? What are you talking about? Who's dead?" She knew the answer before Alexis could force out his name.

"Damon, Keisha. Damon's dead."

Keisha's heart stopped beating. There was no way she'd heard that right. Then she remembered Junior and the gun. "No Alexis, he ain't dead."

"Yes he is. He was shot...he was shot and killed this evening." Her voice was strained. "I'm so sorry, Keisha. He's gone."

What is Forever?

"But I went to the police today. I took out a warrant. Junior's already in jail. How can Damon be dead?"

"It wasn't Junior. He didn't do it."

None of this was making any sense. "If Junior didn't do it, then how did he get shot? Who would shoot Damon?"

"It was a guy named Gabe. He was Tara's ex-boyfriend or something."

Keisha lost the power of speech. The realization of this information crept over her.

"Keisha are.you there?"

She opened her mouth to answer, but couldn't. There was just a sick whimper.

"Keisha? Are you all right?"

Keisha looked at the phone in her hand. What the hell kind of question was that? Her mouth worked soundlessly. She closed her eyes and took a deep, shuddering breath. Finally she was able to get out, "Are you at Damon's?"

"Yes. I just got here."

"I'll be there in a few minutes."

She went through the motions of putting on some sweats and brushing her teeth. She went about the activities with her mind in a fog. She didn't think about what she was doing, she couldn't think at all. She was on autopilot. Once she was dressed, she found her self in front of Ebony's room. Oh God. Her poor baby. What in the world would she say to her? How could she ever explain that her daddy was dead?

She stepped into the room and savored the innocence on her baby's face. Keisha knew in her heart that Ebony's life would never be the same. She sat on the bed. Ebony stirred but did not wake. Tears came to Keisha's eyes when she

274

remembered of all the special times her baby and Damon had shared. She quivered when she thought of all of the special times in the future that had been murdered with her father. Anger filled her heart. She was angry for her daughter's loss, and for her own.

Keisha slipped a coat on the sleeping angel. She was careful not to wake her. She wanted to put off having to explain what had happened for as long as she possibly could. The child was a deep sleeper and never opened her eyes. She slept while Keisha carried her to the car and buckled her into her car seat. As Keisha drove to Damon's she saw her daughter in the rear view mirror. Her head was cocked to one side and the corner of her mouth was wet with drool. Keisha had never seen her look so much like her father.

She drove on.

"Damon, if you can hear me, I promise you that I won't ever let her forget you. She will always know who her daddy was and how much he loved her. I swear that to you."

She drove the rest of the way to his house in silent tears.

CHAPTER 25

Tara sat on the floor staring at the bottle of vodka. Her hands trembled in her lap as she wrestled with the desire to turn the bottle to her lips.

After the paramedics removed Damon's body, the police officers took her and Alexis down to the station to fill out reports. It was hell going over and over the story for them. They seemed less than devastated about Damon's death. All of them except that cop James. He really seemed shaken by it. The others angered her to no end. They treated her like she was the one who pulled the trigger. It didn't help that in a way she felt like she had.

After hours of questioning they finally took her home. She and Alexis both sat silently in the back of the police cruiser. Tara just didn't know what to say, so she said nothing. Alexis managed to tell her to take care of herself once she reached her car. Tara couldn't even force herself to respond.

Once the BMW was out of sight she made a beeline to the liquor store around the corner. Once back in her living room the weight of everything that had transpired forced her to collapse to the carpet. She set the liquor on the coffee table and stared at it. She had never wanted, no *needed* a drink so bad in her life. She knew, however, that taking it would be like a slap in Damon's face. Guilt wrapped itself around her like a blanket.

What is Forever?

As she tormented over it the telephone rang. She was surprised at herself when she answered it. There was no one she wanted to speak to at that moment except Damon.

"Hello?" Her voice was frail.

"Ms. Johnson? This is detective Rodriguez, I'm very sorry to bother you but...well we found Mr. Gabrielle Conrad."

Her anger rekindled itself at the sound of his name. Her voice was low and primal. "Good. I hope you throw his ass in the electric chair tonight!"

"I'm afraid there won't be any need for an electric chair. We found his body at his office. He hung himself."

The world seemed to spin out of control. For a moment she thought she would black out.

"Miss Johnson? Miss Johnson are you there?"

It took a second for her to find her voice. "Yes, I'm here."

"I apologize for doing this over the phone but you told us that you wanted to be notified the moment we found him." There was sadness in his voice. She could tell that this was a call he hated to make. "Ma'am, you're listed in his wallet as his next of kin. We need you to come down to the hospital and identify the body. It can wait until tomorrow if that would be better for you."

"Thank you. Yes tomorrow would be better."

She wanted to cry but no tears fell. Cold emptiness intertwined with guilt. Gabe was dead now, too. She looked at the bottle again and licked the dryness from her lips.

Tara's hands trembled as they reached for the liquor. The bottle contained the only medicine that could numb her pain.

What is Forever?

She grabbed it and pulled it toward her lips. At the last moment she flung it against the wall. The alcohol left a winding trail as it dripped to the floor. Tara stared at the broken shards of glass. They reminded her of her life. She was a wreck, maybe even crazy. She just refused to be a drunk.

CHAPTER 26

Alexis hung up the phone. She was totally drained. She was glad that Keisha was coming over. She didn't want to be alone.

By the time Keisha rang the doorbell she had fallen asleep. She dreamed she and Damon were standing at the altar about to be pronounced man and wife when Keisha and Tara suddenly appeared and riddled him with bullets.

The doorbell startled her awake. She was relieved to have been awakened from the terrible dream until she gained her bearings and remembered that real life had not been any kinder. She let Keisha in. She took Ebony upstairs to her room, then came back down to Alexis.

The women hugged each other like they had always been the best of friends. They held on to each other as though their lives depended on it. Tears fell, bodies convulsed, but still they held on.

Eventually, reluctantly, they released each other. Alexis could see that Keisha was trying to pull herself together.

"What happened?" she asked.

Alexis told Keisha everything that had transpired since they dropped Ebony off. She didn't leave out a single detail. She told Keisha about Damon's relationship with Tara. She explained their run-in with Junior, then went on to describe in detail how Gabe had shot Damon at Tara's apartment.

"That bitch. It's her fault my baby don't have a father no more. I told him he should have stayed away from that crazy

279

bitch." Keisha looked at Alexis. "Why'd y'all even go by there in the first place?" There was a bite in her voice.

Alexis knew that Keisha was only trying to find someone to blame. She needed to put this tragedy on someone. Alexis understood because she had done the same thing to Tara. In the hours that had passed since the shooting she had come to realize that there was no one to blame. Except maybe Gabe. If Damon had not given his life, Tara would be dead. Damon would have never been able to live with that. He could never allow someone he loved to die in front of him without his trying do something. He had to try to save her, and he did.

Damon was born to be a hero. That was his greatest gift and his greatest flaw. He always had to look out for the next person. It was what made him Damon. He was meant to be a hero. It was in his blood, in every fiber of his being all the way down to the smallest strand in his genetic code.

It was the reason he had almost been killed by Junior that same day. Alexis was tempted to remind Keisha of that fact, but decided against it. Keisha was in pain and she needed to vent. Eventually the realization would hit Keisha as well.

"You're hurting. We both are hurting. We're confused and scared. There's no need to point fingers. No matter who they land on, Damon's still dead." She dabbed her eye with a piece of tissue she was holding.

Keisha seemed to want to respond but she remained silent.

"Have you told Ebony yet?"

"No. I don't know how. How do you tell a four year old girl that her daddy's gone forever? That he won't ever pick her up again or tell her he loves her?" Her tears came again, a steady stream flowing from her eyes. "I just don't know what to do. I grew up without a daddy. I know what that can do to a girl. How am I gonna raise this child by myself?"

Alexis put an arm around her friend's shoulder. "I don't know Keisha, but I know that if you let me, I'd like to be there to help."

Keisha forced a little smile to her lips. "Oh Alexis, you know that you're stuck with us. From now on we're family."

They hugged again. When they separated, a different look came across Keisha's face.

"I am so very sorry for you. You should be getting married in a few days. And here I am going on like I'm the only one who's lost him. At least I have a part of him in Ebony." She seemed to regret her choice of words. "I mean *we* have part of him with Ebony."

"I understand what you meant." She put her hand on her stomach. "We may both have a piece of Damon."

Keisha's eyes lit up with comprehension, then true happiness. "Alexis, are you-" she slapped her hand over her mouth and pointed at Alexis.

"I don't know yet. I forgot to take my pills a couple of times. I'm praying that I am, though."

"Don't worry, cause I'm gonna pray too girl." There was nothing but sincerity in Keisha's voice. "I was gonna tell y'all this at the wedding..." She looked at Alexis with an apology in her eyes.

"It's all right, Keisha. Wedding is not a bad word. What were you going to say?"

"I registered for school today. I'm going back."

What is Forever?

"That is so wonderful." Alexis squeezed Keisha's hands. "You know, he would be so happy about all of this."

"I'll bet he does know. You know how nosy Damon was. He's probably sitting up there right now, watching us."

Alexis looked toward the ceiling. That was a very comforting thought.

"Keisha will you stay tonight? I just don't want to be here alone."

"Yeah, I'll stay," she said softly, "if you help me tell Ebony tomorrow."

"I'll be right beside you."

They sat and talked for over an hour before they were both overcome by exhaustion and fell asleep on the couch.

Alexis came to first. She checked her watch; it was 4:00 am. She retrieved the same comforter she had put over Keisha the other night, and once again covered her. Alexis walked into the bedroom for the first time since she had returned home. The bed was still unmade and Damon's pajama pants were lying across his pillow. Alexis slipped into the bed and lay her head on Damon's pillow. She could still smell him. Once again the tears flowed from her eyes.

She just couldn't stay on the bed. She walked to the bookshelf. She ran her fingers over the leather bound journals he had collected. She pulled the latest book from the shelf. Still sobbing she opened his journal to the last entry. The sight of his handwriting filled her with emptiness and loss. She rubbed her hand along the page contemplating that he had only written these words a few hours earlier. She read:

What is Forever?

Dear Mom & Dad,

As always, I still miss you terribly. You would not believe the week that I have had. I am still too exhausted to tell you about it. Just let me say that sometimes I feel so lost and confused. I have a beautiful fianc'e now. Mom I know that you would like her. She reminds me so much of you, at least what I remember of you. And Dad I know that you would take one look at her legs and say "son ya done good." I swear I wish I had the both of you here to guide me. I just want everything to work out with Alexis (that's her name by the way.) She's everything I ever wanted in a woman. I want to spend forever with her.

But there is my problem. I have told two other women that I would be there forever, and needless to say we are no longer together. It's not that I didn't love them. I did, for different reasons and in different ways. But for one reason or another we didn't make it

What is Forever?

to forever together. I still feel guilty about that when it comes to both of them. I believe that's part of the reason that I have tried to remain friends with them. That's not always an easy thing. It sometimes interferes with my relationship with Alexis. I don't want to blow my future by holding on to my past.

I love Alexis and I'm going to marry her. But how do I make sure it lasts forever? I mean that's the real question, right? WHAT IS FOREVER?!?

I Miss you and I love you always,
Damon

She closed the book. She wished she could talk to him. She wanted to tell him that he had been there for all of them. He'd somehow been able to keep his promise to Keisha and Tara and still remain true to her. She wanted to give him the answer. It was so clear to her. She lay back on the bed and fell asleep. She dreamed sweet dreams of she and Damon and their son.

When Alexis walked to the podium she looked out over the crowd and her heart was filled. She opened her mouth to speak, but no words came out. A single tear rolled from her left eye.

"That's all right Sister, take your time," someone spoke out from the mass of people.

"Today should have been my wedding day." She paused to will her tears from falling. "Instead I am burying the man that I love. I won't point fingers and I refuse to have ill-will toward anyone or anything that led to his death." She choked on the last word but got it out. "Damon would never abide by that. Damon was a man with a forgiving heart...a loving heart. I have vowed to myself to make my heart more like Damon's. I would be remiss if I didn't advise you to make yours more like his also."

"Amen, Sister. You sure are right about that."

"I cannot express to any of you how much I am going to miss this man. I feel as though I have lost a part of me. But before he left, Damon gave me a part of him that I will cherish forever." She subconsciously put her hand to her stomach as she looked at Keisha in the audience. She saw Keisha hug Ebony a little tighter as she returned the knowing look with a slight smile on her lips and nod of her head.

"Damon gave me his love. It is the greatest gift I could have ever received. He and I had a great relationship. I believe we were soulmates, but like any relationship, ours had its bumps. One of the few regrets that I have today is that I spent any time at all allowing jealousy to seep into my heart. As many of you know, I am not the first woman that Damon loved. As a matter of fact, I know that he loved at least two others. Before he died I allowed myself to become

285

What is Forever?

jealous of the relationships that he had with those women. I didn't like the fact that he had love in his heart for them.

"So Keisha and Tara, I'm sorry. I'm sorry that it took this happening for me to truly realize that Damon's heart was big enough to hold love for all of us. He was just the kind of person who was not forced to push someone out of his heart in order to let someone else in. We all should strive for that."

The church had become silent. She continued. "I know now that there was nothing wrong with his loving them. Damon respected our relationship and the love that he and I shared. He was a good man who never did anything that would have hurt me. He loved me in a way that filled me up. He loved me sincerely, faithfully and fully. Just as I loved him. Damon once asked the question: "What is forever?" Because of knowing and loving him, I know the answer. God gave us only one thing that transcends time and space, one thing that we can pass on to our children that they can never lose...the one thing that is forever is love."

"Amen, Sister."

What is Forever?

Quick Order Form

Telephone Orders: 336-923-2849

E-mail: mciverjoel@4unitypublishing.com

Postal Orders: 4 Unity Publishing
              PO Box 548
              Pfafftown, NC 27040

Name:_____

Address:_____

City: _____St_____Zip_____

Telephone:_____

E-mail: _____

Sales Tax: Please add 7% for orders shipped to North Carolina addresses.

Shipping: $4.00 for first book and $2.00 for each additional.

Payment: ❑ Check   ❑ Money Order

What is Forever?